LOVE, 24 AD

Gates McKibbin

For further information go to:

www.lovehopegive.com

Cover and text design by Kenneth Gregg

Cover artwork by Serena Barton

www.serenabarton.com

Copyediting by Sally Hudson

ISBN 9798520295976

Printed in the United States of America

First Edition

CONTENTS

DEDICATION

My mother was an avid reader of romance novels. She delayed applying for a library card until my youngest brother was in school, since she knew that once she dipped into a paperback she would never accomplish everything a family of seven needed her to do. Two of her preferred authors were my favorites as well. We spent hours on the phone recounting what we enjoyed most about their latest releases (gloriously male protagonists included).

Mother isn't here to read the stories in the *Love Hope Give* series, but I dedicate them to her nonetheless. They aren't what she typically checked out of the library, but she might still have enjoyed the adventures of Grace and Luke.

FOREWORD

The four novels in the *Love Hope Give* series arrived over a two-year period when I was living among ancient redwoods in Marin County, California. Whenever I had a free day on a weekend I would park myself on the sofa with a blank journal and a pen, ready to write whatever came through me. By the end of the day the pages would be spilling over with words, most of which I couldn't recall.

I never learned to type without looking at the keyboard – a particularly fraught process when handwritten material must be entered into the computer. So I used voice recognition software to transfer the narratives from my journals onto the hard drive. Reading each novel aloud was a fascinating process, since I had no idea what would happen next. I discovered the story arcs not as I was writing them, but as I was reading them afterward.

I shared early drafts with a few friends. One of them who lives in Portland told me a portrait caught her eye when she was visiting the art studio of her friend Serena Barton. It had an uncanny resemblance to how she envisioned Grace in the first novel *One, Beyond Time*. When we visited the studio a few weeks later, Grace was indeed waiting for us.

Serena gave me permission to use the portrait on my book cover. She also agreed to create artwork for the other three novels. As I was describing the storyline in *Love, 24 AD* she stopped me saying, "I may have a few pieces that would work." She hopped on a stool and retrieved three canvases from an upper shelf. "How about these?"

Incredibly, Serena had captured Grace in her three subsequent incarnations even though she knew nothing about the stories. Clearly she and I had connected in the realms beyond time and space. I purchased all four portraits on the spot.

May the *Love Hope Give* series fill your heart with your own deep inner knowing that anything is possible when love is your guiding light.

PART ONE
GRACILA AND LUKAN

They said that lightning parted the sky at the moment of my birth.

My first wail was accompanied by a clap of thunder so vehement, it shook the walls of the birthing hut. These messages from Mother Nature foretold a life of brilliant light and ferocious service. I had been conceived of love during the Beltane celebrations, a most auspicious time. The union of the divine masculine and the divine feminine occurred amidst ritualistic singing, dancing, chanting and intoxication with love. The fires burned bright when male and female came together to create me.

It rained in torrents as my mother labored to bring me into the world. The women collected the water in cauldrons made of hollowed out tree trunks, cut into formidable slices using more magic than muscle. This water, a welcoming gift from the Mother, was heated over a crackling fire in the hearth. Herbs fragrant with the life that surrounded us were steeped in the water, creating an aromatic pool for my entrance.

Soon after I was freed from the loving womb of my mother, I was placed in this fragrant bath. Fresh rain was added to create the perfect temperature for my nearly total immersion. I splashed and kicked, comfortable in a fluid that felt familiar. Smiling faces looked down upon me, joyous that my birth had proceeded smoothly. I was full of vitality.

The women washed and dried me thoroughly, wrapped me in the skin of a red fox and placed me in the waiting arms of my mother. She was weeping sweet tears of gratitude and fulfillment. So many times she had attempted to give birth, only to be disappointed at the loss of her child before three new moons. Mother had all but given up hope when she conceived once again. She had lain with her lover of many years, a chieftain over numerous neighboring tribes, throughout the days of Beltane. They loved not so much to conceive, but to give themselves over to each other and the imperative of uniting the masculine and feminine in their potent divinity.

The potency was real in another way. As my mother and her lover lay together after a union that brought them to exceptional oneness, he whispered, "Gracila is within you now. In almost ten moons she will be born, perfect and powerful. She will be blessed with the best we have to give to each other and to her. I am honored to be the father of your child – our daughter."

My mother cried into his chest, undone once again by the tenderness of this man. He ruled many with an equal measure of force and fairness, both resulting from his clarity of purpose.

"It is I who is honored," she replied. "To be loved by one such as yourself without regard to whether I have given you a son, is to be shown the path that leads to the source of all love. To know that you foretell the birth of a daughter you will welcome into the world so unreservedly fills me with contentment. May your vision become real, and may our daughter contribute much to the world."

"If she is anything like her mother, she will leave it transformed," he assured her. "And now, my love, sleep with me wrapped around you, that the budding life within you may know from this moment on that she is loved and very much wanted by us both."

My parents slept serenely that night, graced as always by the steadfast nature of their togetherness. This time, however, they shared the knowing that at long last a child was on the way.

I was peacefully at home during the months I remained in my mother's womb, nurtured by her life-giving sources as well as her love. Even so, I was transitioning from the realms of spirit to those of compromised and challenging consciousness. Midwives resonant with the ebb and flow of feminine forces assisted with my arrival. Thus I was more comfortable with my new lifetime than I might have been otherwise.

I knew only love during the first many years of my life. But then, really, I knew only love during all of that life. I faced tumults and threats enough for many incarnations, but those tribulations were nothing given the love that surrounded me. I felt it from the moment my sprit settled into my mother's vessel, and I knew it as the predominant aspect of my being until I breathed my last.

This is a story about love, given to me by many and returned to them and others with gladness. I share it with you as my gift to your own loving nature.

∞ ∞ ∞

The year was 24 AD, the location near what is now Glastonbury, Somerset, England. I lived in a community of women healers who existed in harmony with Nature first and humankind second. Of course, people are aspects of Nature – not separate from it. Perhaps I distinguish human behavior from other forces of Nature because people so consistently act contrary to her benevolence.

Lest I signal the wrong image, I hasten to add that our life was nothing like that of nuns in the convents that sprung up centuries later. Significantly different principles and perspectives guided our daily activities. The women who created our circle of sisterhood structured their lives in perfect alignment with the pulses and phases, seasons and synchronicities of Mother Nature. Their inner tides flowed with the actual ones; their courses waxed and waned with the phases of the moon; their capacity to create resonated with the imperatives of divine love and light.

These women chose to live apart from tribal life, forming a self-sufficient extended family that consisted by design of just one gender. Males born to the women in our community were raised among us and taught the ways of the feminine, that they might remember them when they were introduced to the male-dominated tendencies outside our circle. Men, on the other hand, were rarely present, except to participate in rituals, most of which occurred away from the children.

Young boys learned to recognize the callings of Nature, be they from the rustling leaves, the sound of the wind blowing through the canyon or the song of an owl for its mate. They understood that to ally oneself with the natural order was to create accord that sustained life without control or manipulation. They learned that the forests are full of the little ones, spirits who reside there in exuberance and innocence.

They were taught that to use their knowledge and capacity to take by force what was not theirs or to destroy needlessly was an abuse of their power. They became adept at living in the world without being compelled to dominate others through violence, as was the tendency otherwise.

When young males came of age, they were honored in a ceremony acknowledging their maturity. Each was given a talisman created by his mother of clay and leather, stones and feathers, and blessed by everyone in the community. It symbolized the perfect balance between the masculine and the feminine.

These ceremonies were simultaneously sorrowful and hopeful. Sadness followed from the departure of a loved one who was about to venture outside the confines of our community. Hope emerged from our optimism that we were contributing another wise, compassionate, thoughtful man who might guide the tribes to peace and cooperation.

Most men of the light were born into our community. Tribal chieftains who came from within our midst led with an even hand and a commitment to integrity. They fought courageously whenever their people were attacked and won many battles through their superior physical courage and spiritual discernment.

Our lineage derived directly from those who arrived on board a ship that landed on our shores long ago, before life was as it is now. It brought strangers with immense capacity rooted in their ability to balance the energies of the divine masculine and divine feminine. That wisdom, handed down for millennia, informed the creation of Standing Stones throughout the land. It also provided the insight that guided communities of women such as ours.

Communities of men were founded as well, but they began to dissipate due to the constant threat of invasion by other tribes. Those dark forces could not penetrate our community.

∞ ∞ ∞

My first dozen years were tranquil, not because I was innocent and had no responsibilities, but because I was profoundly aware of my connection with Mother Earth and the untold blessings she granted us each day. Of course, she was accompanied by Father Sun. Without him nothing could grow, however rich our Mother's soil was. I acknowledged Father Sun with gratitude, but I felt at one with Mother Earth. I was safe with her. I overflowed with renewed excitement each dawning day, anticipating endless opportunities to play with my friends and the spirits in the surrounding forest.

One night during my twelfth year our village was blanketed in snow. We awoke in the morning to find our circle of roundhouses transformed into a magical wonderland. Everything was pure white, with nary neither a footstep nor an animal track on the ground. The pristine beauty of this monochromatic world mesmerized me.

Everything looked the same, and yet it was utterly changed. Had I perhaps flown to the distant realms where I traveled so often in my sleep and decided not to return? (I could understand why; the adventures I experienced there were most appealing.) Had I slept for a long time while Mother Nature shifted the geography of our community? Had I not awakened at all – was I still asleep, dreaming this perfection into being?

Looking at the snow, I had a memory of a distant experience long before this lifetime, when I was surrounded in white. My recollection was at once vaguely recognizable and strangely mysterious. I remembered being in a flying vessel with eight points, as crystalline as the snow, moving faster than any bird.

I sensed that everything was about to change as it had then, and who I was to become would make me even happier than I had been so far. Spontaneously I declared, "I am ready," though I had not an inkling of what I was ready to do or who I was ready to become.

My mother stood behind me as I peered outside. "And what are you ready for, my dear?" she inquired.

"I don't know," I responded, both confounded by and confident in my readiness. Then the eight-pointed star I saw earlier reappeared. It glowed so clearly in my inner vision, I was beginning to wonder if it would suddenly envelop me as it did before. Even if that occurred, I knew I would be safe.

"May I make a picture in the white blanket of snow?" I asked cautiously, uncertain whether I would be allowed to mark its perfection with my design.

"Of course," Mama replied, "as long as you create it right outside. We don't want to disrespect the surprise gift from our Mother with unnecessary footsteps."

The entrance to our hut was oriented toward the east for the equinoctial sunrise. Peering outside, I was blinded briefly by brilliant white glistening in the sun. As my eyes adjusted to the intense light, I marveled at how the snow had softened the lines and curves of everything I saw. I hesitated. My drawing would be small and insignificant in the context of the pristine beauty surrounding us.

Mama interrupted my ambivalence. "Do you want to use the handle of this wooden spoon," she asked, holding it out to me, "or would you prefer your deft finger?"

"Please, Mama, may I use my finger?" I asked hopefully.

"Of course," she reassured me. "But beware. It is unusually cold outside. Perhaps a fur over your shoulders would keep you warm enough."

Mama wrapped me in my favorite rabbit skin. When I poked my head and shoulders outside the flap, the tingle of chill felt strangely reassuring. I busied myself drawing the star I envisioned. I made the lines straight and even, trying to keep it in proportion and not lopsided, though I had no concept of proportion beyond what I saw in the designs of Nature.

As my finger moved through the snow, it seemed to be guided by an unseen force. I watched it create impressions in the smooth white surface, apparently separate from my own volition.

When I was done, I pulled back inside the hut and peered out at my handiwork. It was perfect! How could I have correctly drawn such a complicated shape? I was in awe of the result.

Mama asked casually, "Are you pleased with your design?"

"It is exactly what I saw in my head!" I exclaimed.

Mama peered through the doorway and gasped, "Oh, my sweet, you have drawn something very special. It is more than special – it is mystical. We must tell everyone immediately, before anyone steps onto the snow." Then she chanted a signal to the community that they should stop what they were doing and pay close attention.

"My child has drawn a Merkabah in the fresh fallen snow," she communicated in a voice easily heard over the stillness of the morning. "She accessed a distant memory. This signals the continuity of our lineage from the arrival of the ship that brought people of wisdom to our land untold generations ago. We must create a large

Merkabah in the snow, connecting the eight roundhouses in our village so they may once again form the star that denotes the Divine in us all. Please make a circle around the outside perimeter as you walk from your hut to ours. We will gather here."

Quickly the members of the village assembled. Mama added logs to the fire pit in the center of our roundhouse and surrounded it with boughs and herbs for burning. The women and children formed a circle around the fire, anticipating the ritual that would soon commence. I felt a rush of excitement combined with another moment of remembering. Somehow I knew what was to follow, as if I participated in the ceremony many times before.

Mama began. "We are blessed abundantly by our Mother. She gives us children and food to help them grow, a forest for us to share with the wee spirits and every necessary component of healing. The divine feminine is generous indeed. We offer our gratitude for her presence in our lives and our spirits.

"But we could not survive – or thrive – without the existence of her counterpart, the divine masculine. The complementarity between the two is the building block of our existence, essential to our enlightened consciousness. We are here to strengthen it with our intentions and actions. We are also here to propagate the wisdom that was brought to this land long ago by the wise ones who were our ancestors.

"Today we have a sign that my beloved daughter contains within her the memory of those times. I have long been convinced that she was on the ship that landed here, and that earlier in that lifetime she experienced a transformation within a crystal Merkabah. We now have evidence that such is the case."

11

"The star she drew in the snow is remarkable," commented one of the women. "No more precise Merkabah could be created. Gracila carries the wisdom of our sisterhood. May she honor the divine feminine with her life and find her loving complement, that together they may heal the vast wounds of humanity."

"Blessed be the Mother in us all," intoned the women. "Blessed be our beloved daughter. May she live in joy and peace."

What followed was a ritual I remember only slightly. The burning incense – cedar, juniper and a pinch of precious frankincense from lands far distant – intoxicated me. Chanting began slowly at first. The women danced in a circle around me, swaying in celebration, their voices rising in exaltation. Their ecstasy increased as the fragrance of the incense permeated the hut.

I experienced myself as someone else – grown up and living in an unknown land. I was walking alone on the beach. The sun was shone brilliant gold on the water, and a warm breeze rustled the skirts of my soft flowing tunic.

My heart was full of love at once new to me and completely familiar. It wasn't at all like the love I felt for Mama or the other women in our community. Rather, this love warmed me to the tips of my toes and made my heart beat fast, the way it did when I was running in the woods. I experienced a strange quality of anticipation. Being still so young, I had no awareness of what could make me feel that way.

I saw myself writing something indecipherable in a volume covered in the finest leather. I was nestled between mounds of sand a slight distance from the sea, almost totally hidden. My hand was moving rapidly across the bound sheets, creating shapes on the pages that communicated my heart's deepest truths. Then I realized I had been describing the ritual occurring in Mama's hut. I was someone else writing about what was happening to me precisely then! Shocked by this revelation, my awareness snapped back into my body. Waves of incense floated around me and chanting voices enveloped me. Mama joined me in the center of the circle and knelt down to whisper in my ear. "You were somewhere else and someone else just then, weren't you?" she asked.

"Yes, Mama," I replied. "How did you know?"

"I was there with you, helping you experience the first of many glimpses into that lifetime, then return safely to this one," she explained.

"What do you mean?" I asked, confused.

"We lived before at a different time and place and will live again when this life is complete," she said. "We will come into many lifetimes together, to share our experiences and love each other dearly."

"Will you always be my Mama?" I asked hopefully.

"I will always love you like your Mama," she assured me, "even if you know me as someone else."

Flashes of wisdom sparked my consciousness, even though I had no way of understanding what they meant. Everything had changed since I poked my head outside that morning and let my finger be guided in the snow by a power beyond me. That same power was becoming the defining quality of my existence.

This neither shocked nor concerned me. I experienced many shifts in understanding during my short life, and I assumed this was simply another one. I felt no resistance, hesitation or fear. I thought, "This is who I am now. That's fine. But I am exceedingly hungry and would love something to eat."

Everyone had brought a bit of food, which was shared all around. Then we bundled up in furs and heavy wool cloaks and formed a processional outside, with Mama leading the way. We walked from one hut to another in a line of yellows, greens and browns, each time crossing the center of the circle in the middle of the huts. With our footsteps we formed in the snow a large eight-pointed star – a Merkabah – just like the smaller one I had drawn that morning. When it was complete, we consecrated the star with our chants and offered it to Mother Nature. Even after the snow melted, the vibration of the Merkabah would remain.

The group dispersed, and Mama and I returned to our hut. She sat on the floor next to the fire, drew me to her and held me in her lap, rocking me within the reassuring contours of her body. It was such a peaceful place for me to be, her soft breasts my pillows, her crossed legs the vessel in which I nestled, her arms enfolding me securely. I slept deeply in her loving embrace. My only responsibility was to surrender fully into her love. That I could do.

I awoke rested and ready to help her with our daily chores, which I had been doing since I was a toddler. I took great pride in my ability to assist Mama, and she inevitably praised my thoughtfulness and desire to be of service.

As I was preparing to smooth out the feather and hay mattresses on our beds and cover them neatly with sheepskins, Mama said, "Today there will be no work for you. Instead we will celebrate how beautiful and smart and spirited you are. We will relax and renew."

That sounded fine to me, though I had been hoping that perhaps Mama would allow me to go outside and play in the glorious whiteness that encased our village and surrounding forest.

"First, you will have a hot bath with soothing petals and herbs," Mama announced. "We will wash your hair and clean your body to perfection, even under your fingernails. Then we will dry you in front of the fire, wrapped in our warmest blanket. I will make bergamot tea with honey in it, and you may eat as many pieces of dried fruit as you want. When you are warm and satisfied all the way through, you can put on your embroidered ceremonial tunic and fasten it with your tasseled wool rope girdle. Then I will prepare a big pot of stew, for I am expecting visitors this evening."

"What visitors?" I wondered.

"You will find out soon enough," she replied enigmatically.

"May I help you make the stew?" I asked. "At least let me use the quern to grind the herbs into a fine powder for seasoning."

"If that is your heart's desire, then by all means you may help me," Mama agreed. "But if it feels like an obligation, please tell me. You must honor yourself completely today."

I have never enjoyed any bath more than I did the one Mama prepared for me. The round tub, which had been carved from the trunk of a large tree, was ample enough for my small, supple body. I remained submerged to my neck in warm water, dried rose petals floating on the surface.

When my knees began to cramp from having been bent nearly to my chin, I shifted position and sloshed water onto one of the deerskins covering the floor.

15

Seeing that I was ready, Mama rinsed my hair with fresh water heated over the fire, then rubbed me dry with a linen cloth. She untangled my hair with her favorite comb made of horn and engraved bronze. As I lay on the blanket, she massaged my skin with oil infused with the essence of lavender. I nodded off to sleep, lost to the world.

When I awoke the stew was simmering boisterously in a cauldron suspended over the fire.

"I am happy you had such a luxurious nap," Mama assured me

"But I was supposed to grind the herbs," I lamented.

"And you shall. I left them for you," she replied, pointing to an assortment of dried herbs arranged next to the grinding stone.

Mama sang the old songs while I worked. I tried my best to follow along with her, though I wasn't adept at voicing their complicated melodies and harmonies, and I certainly couldn't remember all the words. Nonetheless, I felt more grown up than I had in the past. Though I would never equal my mother, I was becoming her partner. She stirred the pot and cleaned the hut, arranging our minimal furnishings with care.

When everything was pulverized into soft powder, I called to her, "Could you check to be sure the herbs are ground correctly?"

Mama came to my side. She peered at each precise pile, fingering the herbs in succession and sniffing their lush aromas.

"Such gifts from Mother Nature!" she exclaimed. "You have ground each one to perfection. I will add your powders to the stew, and after they have thoroughly permeated the broth, we will have a taste. The venison, bacon, onions, leeks and cabbage have combined their flavors, and your delicious spices will add the final touch. Now put on the tunic I laid out for you, and I will weave dried roses in your hair."

I couldn't imagine what visitors would warrant a bath and such finery. Beyond that, I was keenly aware that because I would be wearing ceremonial garb, I wouldn't be allowed to play in the snow. But I didn't protest. How could I resist roses decorating my unruly locks?

I rarely considered how I looked or what others thought of me. I preferred to blend into the community and let Mama take charge. But when she completed her ministrations, she handed me her polished bronze mirror. She seldom used it, and I rarely glimpsed myself.

Looking at my image staring back at me, I was aware that somehow I had become my own person. I was an individual unlike any other, though I was not sure who I was or would become.

∞ ∞ ∞

Night was about to fall. Mama added wood to the fire, making a special effort to keep the hut toasty warm. I felt my cheeks flush, and not because of the heat, when strange voices invaded our hut.

"We became disoriented in the snowstorm last night," declared a powerful male voice, "and then we lost our bearings again today. When we happened upon your circle of roundhouses, we decided to introduce ourselves and ask for information regarding our whereabouts."

Mama glanced at me then walked to the entrance, opened the flap, looked out, nodded and offered graciously, "Please, come in. Sit by our hearth and warm your weary bones. Just this afternoon my daughter and I prepared a pot of hearty stew that will revive even the hungriest sojourner. I will give you directions as well. But you must promise to stay the night and not set out again before dawn. You can make no good progress today, since it is already dusk."

"We gratefully accept your offer," commented the man, "and we ask only that you allow us to hunt for you and fill your winter coffers before we leave. It is the least we can do."

"I accept as long as you don't mind if I distribute your bounty to everyone in our village," replied Mama cheerfully. "We live in a communal way, sharing everything without condition."

"Very well," he replied. "It is as you wish."

"Then welcome," Mama invited, opening the flap wide. "Please warm yourselves by the fire."

A huge man ducked low in order to pass through the opening. He had goldenrod hair and a full beard, eyes as blue as the water in our pond, and a body as big as the trunk of the oldest tree in our forest. A red wool cloak draped over his left shoulder was covered with fox furs stitched together. When he stood up after entering, he seemed to occupy our entire hut. This was my first experience of the singularly imposing nature of masculine energy.

I was transfixed by this man. Had a god blown in from the north along with the snow? One thing was certain. He wouldn't melt as quickly as the snow when the sun came out. Most likely he would do quite the opposite in the light of day. He was formidable.

"And who is this with you?" Mama asked, interrupting my fascination with the visitor warming his frozen fingers by the fire. I turned my gaze to the entrance of our hut, where a boy a few years older than I stood quietly. Unlike his father, he was more reticent to partake of Mama's hospitality. "This is my son Lukan," the elder replied. "He is fifteen years old, almost a man. My boy, this fire has no favorites. It is here for us all."

Lukan covered the space in a few long strides and stood by the fire. He was tall for his age and leaner than his father. But his hair and eyes were the same, and his shoulders displayed the promise of a sturdy build in years to come. I observed him with a degree of detachment, since he exuded so little power compared to his father. He glanced down at the fire, apparently unaware of my presence.

"Please, make yourselves at home," Mama offered. "I will fetch two tankards of ale. When you are warmed sufficiently, you may remove your outer garments and place them by the fire to dry. Meanwhile, my daughter Gracila will serve you some stew."

At the mention of my name Lukan's eyes found mine, and we were spellbound. I was not simply looking at someone. I was peering into his soul, and he was entering mine – an experience at once unprecedented and familiar to me. Inexplicably I had just discovered myself in the eyes of a stranger.

"She is far too lovely to be serving the two of us, rough with the grit and grime of travel," Lukan's father commented.

"Please, allow me," I asserted in an unusually forthright way. "It would be an honor to share our simple stew with you. After your long journey, you both deserve to be served."

"If it is possible, your spirit is more beautiful than your physical presence," observed Lukan's father. "We accept your kind offer, but only if in return you allow us to serve you and your mother."

"It shall be so," responded Mama, wrapping herself in her heaviest cloak. "I'll go to our storehouse and return with the mead. Enjoy your stew."

I selected our two largest pottery bowls and approached the fire. "Mama and I prepared this venison stew with vegetables and herbs from our garden," I explained. "It carries magical powers that can mend broken bones and heal aching hearts. But mostly, I think it is delicious. I ground the herbs so their flavor and fragrance could infuse the broth. We made a full pot for you, so please don't stop after the first bowlful." I handed them each a bowl of sustenance and sat down by the fire's edge.

Lukan spoke at last. "You just said you made this stew for us, but you couldn't possibly have known we were about to arrive. We were lost and knew not where we were going. How could you have anticipated serving us this meal?"

"I did not, but Mama did," I explained. "She has many special powers, not the least of which is the ability to see what is about to occur. She has done that all my life. It is so commonplace, I no longer notice when once again she has made ready for what otherwise appears to be a surprise."

"Do you have the same powers?" Lukan asked with interest.

"That I don't know," I responded candidly. "Just today I experienced what Mama calls an earlier lifetime, but I have never anticipated something about to happen in this one."

"Both powers sound wonderful to me," commented Lukan. "Papa, do you have any abilities like that? Do you think I will?"

"As a matter of fact, I do have similar capacities," replied his father. "And you will as well."

"You never mentioned that before. Tell me more," Lukan encouraged.

"For one, I knew we got lost for good reason," admitted his father. "Think of it this way, Lukan. You and I have been hunting together, further and further from our home and under all conditions, since you were old enough to manage a bow and arrow. We know this countryside better than anyone. Certainly a snowstorm wouldn't create such extreme disorientation as we experienced yesterday and today."

"That's true," Lukan interrupted. "We know this land well and have never been lost before."

"Take it one step further," his father continued. "We have ventured throughout this region and yet we never came across this village. How is that possible?"

"I have no idea," confessed Lukan.

"The existence of this community was veiled from us until the proper time for us to present ourselves," declared Lukan's father. "We had to go astray in order to pierce the veil, to happen upon this village on this very day so at this precise moment we would be sitting together by this fire eating this delectable stew. Which reminds me, Gracila, could you ladle another serving into my empty bowl?"

He looked at me, azure eyes glimmering, and I smiled back at him. I filled his bowl with the best morsels in the pot.

"What is the purpose of our being guided here precisely now?" queried Lukan, forgetting his own bowl of stew.

"That is for you to discover," commented his father, "and for me to celebrate."

Mama entered carrying the mead and asked blithely, "Have you been enjoying the stew?"

"That and far more," replied Lukan's father, smiling in her direction.

"This is an auspicious day and a most joyful homecoming," she replied with love in her voice.

"Profoundly, yes," he answered, nodding. "Now, please, place yourself by the fire and let me serve you and your daughter what you created in anticipation of our arrival."

Mama took his observation in stride. "As you can see, we planned for two hungry men and two contented females," she noted. "It appears we made just enough, provided you each enjoy one more helping."

Mama sat down next to him and picked up a bowl. He filled it attentively. Then to my astonishment, he handed it to me. "In commemoration of your day," he observed, beaming.

He filled a second bowl with equal care and presented it to Mama. "Here's to your health, the expansiveness of your powers and the profundity of your legacy, generation upon generation," he said in blessing. Mama poured the honey mead into drinking horns for the men and pottery cups for us, and we toasted this good intention.

Lukan's appetite returned after his first cup of mead. He and his father finished the stew, down to the last spoonful. I looked at them with tender satisfaction. These two travelers had entered our hut unceremoniously and rather than disrupting my life, they completed it. Lukan and I shared an undeniable connection, and his father already held a significant place in my heart.

After the stew bowls were washed in water heated in the pot, Mama asked, "So tell me, where do you live and how did you come to find our village?"

"It's interesting that you should ask," began Lukan's father. "While you were procuring the mead, which is delicious by the way, we were discussing why we didn't come upon your settlement until now. We live some five days' walking distance from here, but we often explore much further. Although we travel deep into these woods, we never glimpsed your village until now. How is that possible?"

Despite his intensity a flicker of humor flew across his face.

"Since you already know the answer to that," Mama chuckled, "I'll offer additional context. Only women and their children inhabit this village. When a young boy is born and reaches the age of ten, he is sent away to be raised by his father. The girls reside here until adulthood, when they can choose to remain in the community or live with a male partner elsewhere.

"Over time this community has achieved a state of grace, which manifests as an extremely high vibration that makes our village invisible to most. When it is appropriate for us to be seen, we align the frequency of our consciousness with that of the person who is to come to us, creating the circumstance you experienced today. No doubt you have been to this location before and seen nothing but a grove of trees, a clearing and a freshwater pond. Is that not so?"

"That is exactly what we encountered!" exclaimed Lukan. "We weren't supposed to know of your existence until today. And when the time was right, finding you was as easy as locating a rabbit's hiding spot or tracking a deer."

"Precisely," affirmed Mama. "Why, then, was today was the perfect moment for you to arrive?"

Lukan looked directly at me, penetrating my heart. I smiled knowingly back at him.

"Because Gracila was ready for me," he observed. Then realizing the implication of his declaration, he clarified, "Or rather, she was ready to meet me."

"Both are true," commented his father. "But for now, let's focus on her readiness to meet you."

Mama looked at me encouragingly, which I took as an invitation to speak.

"Today I discovered aspects of myself that had been hidden from me, just as our village was hidden from you," I ventured. "I drew an image in the snow, allowing my finger to be guided by a force apart from myself. I remembered it from a lifetime long ago, when I sailed here with the wise ones."

"It was a Merkabah," Mama explained to Lukan's father.

"I assumed that," he responded fluidly.

Undeterred, I continued. "As the women in the village celebrated this confirmation with chanting and incense, I experienced myself in that lifetime, writing about this very day as it has unfolded."

"So you do have your mother's remarkable powers!" exclaimed Lukan excitedly.

"Perhaps," I responded tentatively. "The shape I drew in the snow was what brought you here. Lukan, when I drew the Merkabah I was preparing to receive you. Until that moment I was still a young girl. I am still young, but I feel twice as old today as I was yesterday."

Lukan's father smiled at me with satisfaction and a touch of paternal pride. "She is indeed your daughter," he remarked admiringly to Mama. "You have prepared her well. I can only hope I have done equally well with Lukan."

"You have," Mama assured him. "And if either of us missed the mark, their connection is so perfectly aligned, they can easily make the necessary recalibrations."

I was growing uncomfortable with these commentaries about the two of us, made in our presence as if we were not there at all.

"I fear we have offended Gracila by sharing our thoughts. Have we been disrespectful?" Lukan's father asked me directly.

"There has been no disrespect," I replied. "Rather, it is as if you and Mama already know much more than Lukan and I, and you are talking past us as you anticipate what lies ahead. Please allow us to discover it for ourselves. It would be much better that way, don't you think?"

"Lukan, your divine complement just proved herself in my eyes, not that she needed to," commented his father. "But there it is – the voice of the most worthy and exalted feminine coming from one so young. Listen to her well and always, for she is a teller of truths. Beyond that, she should have roses for her hair year round."

"I will heed your counsel, Papa, roses included," Lukan affirmed eagerly. "And now, if the two of you would warm your feet by the fire, I'd like to take Gracila for a stroll outside."

He stood up and held out his hand to help me rise. Heat engulfed my body with his touch. I willed my hand to be in his for all of eternity. Little did I know we already made that commitment over venison stew and silent communion.

"May I help you with a warm wrap?" he asked, more formally than was necessary.

"I'll get it for you," I replied, removing a heavy cloak from a peg on the opposite wall. He deftly draped it over my shoulders as if he had been doing so all his life.

"We won't be long," he assured our parents. "And even if we take longer than you expect, please don't come looking for us. We'll be safe and warm."

Lukan held the flap open for me, and we stepped outside.

"There's the Merkabah," he whispered, pointing to the shape glistening in the light of the full moon. "It's beautiful and perfect, just like you."

"I don't know about that," I replied self-consciously. "But it doesn't hurt for you to see me in that light."

"I'll never stop seeing you that way," he declared, "so you may as well get used to it."

I wondered what was going to happen as we walked. Would he be silent? Would he hold my hand? Would he ask endless questions? Would he reveal his own buried secrets?

That evening I came to understand the intensity of our connection and accept the immensity of our love. Despite our youth our oneness was apparent. We recognized each other from the lifetime before, when I walked the beach and wrote in leather journals. I knew I had met the person who would mature into a man and be my beloved for the rest of our lives. He knew he had met the girl who would blossom into the love of his life, the core of his being. Although we couldn't put words to this, it was our essential shared truth.

He took my hand in his, holding it with gentle resolve. I didn't dare look at him, for fear of breaking the spell that seemed to make us one as we walked together wordlessly. When we approached the edge of the forest, which gave us a measure of privacy, Lukan faced me directly and took my hands in his.

"Gracila, I know who you are, now and in the future. I will love who you will become just as I love you as you are now," he vowed. "I cannot explain this, and I have no more words to express how I feel. But if you agree, I would like you to be my partner and lover and perfect complement throughout our days on this Earth.

"You are young still, as am I. You need not respond now. But when you are old enough to do so, I request only that you consider committing yourself to me as I have done to you."

True, I was too young to make such a commitment for life, and yet I felt the same as he. I let my heart form the words, discovering how I would respond as I spoke.

"First, Lukan, I am only three years younger than you. If you feel comfortable making such a lasting commitment, so can I," I replied.

I had gotten off to a very bad start. My words sounded antagonistic. But Lukan was smiling back at me, apparently expecting nothing less. I took another step into the unknown.

"I can't pretend to understand it, but I know with all that I am – and all that I will become – that you are my eternal love. Let's not get distracted with concerns about commitment and how our lives will unfold. Let's instead rejoice in the gift of our togetherness, knowing it can only expand as we grow."

Those were not my words, yet they eloquently expressed my thoughts and feelings. Suddenly I was transported to the earlier lifetime I shared with Lukan. I saw him standing across from me, older but essentially the same. What I just communicated to him came from who I was before, brought forward into this moment. Then I had another revelation. He had been speaking from that lifetime as well.

"Do you know what just happened?" I asked.

"I believe so," he responded. "We temporarily became who we used to be when we were together in an earlier life."

"I went there with you," I affirmed. "I wonder if the full moon is helping us move back and forth between incarnations."

"Whatever is enabling this to occur, it affirms our love," responded Lukan. "I loved you in that existence as I do now. Nothing has changed, nor will it."

"What shall we do, then?" I asked, acutely aware we were too young to be together as we were before.

"We'll use the time that lies ahead to become the best version of ourselves," he answered with conviction. "That way I will deserve you, and you will be an even more forthright presence in my life."

"Will we see each other?" I queried, already anxious about his departure.

"Yes, of course," he assured me. "But mostly, you will be learning everything you can from the woman you respect the most, and I will be doing the same with my father."

"When can we be together for good?" I begged to know.

"When we both are ready," he answered, refusing to predict the unpredictable. "In the meantime, the months and years will fly past us faster than a fox beating a hasty retreat."

"But there's no retreat into our future," I laughed.

"No there isn't," he chuckled. "We'll be drawing closer together instead of away from each other, even while we're apart."

Looking at Lukan, I understood we were already united in an unfathomable love. I would surrender to it, and make the most of the time that separated us.

Lukan bent down and kissed the tip of my nose. It was a familiar gesture, albeit an unusual first kiss.

"I have no idea why I just did that," he admitted, "because I was thinking how much I would love to give you a real kiss on the lips. But I'll save that for later. For now, your nose will have to do. By the way, it is as cold as an icicle. We'd better return to your roundhouse and the fire, which your Mama and my Papa have no doubt been maintaining for us."

"You used to kiss the tip of my nose when we were together before," I noted, though I was unaware of that memory until I verbalized it. "Thousands of kisses were bestowed upon my grateful nose. Keep doing that, and your kisses will sustain me – and my nose – for at least another lifetime or two."

∞ ∞ ∞

Lukan took my hand and we walked briskly back to the hut. Mama and his father were sitting together by the fire, talking quietly.

"How was your walk?" Mama asked noncommittally, giving us a chance to respond superficially or otherwise. I turned to Lukan for guidance, inviting him to express whatever was to be revealed – or not.

"We agreed that we are blessed to have found each other so soon," Lukan stated with alacrity. "Gracila is the love of my life, and I am her love as well. Of course, it is much too early for us to complete the oneness that has already occurred. So we'll continue to live as we have been, learning and growing all the while. Then when we do come together, we'll bring the best of ourselves to our union."

"Well said, son," replied his father. "We were just discussing how to handle the situation if you two insisted on seeing more of each other from now on. We were hoping you would remain levelheaded even in the context of your discoveries this evening, and I am gratified you chose such a responsible approach."

"During our walk we shared the distinct memory of being together before," I interjected. "Acknowledging the love we brought forward into this lifetime contributes to our patience. We can unite in the best possible way if we take time to develop into the adults we will become."

"Based on what I'm hearing, I'd say you two have little growing up left to do," commented Mama. "Your choices are remarkable in their wisdom and prescience. You are older than your years, as I would expect. With that said, neither of you is mature enough to enter into the relationship that is your destiny. You must wait and as you say, make the most of your experiences between this evening and the day of your sacred union."

"Papa, what would you advise me to do now?" Lukan asked.

"You have ample opportunity to learn the skills and wisdom you'll need to serve and succeed," observed his father. "For now I suggest you allow yourself to experience the sheer joy of having received the precious gift of love. There is no greater honor than that, and there is no greater responsibility than to be deserving of that love."

Lukan had chosen a wise and loving parent, as had I. Most likely his Papa and my Mama shared that earlier lifetime with Lukan and me.

Mama read my thoughts. "Lukan's father and I were the high priest and high priestess in the temples in your earlier lifetime," she explained. "We were lovers in the most exalted sense, strengthening the presence of the divine masculine and the divine feminine on the Earth plane every time we merged physically. We were also intellectual equals, intimate companions and close colleagues. The two of you were our dear friends – family, really. It was a marvelous lifetime, wasn't it?"

"It was," confirmed Lukan's father, "until we were forced to flee before the fall. But even then, we protected the divine wisdom that was the foundation of our existence and carried it forth to the new land we inhabited. Our love gave us great joy each day of our lives."

"Mama, will you two be lovers again?" I asked, unable to withhold the question. "And if so, wouldn't that make Lukan and me more like brother and sister?"

"We considered the implications before we incarnated this time and agreed that our primary purpose was to bring the two of you into the world," Mama revealed. "We also committed to imparting all that we knew to prepare you both for your life's purpose and celebrate your togetherness when you were ready to leave hearth and home. To accomplish that appropriately, we agreed not to be lovers. Even so, we'll always love each other with deep respect and open hearts. Never fear, my love. Nothing will obstruct your union with Lukan."

"But Mama, if you both feel the way Lukan and I do, that's too great a sacrifice for you to make," I objected.

"Lukan's mother and your father were the chosen ones for this lifetime," Mama explained. "We are at peace with this decision. Now that the four of us have come together, I feel nothing but gratitude."

"One more question, Papa," requested Lukan. "Gracila and I were with you two on the ship that set sail when the fall was imminent, were we not?"

"Yes, you were," affirmed Lukan's father. "We invited you to leave the island with us."

"And after a long voyage, we landed somewhere near here," continued Lukan.

"We did," his father affirmed. "We established our village precisely on this piece of land. We lived here together for many years, creating a portal to the realms of the Divine with our meditation and worship."

"That enables this village to resonate with divine light even as it exists on the Earth plane," noted Lukan excitedly. "It's a sacred place, like a temple in Nature, that has remained pure ever since we consecrated it."

"Those are vital insights about this location," Lukan's father verified. "Other power spots exist as well. I'll acquaint you with them in the next few years."

"Can I go, too?" I blurted out.

"You will experience them later, with Lukan as your guide," his father assured me. "Similarly you will share your knowledge as Lukan's guide, taking him to previously unexplored dimensions of divine oneness."

"There is so much to look forward to!" I exclaimed.
"And so much to be thankful for right now," Mama
reminded me.
We raised our containers of honey mead and toasted
our shared gratitude.

∞ ∞ ∞

Mama had a great deal to teach me. Time stretched
out before us like an endless summer of warmth and
glorious, sparkling sunshine. Every day presented me
with a new discovery, an expansive exploration of the
realms of the divine feminine. I learned how to grow
herbs, flowers and plants that had miraculous healing
powers. And then when I became adept at that, Mama
taught me the opposite – that I could heal others with my
well-intentioned love, without relying on powders,
brews or poultices. When I was able to see the perfection
in another, when I acknowledged nothing but his or her
divinity, the portal was open for that person to return to
the birthright of divine perfection. That was the secret of
what others referred to as miraculous healing.

Mama reminded me of the capabilities I had in my
prior lifetime, which were aligned with what I was
learning. She told me often that I was following a
process of remembering more than learning, since I
carried the wisdom deep within me already.

"Did I make a lot of soup?" I asked her out of the
blue.

"When, dear?" she queried.

"Before, when you were the high priestess and I was
with Lukan," I explained.

"Oh my, yes," she told me cheerfully. "You had a
thriving business that sold homemade soup from street

carts. You made twice as much as you could sell so you would have plenty to give away to the needy at the end of the day. Your soups were renowned for their robustness and healing powers. Both derived from your ability to hear plants tell you how to create unique combinations for flavor and health. You also opened healing centers that used the herbs to counteract disease and realign energies enhancing wellness."

"So the stew we made the day Lukan and his Papa arrived, and the herbs you had me grind into powder, were meant to work their magic," I surmised. "The stew helped the four of us find each other, since it was reminiscent of the soups I made before and the healing I did with plants and herbs."

"Absolutely," Mama agreed. "Rather than telling you about it, I thought it would be more enjoyable and meaningful for you to discover this association on your own. Have you been tapping into your earlier life?"

"I get glimpses into it," I replied. "They arrive unbidden, usually when I'm preoccupied with a task I enjoy and thinking of nothing in particular. Then I become the person I was before. I see patterns that connect who I was then with who I am now. Some tendencies I want to correct."

"Such as," Mama invited me to continue.

"Such as her habit of working too hard because she was so committed to helping others," I explained. "I recalled a conversation with Lukan in that lifetime when he commented on how I was sacrificing time with our family in order to serve the community. He asked me to reconsider my priorities."

"And what did you do?" Mama queried.

"I burst into tears when I realized he was correct," I declared. "I asked a number of capable people working with me to accomplish what I had been doing, which enabled me to spend more time at home. It was wonderful and not difficult to do."

"Do you think you are working too hard now?" asked Mama.

I paused. That never occurred to me. I did fill my days to overflowing because there was always so much to do and so many people to help.

"Now that you mention it, maybe so," I observed. "I can change that now, so Lukan won't have to approach me again about rethinking my priorities."

"That's why you have this time with me," Mama noted. "I am helping you make enlightened choices about what you want to carry into your union with Lukan and what you prefer to set aside. This is an opportunity for your spirit to evolve rapidly. Your relationship with Lukan will be unburdened and effortlessly joyful as a result."

Then it dawned on me. "When you tell me I still have a great deal to learn, you are referring to what I can remember about my prior life!" I exclaimed. "I thought all along that learning involved what you and others could teach me."

"There is some of that," Mama acknowledged, "but as you indicate, most important is an in-depth understanding of yourself. My role is more to affirm your own insights than to point out a blind spot or unwanted tendency from your earlier experiences."

"Are everyone's lifetimes closely linked, with similarities between who we were before and who we become in our current existence?" I wondered.

"Yes, for the most part," Mama answered.

"But how does that happen, if we only occasionally remember what occurred before?" I persisted.

"Our experiences form imprints on our soul, which then affect how we approach situations," Mama explained. "We retain unconscious habits and perspectives that cause us to perceive and act in ways that are similar – and sometimes identical – to what is encoded in those imprints."

"How can we change something we no longer want to perpetuate?" I asked, anxious to apply her answer to my own life.

"You always have free will choice," Mama said matter-of-factly. "You are never required to remain mired in a pattern that doesn't serve your own spiritual emergence. One of the primary reasons our spirit takes embodiment multiple times is to enable us to strengthen the Divine within us and release vestiges of fallen consciousness. Over time we perfect our existence until finally we return to oneness with our Creator."

"Did I make many mistakes previously that I must spend this lifetime correcting?" I worried.

"No, my love," Mama assured me. "The key is for you to live in the perfection of your love. Whatever happens, never forget that the only reality is love. All else is illusion. During the most extreme chaos, when others around you are paralyzed by their own fears, remember this and all will be well. Affirm love, and the imprints on your soul will be those born of that love."

∞ ∞ ∞

I would be remiss were I not to offer a few stories of how I spent my early years, before Lukan and his father entered my life. Now is as good an interlude as any to do so.

My mother was the acknowledged leader of a communal sisterhood, though there were no formal means through which she established her leadership. Our circle of huts was populated with a number of highly adept worshipers of the divine feminine. Even so, Mama's wisdom, healing powers and direct access to the loving vibration of the feminine far exceeded the capacity of anyone else in the village.

The women lived this way not because they preferred their own gender sexually – quite the opposite was true – or because they reviled or disrespected men. Rather, their choice reflected their desire to thrive in the untrammeled purity of the divine feminine. Our community was not unlike the temples for priestesses in my earlier incarnation, where women led relatively secluded lives immersed in their spiritual practices.

We resided in a protected vortex emanating the highest frequencies of divinity. This was accomplished through constant worship of the feminine during rituals, chants, meditations, dancing and spontaneous speaking. We also celebrated the seasons and phases of Mother Nature – the moon cycles, the solstices and equinoxes – and participated in annual festivities. Most important of all was the intention we held in our hearts as we went about our daily tasks. Every act was a form of worship, an opportunity to create from love.

We were protected from the encroachment of compromised consciousness because those who embodied it couldn't actually see where we lived. We provided no threat to their greed, hatred or violence because we weren't obvious to them. We were living simultaneously on the Earth plane and in another dimension. Because of our daily practices and the impeccable actions of every member of our community, the vortex that surrounded us remained invulnerable. Only those whose love was pure could see our village and penetrate it.

Despite this extraordinary circumstance – or perhaps because of it – the women in our village ventured out on occasion to provide healing services and minister to the sick, the hungry and the lame. Our healers requested nothing in return, except that no one follow or find them. Over the centuries other tribes welcomed the women on their terms. Since no one knew the whereabouts of the village, messages were sent telepathically when the assistance of a healer was critically needed. Invariably the most appropriate person to serve the ailing or injured individual was on her way.

Our village was situated where Mama established a temple in a lifetime long, long ago. She had left behind a magnificent marble structure, perfectly proportioned and precisely constructed, only to have her new temple composed of dirt and rocks, grass and trees, flowers and birds provided by Mother Nature. More than once she commented that this new temple was more spectacular than the previous one.

During that lifetime women from surrounding tribes stopped by to see what was occurring, then over the centuries they formed our community. It consisted of the souls and spirits of those who chose to honor the feminine uncompromisingly.

Men were allowed into the village, but only if they embodied a vibratory frequency aligned with the community. Women took lovers, sometimes for life and sometimes temporarily. Either way, they were discerning in their choice of a partner. The men who visited were invariably revitalized by the lovemaking in which they engaged. They emanated even more of the divine masculine, which was already considerable. I came to relish the times when a man would appear for a visit with his lover. Somehow everything in our village seemed more vibrant and complete. I assumed it was because he brought necessities from the outside world. As I matured, I realized that no matter how aligned we were with the divine feminine, we still needed the masculine to complement us. These men were catalytic sources of wholeness and abundance in our otherwise seasonal and cyclical lives.

Whenever Mama's lover – my father – was present, I was taken to another hut to sleep and spend my days. Since that was what everyone in the community did when her partner arrived, I thought nothing of it. This meant, however, that I had only a peripheral acquaintance with the man who sired me.

Interestingly, after one evening with Lukan's father I felt more love and acceptance from him than I experienced in all the years I knew my own my father. It's not that he was inconsiderate or uncaring. Quite the contrary, he was generous with his affection whenever he saw me. But he had a more compelling priority that involved privacy with my mother. Their relationship brought him to the village – not the fact that he had a daughter there as well.

I experienced no void in my life because my father was rarely present. He wasn't expected to be there for me, and I could count on everyone else. I grew up in a communal setting comprised of one large extended family. Nothing was lacking.

When I was older, Mama explained to me what occurred during her lover's visits. She told me that the most beautiful way to access and affirm one's own divinity is to create oneness with a lover who complements oneself. Therefore, one's choice of a lover is the most important decision she can make. When the complementarity is there, the oneness the two achieve is transformative. When it is not, the experience is less than fulfilling and under the worst circumstances can create despair and heartache.

"Do you agree with me that Lukan is my perfect complement?" I asked her, the better to avoid my own despair and heartache.

"Definitely," Mama assured me. "The two of you complete each other to perfection, and your love is enduring. He embodies the divine masculine vibration that matches your divine feminine."

"What do those words mean exactly?" I wondered. Assurances were fine, but I wanted to understand them.

"A man and a woman can come together in many ways," she began. "They can be acquaintances who collaborate on shared interests, friends who support one another faithfully, or brother and sister committed to each other because of their lineage.

"They can also choose to become lovers," Mama continued. "This is where the road of friendship forks and takes a different direction. To accept a man as your lover requires you to make yourself available to him physically. The two of you unite as one when he pierces your body at the entrance to your womb. You welcome him, and he fills you with his power and his seed. That is how babies are conceived."

As Mama described this process, I experienced intimations of my union with Lukan when we were lovers in an earlier life.

Mama saw this dawning recognition and carried on. "But that is not the most important aspect of your coming together. With your divine complement, the act of physical love opens the portal for the two of you to merge spiritually, becoming one being, one force, one essence. You join so completely, the 'you' who used to be vanishes, as does the 'he' who used to be. You are reborn into oneness."

"I remember that feeling from before," I told Mama. "Do you think Lukan and I will experience it again?"

"The two of you are essentially the same as you were in that lifetime," Mama observed. "And yet neither of you has remained static. You are both growing and changing and reaching even more of your potential. You will bring that into your relationship. Do not wish that it be exactly as it was, for you are each growing and changing. Have the courage to contribute your own individuality to your partnership – and welcome his with all your heart. Celebrate his ongoing emergence, and allow him to recognize and celebrate yours. Then your oneness will become ever more profound."

"Do you feel such profound oneness with my father?" I asked.

"Yes, I do, and it makes my heart sing," Mama affirmed. "But our capacity to merge doesn't equal what I had with the spirit who is now Lukan's father, when we came together in our earlier lifetime as priest and priestess."

"Do you love him more than you love my father?" I prodded.

"I wouldn't say I love Lukan's father more," Mama replied candidly. "Rather, I love him in a different way. We will be the closest of companions in this lifetime, since we committed to bringing the two of you into the world and preparing you for the lives you will share."

"But you gave up so much," I objected.

"Our commitment was critical for this lifetime and many others to follow," Mama stated vehemently. "What you and Lukan do – who you are – in this incarnation will influence future lifetimes when you both will greatly impact the world.

"You needed to have us as your parents. We gratefully volunteered for that role. The fact that we won't be lovers this time is a small consideration in the larger context of our involvement with you and Lukan."

"And my father?" Once more I searched for clarity.

"Your father loves you dearly and is proud of you," Mama assured me. "He spends time during his visits asking about you and listening as I provide every detail."

"So he does care," I commented.

"He cares with all of his being," Mama confirmed. "Why else would he bring you a wonderful gift each time he is here – a doll made of leather, a carved box for your bronze pins? He creates something for you with his own hands in the interval between visits."

"I haven't thanked him adequately," I acknowledged. "I always felt he was so interested in you, I didn't matter."

"You matter a great deal to him," replied Mama, giving me a warm hug. "I'll make sure you spend more time with him when he is here."

Mama made that possible, but my experiences with him lacked something. It didn't take me long to realize I already had a father whom I loved dearly – Lukan's Papa.

∞ ∞ ∞

I saw Lukan only once during the time between our initial meeting and our sacred union. He and his father returned when I was seventeen. Five years had passed since their first visit. Although I had become a woman by then, I was not prepared for who Lukan had grown to be.

Winter was still blowing across the land, bringing with it bone chilling temperatures and almost impossible conditions for travel. As much as I longed to see Lukan again – I was beside myself with anxiety and excitement – I wanted no harm to come to him or his father during their journey. I would rather they waited until the spring thaw than jeopardize their safety by making the trek now. Mama assured me nothing would keep them from arriving at the divinely ordained time.

I spent countless hours that winter sorting, scouring, combing and spinning the wool for a tunic I was making for the occasion. I selected berries for color, which I mixed with a copper mordant to help the dye adhere to the wool, and carefully followed guidelines for which days of the month were best for dyeing. The periwinkle blue wool that emerged from the dyeing vat was soft and subtle. I wove the yarn into two rectangles of fabric then sewed them together and added cast bronze buttons at the shoulders. Finally, I braided purple wool and leather to create a belt with a bronze belt hook, compliments of Mama. I was ready to see my beloved again, robed in an expression of my joy.

On a day more beautiful than we had seen in at least two moon cycles, I heard their voices. Mama and I were sitting in meditation, surrounding them with our prayers to help ensure their safe and expedient journey. I looked at Mama and she nodded, eyes sparkling.

"You may welcome our guests," she suggested.

I approached the entrance to our hut and pulled back the flap. Peering out, I saw two huge men standing outside. Lukan's father I recognized, although he had more gray in his beard and the creases in his face had deepened. The other one was the same size, large and muscular – vital in an undeniably masculine way. Was that really Lukan? If so would he recognize me?

Our eyes found each other and we merged, swimming in a calm pool of togetherness. My awareness left my body and became part of him. We held our gaze of infinite love, timeless, until his father commented wryly, "I see nothing has been lost in our absence."

Lukan chuckled and, allowing me to collect myself, responded cheerfully, "After five long years, Gracila and I managed to pick up right where we left off."

"I expected as much," noted his father jovially.

I resumed my duties as hostess and official greeter, not that they were necessary. "Please do come in," I said, standing aside to allow them to enter. "We haven't made the stew yet, since we weren't sure when you'd be arriving."

"I suspect your Mama knew full well when to expect us," observed Lukan's father, "but she feared that starting the stew would thrust you into intolerable waves of anticipation. So she kept you appropriately in the dark."

He gave Mama a hearty embrace and kissed both cheeks for good measure. "If it is possible to become more beautiful than you were before, I believe it has come to pass. There's good reason you are known for consistently accomplishing the impossible."

Mama smiled back at him. "You exaggerate, but I'll accept the compliment and remind myself that you have seen nothing but the harsh, cold face of Mother Nature on your journey here. An old hag would seem beautiful in comparison. Warm yourselves by the fire while I fetch some mead."

"Let me go with you, since I'm still dressed for the cold." offered Lukan's father. "Perhaps you can take me on a tour of the village while it is still daylight."

With that they were out the door, the flap closing quickly behind them.

Lukan and I gazed at each other. I wanted to run to him, but I hesitated.

"You have been in my heart every moment of every day," he said, sweeping me into his arms in a fierce embrace. "You have accompanied me on hunts and sat with me through Papa's many gatherings. You have given me strength during endless training as I learned how to defend our land and customs. And at the end of the day, you were the last thing I was aware of before I fell asleep."

Tears welled up from deep within me. If I allowed a single one to spill onto my cheeks, I would be incapable of stemming the tide.

"Lukan," I sighed, "I tried with all my might to be strong and self-sufficient. But in my heart all I wanted was to be with you, to have you hold me. Now that you're here, I don't know how I can endure another parting."

With that I surrendered to a flood of tears, splashes of relief and happiness and gratitude for this end to our separation.

He held me steadfastly and patiently. I would come to know his love in precisely this way, for no one could be more steadfast or patient than Lukan. He must have grown quite warm, standing in our hut with layers of wool and fur still covering his body. But there he was, holding me securely with no thought but to be there for me and with me.

The tears subsided and the deer hair woven with the wool of his cloak was scratching my cheek. I lifted my face from the wet folds and peered at him tentatively. The tenderness in his gaze crept into my heart, and I began crying all over again.

"This will never do," he said, kissing the top of my head. "If you cry every time I look at you, I'll be reduced to gazing at the floor. And it is far less interesting than your glistening green eyes and mass of auburn hair. Oh, my marvelous Gracila, you are so beautiful!"

His voice soothed me, and the tears vanished just as quickly as they had arrived.

"And you, my dear Lukan, grew into quite an impressive man," I reported appreciatively.

"Don't be overawed," he rejoined. "You might wait to pass judgment until the badger furs I am wearing beneath this massive cloak have been removed."

"You must be suffocating!" I exclaimed.

"It's getting pretty warm under all this," he commented, pulling off the layers. "Clearly I've been preoccupied with an important undertaking."

Lukan folded his outer garments and stacked them out of the way. I watched him, comfortable in his tall, lean body, remembering how his long arms felt around me.

"I'll admit, the furs did add something," I quipped. "But you look even more appealing without them. I have a suggestion. Why don't you take those recently unburdened arms of yours and surround me with them all over again?"

I made my way to Lukan, as joyful as a young colt on a spring day. We held each other for a long while. I listened to his heart beating, strong and steady and also very like him. I matched my breathing with his. Then he pulled back slightly, releasing me from his firm grip. He took my face in his hands and studied every detail of it, as if to memorize it for all eternity. I felt seen and understood, cherished and respected.

Lukan affectionately kissed the tip of my nose, recalling our walk in the snow the evening we first met. Then his lips were on mine. He touched them softly and with such gentleness, I wondered how someone so physically imposing could be that tender. I leaned into him and his kiss, hungering for a deeper and more complete joining with him. And with that we were both undone.

We kissed each other passionately, our desire increasing. I urgently pressed my body against his. It was everything I could do to keep from inviting him to lie with me right there in the middle of the hut.

His hardness arose against my belly. He, too, desired more than our kisses. His lips left mine and graced my eyes and cheeks and nose with their sweet caresses. The imposing part of him lower down grew more insistent.

"It's hopeless," he announced. "If I keep kissing you and feeling your body so soft and enticing against mine, I won't be able to contain myself. And since the time hasn't yet arrived for our sacred union, I must stop."

"Are you always this considerate?" I asked, still in a haze.

"Only with the people I love," he replied, "in which case I can be unbearably attentive."

We pulled apart. Taking my hand, Lukan led me to the fire. We sat next to each other, watching the flames dancing and the embers popping. He put his arm around my shoulder and began massaging my muscles with his thumb. It was an act of intimate familiarity, something a man would do with his love after perhaps ten or twenty or thirty years together. And yet there he was, kneading the tension from my body, after having been with me for only one day five years ago.

"I can't fathom what those strong fingers of yours will do with my feet," I commented, punching him playfully in what I discovered was a rock-solid abdomen.

"Feet are my specialty," he declared, "unless you are ticklish, in which case I could very well cause you to lose your senses completely."

"May I be reduced to losing my senses perpetually, in and out of lifetimes," I replied.

"That, my love, is a certainty," he replied, giving my newly relaxed shoulders and extra squeeze of reassurance.

At that the flap opened, and Mama and Papa entered the hut. "Sorry we took so long," Mama commented. "We stopped in to visit one of the women in the village. She had just made winter cakes with dried apples and nuts, and we couldn't refuse a taste."

"Thank you, Mama, for giving us time to adjust to each other," I quipped.

"I might have surmised you would allow me no pretense," Mama responded amiably. "And I should have known none was necessary. We all know each other too well for that. But after an absence spanning half a decade, I wanted to be cautious."

"No need for caution," commented Lukan, "except where Gracila's kisses are concerned. I got so caught up in them, I almost forgot that our sacred union is still a long way off."

Hearing that, I realized there would be no secrets among us. Then it dawned on me that Lukan's openness with Mama and Papa confirmed he intended to honor our agreement. Nothing would be concealed, nor could it be.

Mama and I busied ourselves making stew while Lukan and his father lounged by the fire drinking mead and chatting casually with us. Occasionally I glanced at Lukan, who was watching me intently.

As I was pulverizing the herbs into fine powder, I sent my love into each arc the stone in my hand made in the quern. I felt the herbs come alive, thinking to myself, "This will be a delectable repast if I have anything to do with it!"

"We are preparing for a Roman invasion from across the channel," Lukan's father announced, interrupting the stream of love I was sending into the herbs.

"How soon do you expect it to occur?" asked Mama.

"Perhaps this year, but most likely the next," he replied.

"And will you be there to meet them?" Mama inquired, clearly concerned.

"We are calling for a gathering of kings and tribal chieftains to agree upon an approach all can support," he explained. "Our strongest defense lies in our unity. If we cannot achieve that, I may consider a less confrontational strategy. The Romans have a far superior force in numbers, training, tactics and weaponry. It would be foolhardy to take them on if we had little possibility of success."

I looked at Lukan, wondering if he would be among those sent into battle. I wished with all my heart that wouldn't be necessary.

"I have almost completed my training," he revealed, "and will be ready when I am needed."

"That is for me to decide," declared his father. "I have no intention of sending myself or my son into battle for no good reason. I fully support your rigorous training, Lukan, but I cannot agree it will lead you into armed combat."

"Don't misunderstand me," Lukan urged. "I find violence abhorrent, especially since it is usually caused by a handful of power mad men whose only source of satisfaction is to conquer and harm. I am loath to give up my life trying to deter those who stupidly desire nothing but to dominate others."

"Well said, Lukan," affirmed his father. "We are in agreement, then."

"So far," Lukan responded. "But I won't stand by feebly and allow others to wreak havoc on our way of life. We have maintained a relative peace for more generations than can be counted. We live simply but well. We maintain rituals and traditions from the past, keeping their spark of spirit shining bright.

"I refuse to sacrifice our way of life without first giving my all to defend it. And if an effective defense is not possible, then I am willing to consider negotiation and diplomacy. Perhaps we can still preserve the essence of who we are, even under occupation by a force from afar."

Lukan's father gazed at him thoughtfully. "You have developed into a wise leader," he observed. "I will leave the judgment to you regarding your role in what lies ahead. Please forgive me. Sometimes I forget you are no longer a young boy. It is not my responsibility to protect you."

"I hope I embody the best that you have taught me," replied Lukan. "If I am half the man you are, I will be blessed far more than I deserve."

His father's eyes grew misty. Mama and I were witnessing a candid, loving exchange between father and son – a rare privilege.

Lukan's father gazed at Mama and me, "Thank you, dear ones, for the gift you have just given Lukan and me," he acknowledged.

"And what gift is that?" queried Mama.

"The gift of the divine feminine in the nurturing space you create here," he clarified. "Lukan and I would never have shared such an exchange anywhere else. I am grateful to you both for making it possible."

"It was an honor to be included," responded Mama. "I glimpsed in you new facets I hadn't seen before, and I thought I knew you well."

"You do, my dear," he affirmed. "It's just that I continue to evolve. How could I not with Lukan at my side?"

The men napped while the stew simmered. Mama and I whispered briefly so as not to disturb them.

"All is well?" she asked, allowing me to choose how much I was ready to reveal to her.

"I love Lukan so much, I think I will burst," I revealed.

"You two have managed to grow together flawlessly, even during a protracted absence," observed Mama.

"Hasn't he become handsome?" I asked, expecting no disagreement.

"He is as wondrous as the sun and the moon together," she affirmed. "I see a great deal of his father

Love, 24 AD

in him, and yet he is his own person. His father is so
proud of Lukan, he is absolutely beaming."

"I am beaming as well," I added, "but for different
reasons.

Their visit was much too short. But then after seeing
Lukan again, nothing could have satisfied my need to
experience more of him in my life. I loved him deeply,
and I was also very much in love with him.

Our union would occur the following year during
our celebration of the spring equinox. This moment,
along with the autumn equinox, represented the perfect
complementarity of the divine masculine and the divine
feminine in Nature and humanity. It was considered the
most auspicious moment for a sacred union.

I would have to wait sixteen moon cycles until
Lukan's return. I stayed busy, the better to keep our
time apart from feeling like sixteen seasons.

I had much to prepare. Mama and I gathered and
made household necessities – wooden ladles and
dippers, pottery bowls and cups, willow baskets in
various sizes and shapes, a hammered bronze bucket
and my very own quern. We also collected herbs and
healing remedies, for I was almost as proficient as Mama
at healing illnesses, disabilities and chronic physical
difficulties. That spring we planted a larger garden in
order to harvest herbs in the fall and have ample cuttings
the following spring with which I could start my own
garden.

Finally, Mama filled my clothing chest with a
rainbow-colored wardrobe she created lovingly for me.
Some of the designs were reminiscent of what we wore
in our earlier lifetime. The tunic-shaped leines in
gossamer linen and wool were so soft, I wanted no more
of the rough homespun I typically wore. Each leine was

decorated with fringes, bright tapestry borders and elaborate needlework. The chest contained more serviceable garments as well, which Mama suggested I wear when I prepared pots of stew for my husband-to-be.

∞ ∞ ∞

Sometimes Lukan appeared before me as I slept. His palpable presence would startle me awake, after which I lost my connection with him.

One day as I was tilling the thawing ground for our garden, I realized if I willed myself to remain asleep when I felt Lukan's presence, perhaps we could enjoy being together for longer periods of time. That night before I went to sleep I invited Lukan to visit me.

The moment I fell asleep he appeared, hovering over me and whispering, "I am here, my love."

"I miss you so much," I responded. "How will I ever manage to wait another full cycle of seasons before our union?"

"I am lamenting the delay as well," he admitted. "Tell me what you've been doing, down to the smallest detail."

Communicating with him as we slept strengthened our connection. Then one night we merged so completely, I lost my individual identity. We were one spirit. There was no "he" and no "me" – not even an "us."

We held this oneness long enough to appreciate that something extraordinary had occurred. We remained silent afterwards. Then he bid me farewell and promised to return the next night.

We experimented with meeting in other locations. I had never been to his village and was unclear about where it was located. But he suggested I simply trust I would find him, and to my delight I did. Our spirits met in secluded spots throughout the countryside, none of which I had seen before.

We experienced each other's presence when we were awake as well. Usually when my mind was effortlessly in the flow, I would sense his arrival, accompanied by a rush of energy through my body.

As I filled my trunk with necessities and a few luxuries, Lukan also prepared for our union. He enlisted the best craftspeople in the area to design and construct our home on a grant of land from his father.

Much later, when I explored our previous lifetime in greater depth, I recalled he was the one who found our houses. Aspects of our second home during that life were evident in the welcoming warmth he created for us this time.

Perhaps I should explain a bit about that prior lifetime. The highly developed civilization in which we resided was influenced by inconceivably sophisticated technologies. It was considerably more advanced – culturally, technologically and scientifically – than the one I have been recounting. On the surface they could not be more opposite.

Mama and I were living in a tiny village, grinding herbs in a rudimentary quern. In our prior incarnation the frequencies within the physical body could be recalibrated to avoid aging. Our current home was a mud and wattle roundhouse, whereas our earlier residences had marble floors inlaid with intricate mosaics. A superficial assessment of the two lifetimes would conclude that we devolved from a supremely sophisticated society to a decidedly primitive one. That would not be incorrect, but it also wouldn't be the whole story. The technologies available then may have been lost, but the mystical wisdom was preserved. The most important aspect of our previous existence – our capacity to invoke and embody the highest spiritual emanations – remained constant. The community of women worshiping the divine feminine into which I had been born was no different from that of the temple priestesses during my earlier life. Mud or marble, it didn't matter.

Love survived even if civilization did not. And since there is no reality other than love, what was lost? Nothing really. Nothing at all.

"Were you ever at the house Lukan and I lived in before?" I asked Mama one autumn afternoon as we were harvesting gourds. My visions of a glorious home by the sea seemed every bit as preposterous as they were apparently real.

"I went there often with Lukan's father, who was the high priest, long before Lukan discovered it for the two of you," she revealed.

"Was it your home before it was ours?" I asked, intrigued.

"It was a sacred place where we performed potent rituals," Mama explained. "We united the divine masculine and the divine feminine perfectly and lovingly in order to strengthen the balance of the two in mass consciousness. That in turn affected people's decisions and actions."

"But that didn't prevent the fall," I averred.

"No it didn't," she confirmed. "Nonetheless, we managed to neutralize the impact of fallen choices for a long time. In the end, however, the dark forces gained a stranglehold on human perceptions and behavior. Even our most concerted efforts were futile."

"When destruction was imminent, we left together on a ship bound for unknown shores," I continued.

"And landed precisely in this location," she verified.

"It was by the sea instead of inland as it is now."

"How did Lukan and I come to occupy the house?" I asked.

"A plan to overthrow the temple hierarchy arose from within the priesthood," she answered. "This breach of trust so compromised the vortex protecting the house, we vacated it. Lukan came across the house seemingly by accident and purchased the property. Of course, it was destined to be your home all along."

"Did Lukan and I have children?" I queried.

"A girl and boy came into your lives unexpectedly," Mama told me, "but you did not give birth."

"Why not?" I wondered.

"You were unable to conceive," she said simply.

"Do such conditions carry over from one lifetime to another?" I prodded.

"Sometimes, but not always," she answered inscrutably. "We'll just have to wait and see."

∞ ∞ ∞

The time for our sacred union finally arrived. It was still quite cold. I was hoping for an early spring so I could weave fresh blossoms in my hair. I wanted something reminiscent of what Mama created with dried roses the day Lukan and his father first appeared.

Everything was ready. The roundhouses were cleansed and freshened not so much to sweep accumulated dust from the months just passed, but to recharge the spiritual power of the circle. We chanted the entire night before the expected arrival of Lukan and his father, calling in the most benevolent spirits to bless our union. We welcomed those beings with pots of aromatic mulled juice and wine, which we drank to infuse our bodies with their presence.

Early the following morning, just after the chanting concluded, Lukan and his father rode into our circle of huts, gratified their long journey was over. They quaffed bowlful after bowlful of the mulled wine, thawing from inside out.

It was odd, seeing Lukan this time. We were accustomed to meeting in the nether realms, and now that he was physically present I had trouble finding my bearings with him.

I didn't expect him to have changed so much. When he and his father visited the previous year, it was after an absence of five years – twenty seasons. I knew he would be different then. But it had barely been four seasons since I last saw Lukan, and he had transformed just as much again. An unmistakable confidence and self-assuredness defined him. His face was chiseled, his torso muscular. He looked like a character from mythology to me, all blonde and agile and potent. Next to him I felt like a weed in the garden – one he would most surely find sadly wanting.

He perceived my uncertainty. Rather than responding to it, he finished his third bowl of the hot, fragrant liquid, set it down, then as gracefully as an elk strode over to me.

"Hello my dear," he said in greeting, bowing low. "May I offer you my hand for a dance today and for our marriage tomorrow?"

He brought me to him for an exuberant embrace and held me for a long while. As I melted into him my insecurities vanished. He was there, in the flesh, holding me with his considerable might. All I had to do was receive his love.

He kissed me on both cheeks then led me in an impromptu dance around the inner perimeter of our huts. The women clapped and chanted to the rhythm of his footsteps. Soon the entire village erupted in a spontaneous celebration of his arrival and our impending union.

Lukan created this moment, transforming my timidity into joy.

Papa requested a dance with me, inviting Lukan to lead Mama in a rhythmic procession. Both men were graceful, physically strong and comfortable in their oversized bodies. Lukan and Mama danced and chatted like long-lost friends, which from a perspective spanning lifetimes, indeed they were.

Mama suggested that after their long journey, Lukan and Papa might want to retire for a meal and some rest. They admitted they were weary and hungry. Mama and Papa entered our hut but Lukan held me back.

"You are so beautiful," he whispered to me. "In the past year as we met energetically, I feared I was conjuring an unattainable goddess. But you far surpass my vision of you when my longing was the greatest. You are glorious."

"You are the glorious one," I replied. "I took one look at you and decided on the spot that given your perfection, you'd find me singularly plain and uninteresting."

"Oh really!" Lukan exclaimed. Then he grabbed me in a mighty embrace and kissed me ardently. My knees were on the verge of buckling.

"It might help if you would breathe," Lukan murmured between kisses. "I don't want you to expire before we're united. I've waited too long to allow that to happen."

I kissed him back – a long, slow, sensuous kiss – making sure I was breathing the entire time. He pulled away, kissed the tip of my nose playfully then said, "We'd better go in before our parents wonder if we're consummating our union without benefit of ceremony." Opening the flap, he helped me into the hut, where Mama was serving stew.

I watched Lukan as he napped that afternoon. Soon he would be sleeping next to me. I would feel his breathing and sense his protective warmth. The prospect of his body alongside mine was beyond inviting.

That evening Mama and Papa set a special place for us across from them. Papa poured honey mead for us then lifted his drinking horn in a toast.

"Here's to my beloved son Lukan and my daughter-to-be Gracila," he announced. "May you find in each other the flawless love and unmitigated joy of the Divine. May you become ever more completely one. May your union be fruitful in all ways, and may the love you share expand throughout the realms of Creation."

I beamed with gratitude that such a marvelous man was soon to be my Papa. His blessing meant everything to me. I loved him dearly.

Then Lukan raised his drinking horn. "To Gracila, my one and only love. May you always have a place in your heart for me. May you welcome me home at the end of the day and awaken me with your kisses every dawn. May you find me worthy of your love, and may you cherish our union eternally."

What an honor to be loved by this man!

Mama was next. "May my dearest daughter Gracila and her beloved Lukan find in each other a pool of serenity and sanctity. May your love express the wisdom of the seasons: ongoing rebirth, planting, growing and harvesting, each experienced with joyful anticipation, acceptance and abundance."

Although it was my turn to offer a toast, I had no idea what to say. I raised my cup, looked at Lukan and surrendered myself to the moment. "To my dearly beloved Lukan and my most precious Mama and Papa. May we experience our togetherness as a family, each of us providing mutual support and abiding love. And in this most sacred context, may Lukan and I learn the meaning of love, shared with purpose and passion."

A pyramid of light enveloped us. My spirit left my body and met the spirits of Mama, Papa and Lukan. We ascended the pyramid together. When we were about to enter the apex, Mama merged fully with Papa and I with Lukan. We floated to the tip of the apex, two spirits formed from the prior union of two and two. Then we became one, and finally even that separateness vanished. We were divine essence, at one with Source. I was floating in nothingness, infused with sublime love and pristine light.

Eventually we returned to our separate spirits. Then we slowly and gently reclaimed our bodies, which remained safe and warm by the fire. I gazed upon the three people I loved most dearly. Each of them was exquisite, more precious than ever.

Lukan took my hand in his. "We just experienced our sacred union," he commented tenderly. "Mama and

Papa, thank you for blessing us in this way on our last evening together before the ceremony. You have given us the gift of oneness, not just with each other but also with you and our Source. May we be ever worthy, and may our oneness expand throughout the land, touching all of Creation."

Our union, consecrated by our parents, was already complete. I could not utter a word. Instead I squeezed Lukan's hand and allowed my tears to fall in happy profusion.

"Gracila, your Mama is as adept as she always was, if not more so," Papa observed. "No doubt you inherited her capacities and learned all you need to know at her side. Lukan, you are fortunate to be united with such an exceptional partner. Respect her always, and leave ample room for her immense spirit."

"I will, Papa, always and forever," Lukan vowed fervently.

That night Lukan and his father slept in the roundhouse of another member of the community. He and I were to awake the next morning under separate roofs, knowing that from that day on we would sleep together.

∞ ∞ ∞

That morning Mama did a ritual cleansing of my body and massaged it with rose oil. Even without flowers braided into my hair, I was a walking rose garden.

I wore a floor-length linen bridal tunic embroidered with a border of geometric designs interspersed with glass, pearl and amber beads. A light wool cape in deep purple was pinned at the shoulder with a large bronze brooch featuring Matres, the Mother Goddess. A delicate bronze headband held a whisper thin veil in place.

The ceremonial hut was decorated with pine boughs and dried lavender. A fire danced in the central pit as I entered with Mama. My beloved and his father were waiting expectantly.

Lukan wore a long-sleeved, thigh-length forest green tunic decorated with fringe and belted at the waist, long brown wool trousers and a blue and green plaid cape pinned at the shoulder with an imposing gold brooch. He fairly erupted with love and no small measure of power.

We walked to the center of the circle, surrounded by members of the community. They intoned a prayer to bless our union with everlasting love. Then Mama and Papa stepped forward and stood opposite us. Mama was holding a narrow length of wool cloth, embroidered with sacred symbols honoring the interplay between the feminine and the masculine. Papa held a bronze incense burner containing cedar, juniper and frankincense.

Papa raised the smoking incense and walked in circles around Lukan and me, forming a figure eight. He intoned a blessing, "Dearest Lukan and beloved Gracila, you are at once two and one. You are male and female, joined in sacred union. You are also the embodiment of the divine masculine and the divine feminine, capable of oneness because of your perfect complementarity. May your union strengthen your love, hold you in the embrace of Mother and Father God, and fill you with the light of your individual and shared spirit. Peace pervades all; love is all. The Divine resides within you eternally."

Lukan took my hands in his and stood facing me. Mama held the strip of embroidered cloth high and prayed, "May the union between Lukan and Gracila be one of mind, body and spirit. May all those present, both physically and spiritually, commit to their union, that it may blossom and prosper."

Then she wrapped the cloth around our wrists, binding us together.

"Dearly beloved Gracila and Lukan, you are about to be joined in sacred union," Mama announced. "You come together freely and by choice, knowing your love is strong and steadfast. Lukan, do you commit to loving Gracila with all that you are, all that you do, all that you say and all that you pray?"

"I do, with a glad heart," replied to Lukan, his voice as clear as a rushing river in the spring.

"Gracila, do you commit to loving Lukan with all that you are, all that you do, all that you say and all that you pray?"

"I do," I replied, "with all of my being."

Mama and Papa joined hands and held them above our heads. Papa affirmed, "May this union be exalted in every way, and may my son and daughter live out their days together in harmony and tenderness."

Mama prayed, "May my daughter and her beloved find contentment in the simplest of pleasures, and may their joy be profound and everlasting."

They raised our hands, still joined by the cloth. A cheer erupted from everyone present. We were united.

A spirited celebration ensued, with a grand feast – everything from roasted boar and pheasant to a cauldron of stew and stacks of honey cakes – accompanied by much drinking and dancing. Lukan and I enjoyed ourselves immensely. As the energy began to wane, Mama and Papa approached us smiling broadly.

"It's time for the two of you to celebrate alone," Mama suggested.

"May your first night together bring you closer in love than you ever thought possible," affirmed Papa.

"Now, go!" urged Mama.

We thanked those who shared the day with us and took our leave.

∞ ∞ ∞

Mama made arrangements to stay in the hut of another that evening, and Papa slept where he had the night before. Lukan and I were to spend the night in the place that was home to me all my life.

One of the women in the village left the gathering early to attend to a few finishing touches. We were to settle into Mama's bed, since mine was too narrow for us both. It had a raised oak frame and a woven hazel sleeping surface. The mattress feathers were fluffed, and a new sheepskin was placed on top.

A tankard of mead and two cups were sitting on a table at one end of the bed, along with seed cakes and a bowl of nuts. A crackling fire in the center produced so much heat I mused we'd be lying on top of the sheepskin instead of underneath it.

"At last!" exclaimed Lukan.

"Let's see, how long have I been waiting for this moment?" I responded lightly, trying to suppress my insecurity. Then in a flood of honesty I added, "Now what?"

Without a word, Lukan took me by the hand and walked me over to our bed for the night.

I half expected him to consummate our union immediately. Instead he whispered to me, "I want nothing more right now than to hold you in my arms, quietly and peacefully. I want to feel you breathing and experience your warmth next to me. I want to fall asleep and wake up holding you, then rejoice in the great blessing of our oneness."

My apprehensions faded away with these words of love and reassurance.

"Please lie with me," he offered, sitting on the bed and bringing me to him. We were both still fully clothed. He eased me onto the bed next to him. He put his arm around me and drew me to him, my cheek on his chest.

"I want to memorize you," he murmured, "to know you by touch rather than in the ethereal way we met this past year. And here you are, in the flesh, lying with me, my dearly beloved Gracila, my wife."

We kissed. A surge of primordial need came over me, more forceful than even my most passionate fantasies. It was as if I were experiencing the ardor felt by every lover who ever existed, quickened within me through some unknown power of Nature. I clung to Lukan, trying to imbibe all of him with my kisses.

Lukan's hands explored my body tentatively. He kissed me with feather-light gentleness then pulled away slightly.

"I want to know you little by little," he whispered. "I want our passion to last all night – not have it spent in one burst of fire. I want to move with you and make all of you familiar to me."

"All that I am is yours, and all that I am is us," I replied. "I came into this lifetime to be with you, and our days and nights together have finally begun. Take pleasure in my body, as I most certainly will in yours. However we choose to spend this night, remember there will be many more to come."

A look of concern swept across his face. Something was worrying him that he hadn't revealed to me.

"What's wrong?" I asked. "Tell me what you were just thinking."

"It's not something for us to discuss tonight of all nights," Lukan warned.

"On the contrary, tonight of all nights is exactly when we should do so," I insisted.

"Oh, my beloved Gracila," he sighed, "just when I believe nothing could make me admire you more, I see another facet of who you are and fall even more deeply in love with you."

I couldn't tell if he was trying to avoid disclosing his thoughts by changing the subject, or if he merely stated his truth in the moment. Rather than responding, I chose to remain silent in the intimacy of his embrace. I couldn't force him to speak what was on his mind and in his heart.

We lay together quietly. I was about to doze off when he drew a deep breath.

"I may be leaving soon after we arrive at our new home," he revealed. "I have been asked to join a group of chieftains and soldiers preparing to meet the invading Roman army when it lands on our shores. I have trained well and have the necessary stamina and expertise. But we will likely be outnumbered and overpowered by their superior weaponry and manpower. I may not return."

"How long do we have before you depart?" I asked desperately.

"One full moon cycle if we are lucky," he said. "Beyond that we are in the hands of powers far greater than our own."

A despairing sadness filled my heart, but I willed it away. "Whatever happens, we have each other now, and we will have our love throughout eternity," I affirmed. "Nothing, not even death, can separate us. We will be united always, whether you are with me here on Earth or have joined our guiding spirits in the netherworld."

"Gracila, my most precious one, you have my devotion until the end of time and back around again," Lukan vowed in return.

"Why such a short span of time?" I asked playfully.

"It's the best I can do for now," he chuckled. "But you never know, I may be moved to declare something more significant after we have lain together a while longer."

Then Lukan swooped me into an exhilarating embrace and kissed the tip of my nose.

"Is that all you can conjure up?" I teased.

"Give me a moment," he retorted. "I'm about to work some real magic."

We undressed each other hastily but with care and lay together under the fur, experiencing for the first time skin upon skin, curves against muscle. Having grown up around women, I was unaccustomed to such sheer physical strength. For a brief moment I wondered how any person or weapon could extinguish his life force. Then I set that thought aside and let my hands trail over his chest and his back.

"The great benefit of preparing for battle is that it enhances my endurance," he commented dryly, once again intercepting my thoughts. "Those muscles are good for many things other than hurling a sharp piece of iron at an unfortunate Roman."

"And what might those other uses be?" I asked demurely.

"This, perhaps," he suggested, rolling onto his back and pulling me on top of him.

I stretched my body along the length of him, marveling at how magnificent every new experience of him was. The hair on his chest tickled my nose, which I loved. His toes played with mine, acknowledging he was fully aware of every last inch of me. Lukan kissed the top of my head then pulled me up face-to-face with him.

"Let's see," he mused. "Your toes are now just below my knees. My own toes will have to survive by themselves whenever I kiss you."

His lips met mine, and I flowed with him into uncharted waters. Rather than trying to anticipate what would happen next, I gave myself over to the moment. I trusted Lukan completely. Whatever transpired that night and, hopefully, for many others stretching far into the future, would be the expression of our love.

Lukan ran his hands down my back and cupped them around my hips. "You are so soft, everywhere," he whispered. "I had no idea what you would feel like."

"Does that mean you have never been with anyone else?" I asked, setting aside my earlier commitment not to query him on the subject.

"I have known no one before you," he said simply, "and I desire no one but you."

"Then, how will you know," I began only to be interrupted by Lukan's kiss.

"I'll know partially by instinct and partially thanks to Papa's most explicit instructions," he replied honestly.

"And what were those most explicit instructions?" I ventured to ask.

"Papa gave me a clear picture of how our bodies fit together," Lukan revealed, "but he said that most importantly I should be gentle, love you with all my heart and let Nature take her course."

"Her course has brought us very close together," I whispered in his ear.

"That's true," he agreed, "but there are even greater degrees of closeness."

"Oh, really!" I exclaimed, feigning innocence. Mama explained everything quite thoroughly to me as well. "I expect you to explore all possibilities with me."

"Throughout the night," countered Lukan, "even if I need a quick nap between discoveries."

As his hands massaged my buttocks, I felt a quickening inside my womb. A slow, deep ache began in a small area within me and then expanded into my entire inner vessel.

"I ache for you, a longing that can only be filled by you," I murmured.

His shaft hardened against me. "Obviously, I long to be inside you as well," he whispered.

We explored each other slowly, indulgently. I relished this prelude to our physical coming together. In fact, I wondered how it was possible to experience greater oneness. But as he moved me beneath him and entered me gradually then completely, I experienced a truly sacred union. We rode wave after wave in ecstatic oneness.

"I want to become lost forever in this pool of bliss I found within you," he murmured. "Nothing could be more beautiful or more enticing."

We lay in each other's arms, satiated. I had an errant thought, which was to somehow kidnap this man and never let him out of my sight, after which I would seduce him each morning, every evening and often throughout the day.

Stirring finally, Lukan lifted himself slightly. "I must have crushed you in my display of mighty manly magnificence!" he exclaimed, smiling broadly.

"Well, if you did, it was at my insistence," I teased. "If any part of my body is crushed beyond recovery, you must kiss it for a very long time. Kissing assists in the healing of all things, you know."

"Are you sore?" he asked, concerned. "I hope I didn't hurt you."

"If you are wondering whether to leave me and roll over on your back, the answer is, 'Please don't.'" I urged. "I love the feel of you inside me and on top of me and wrapped around me. I love it so much that I respectfully request you remain exactly where you are, as you are, until perhaps harvest time. That is only six or seven moon cycles from now. Is that too much to ask?"

"Not at all," he replied ceremoniously. "I am more than happy to oblige." Then he kissed my eyelids, my nose, my mouth, my ear lobes. Each touch of his lips was a joy. Even his playful kisses sent heat to my heart. One thing led to another.

"See?" I chirped. "I told you I didn't want you to leave yet. Now you know why."

"This time, my love, I promise to take things more slowly," he offered.

"Only if you do so just at the beginning," I replied. "I like not so slow as well. Or hadn't you noticed?"

We made love throughout the night, with intervals for snuggles by the fire, pauses to replenish our energy

with food and a nap, and conversation to weave it all together.
At dawn I was finally ready for a really good night's sleep. I was lying on my side, curled up. He was behind me with his knees bent into mine, his arm around me, his hand cupping my breasts. I stirred as light filled the room then settled back into our splendid sleeping arrangement. It was my favorite so far.

"If it's possible to name something I love more than making love with you all night," he observed, "it might well be waking up with you the next morning. I am totally at peace."

"More likely, you're mistaking exhaustion for peace," I quipped.

"I'm not all that tired," he reported. "In fact, I may be about ready to help you reach yet another incomprehensibly ecstatic state."

At that I flipped over to face him, my eyes wider than an owl's. "You can't be serious," I said, tapping him lightly on the chest. "But if you are, I am without a doubt the luckiest girl ever to have joined with someone in sacred – and perhaps not so sacred – union!"

We reveled in each other one more time. Halfway through our lovemaking, I couldn't resist saying, "After a little more practice, I may discover what I am supposed to do whenever you kiss me."

∞ ∞ ∞

When we finally emerged late that afternoon, Mama and Papa were just leaving for a walk in the woods. Lukan and I were dressed warmly, so we asked if we could join them.

"By all means," answered Papa. "Considering how much sleeping you have been doing and how little exercise you have had, a bracing walk will do you both some good."

But Mama had other things on her mind. "You both must be hungry," she said. "Would you like something to eat before we venture out?"

"We can share a meal with the two of you when we return," I suggested.

Since Lukan and I were spilling over with happiness, Mama could confidently surmise everything went well the night before. Later that evening I assured her privately that I couldn't be more enchanted.

Lukan, Papa and I remained in the village a few more days. The men went hunting supposedly to refill the village coffers. But another reason for their forays into the countryside was to give Mama and me time alone together. I was about to leave her home, where I had spent my entire life at her side. It would be a bittersweet parting for us both.

"I can see what a perfect love match you and Lukan are," Mama told me as we were packing my traveling trunk with items for my new home. "Already you love each other dearly and respect each other deeply. The life you will share can only get better."

"How can anything be better than this moment?" I asked, doubting that greater bliss or contentment was possible.

"As the years unfold, which they undoubtedly will," Mama paused, "you will find the sweetest joy in the simplest of pleasures. The way your forehead fits just so in the curve of his neck, the familiar feel of his arm around you as you sleep through a cold night – those moments warm the soul and keep the embers of love burning throughout your days.

"Over time the most complete oneness you experience with Lukan will occur when you are doing familiar things together – knowing imperceptibly how the other will move, picking up where the other left off, be it a sentence or a shared endeavor. That is the beautiful dance of love you will share later in life."

"Like what you have with Papa?" I asked. She responded by surrounding me in her arms.

"Only someone who can love the way you do would see what he and I have together," she said. "Yes, that is the love we share. It is enduring, timeless, just like the love between you and Lukan. It carries us through and between lifetimes."

"I understand, Mama," I replied. "Now the two of you can perhaps see and share more of each other, since Lukan and I will be gone from your nests."

"Don't forget, my dear, he is leading the force that will meet the Romans," Mama noted. "You and I both must be alone, hopefully not for long."

"When there is a choice between love and hate, freedom and domination, why would anyone opt for anything other than love and freedom?" I asked.

"Those who choose otherwise know little about the power of love," Mama stated flatly. "If you have love in your life, profoundly and steadfastly, why make war on others?"

"So it comes down to lovelessness," I observed. "Is it as pervasive as it seems to be, given the violence that interrupts our peace?"

"Divine love is always available to us," Mama affirmed. "But many people can't open themselves to love, divine or otherwise. It makes them feel vulnerable."

"Vulnerable?" I questioned. "Love makes me feel the opposite – invincible or at least heading in that direction."

"Let's affirm that the love Lukan and his father carry with them will make them invincible, if not also invisible, on the battlefield," proposed Mama. "And if battle can be avoided altogether, even better. Perhaps there is a diplomatic way to settle the issue."

Our departure the following day was heart-wrenching. Mama tried to remain strong and positive, but in the end tears of grief burst forth. I plunged into the same emotional abyss, and we wept together, embracing each other with all our might.

As our flood of tears became more torrential, Lukan and Papa encompassed us in their embrace. That caused Mama to cry all the more.

Knowing her well and loving her dearly, Papa knew what to do. He pulled her away from me gently and embraced her in his huge arms. She pressed her head against his chest, and her sorrow took its leave.

"My love, you must cry tears of joy only," he told her soothingly. "Our lives are blessed far beyond our worthiness to receive such beneficence. The four of us have come together once again. Your beloved daughter has been united with her eternal love. You and I share an equally enduring love. Our journey continues."

Mama nodded, but still she kept her cheek pressed against his chest.

"Don't squander a moment worrying about Lukan and me," Papa urged. "We will be safe. We will both live long lives – long enough to cause the two of you to rue the day you became entangled with us."

A low chuckle surfaced from deep within his throat. "You and I have many more adventures to share before either of us completes this lifetime. As for Gracila and Lukan, they have only just begun. So cry tears of joy all you want. Anything other than that is unnecessary. You have your daughter still. She carries you in her heart. You have Lukan's devotion. And you know you have my infinite love."

Mama brightened, regaining her composure. She gave each of us a hug and kisses then insisted, "You must be on your way so you can travel an adequate distance before nightfall. Be safe and know that you go with my love."

With that benediction we departed.

∞ ∞ ∞

Our trip was without incident. The most memorable aspect of it was my awakening to the tone and feeling of life outside my village. I was accustomed to living in uncompromising harmony with Nature and the people around me.

Being thrust into a world pervaded by different energies and inclinations was a shock. Mama did her best to help me anticipate what was ahead, but her descriptions couldn't prepare me for the hardship I observed on our journey.

"When you meet the Roman invaders, are these the conditions you are ready to give your lives to defend?" I asked after we passed a particularly desolate area.

"Clearly life outside your village leaves you unimpressed," Papa commented.

"Are the people happy?" I wondered.

"Many of them are," Papa observed, "most notably those who follow the old spiritual traditions. They lead simple but fulfilling lives composed of more than hard work and perpetual discomfort. They have adequate homes, sufficient food and mutual support from their neighbors. Many live much like your Mama, except they don't have the advantage of existing apart from the world."

"But still I don't see in their faces anything worth the violence that might be required to protect their way of life," I insisted.

"I understand and respect your opinion," Papa replied evenly.

I felt dreadful for having expressed such doubt. I challenged not just their lives and culture, and now mine as well, but also their commitment to defend it. They seemed to take my questioning in stride, as if it didn't surprise them in the least. Nonetheless, I kept my contrary opinions to myself for the remainder of the journey.

When I was about to conclude we were traveling to the end of the world, we arrived at our destination. "We're home!" Lukan exclaimed. "Welcome to your new residence."

He helped me down from my horse, and Papa unfastened the ropes that secured my trunks in the cart.

"Lukan, this can't be our house!" I exclaimed in disbelief. "You told me it was slightly larger than Mama's hut. But it is enormous. What will we ever do with all that room? And what about the roundhouses?"

"Families who maintain the property live there," Lukan said matter-of-factly.

"What help do I need?" I asked. "I know how to keep a household."

"I'm sure you do, but your new life will include some assistance," he replied casually.

Papa grunted under the weight of the first trunk, and Lukan helped him wrestle it from the cart. I opened the gate and stepped aside so they could pass through it and on to the house. They continued up the stone path while I stood in the same spot, surveying what was before me.

What Lukan called "our house" was more like a small village. There were five buildings in all, about the same distance from each other as the huts in Mama's community. But the home Lukan built for us was too big for a young couple.

Reading my thoughts when he returned for another trunk, Lukan commented, "Hopefully it won't be just the two of us for long. Obviously I am planning on having a big family."

"Until then, we'll have to make special arrangements just to find each other!" I laughed.

"Come, let me show you around," he suggested.

We held hands as we walked up the path. Care had been taken to prepare the garden for planting in the spring. "How much land do we have?" I asked.

"Let me put it this way. You can create a garden that extends farther than the eye can see and still not have tilled much of our land," he explained. "It's a large holding. But for now, let's take a tour of our humble abode."

He led me across the threshold and into the first room, then followed me inside. Fabrics, furs and furniture unlike anything I had ever seen created beauty everywhere I looked. The walls were lime-washed to perfection, and the chairs, stools, tables and shelves exhibited superb craftsmanship. A huge river rock hearth at one end apparently had no purpose but to provide warmth.

"This room is more spacious than our hut," I remarked. "And yet I see no indication that it is for sleeping or cooking."

"The cooking takes place in here," Lukan replied, leading me into a separate room that also included a long table with benches for dining. Papa was sitting at the table, having already dug into roast boar, fresh baked rye bread and a tankard of dark mead. "How does the place suit you?" he asked between bites.

"I had no idea such a home could exist. How can it possibly be ours?" I replied.

"I love you like a daughter and wanted you to live where you could be truly happy," he revealed.

"Does Mama know about this?" I wondered.

"Not exactly," Papa admitted. "I told her we'd taken a few extra measures to assure your comfort, but I didn't go into detail. Why do you ask?"

"She helped me collect what we thought I would need," I explained. "We both assumed my new living circumstances would be modest."

"She trusts you are in good hands," he replied. "We did our best to anticipate what you would like."

The next room contained our sleeping quarters, which also featured a substantial hearth. How extraordinary that a house would have three fireplaces! Realizing how much time and effort would be spent collecting wood for them, I mused to myself, "Now I understand why I might need assistance, especially if Lukan is away."

A custom made bed long enough to accommodate Lukan's height dominated the room. Hanging on the wall behind it was a weaving of the sun rising over a hillside, bordered with the symbols of various Celtic gods. In one corner stood a delicately carved table, with a matching mirror and comb, an inlaid wooden box and various small covered pots arranged on top. Two large trunks, a second table and pegs on the walls completed the interior.

The final room in the back was smaller and empty, still waiting to be assigned its purpose. "For the children, or however you want to use it before they arrive," Lukan explained.

"So we are to have our privacy away from the children once they are old enough to sleep by themselves," I noted. "What an interesting idea! I could become accustomed to that. Thank you for creating this wonderful home for us."

We joined Papa in the kitchen and nestled into the food ourselves.

"This is delicious," I commented. "Who made it?"

"Your cook no doubt," remarked Papa.

"Are you saying someone will cook for us?" I asked in disbelief.

"Yes, along with a few others to help with additional tasks as needed," Papa informed me.

"And what am I to do?" I wondered aloud.

"Keep my son blissfully happy, for starters," suggested Papa. "He becomes like a bear when he is worried about you."

I stood behind Papa and hugged his sizeable shoulders. "I love you dearly," I declared. "You have welcomed me into your life, blessed my union with your son and enabled us to begin our marriage in this beautiful home. Thank you for that, and not incidentally, for loving Mama as you do."

Love, 24 AD

Part Two: Vespasian

PART TWO
VESPASIAN

The next morning Papa left on what he indicated would be a short journey to his own home. Lukan and I waved goodbye and returned inside to sit by the cooking fire.

"Who is your father, really?" I asked, unable to contain my curiosity. "If you were given the wherewithal to build a home such as this, I can only assume Papa has considerable resources at his disposal."

"He does," Lukan admitted, "but not because he abuses people with his power and influence. Papa is the most compassionate, magnanimous person I know."

"That's a fair statement," I said. "But who is he?"

"My father is the most highly respected of all the chieftains in the land," Lukan revealed. "His holdings are considerable. He gained them from inheritance, not bloodshed. His sole purpose in life is to keep the peace and enable those in his care to live meaningfully and fruitfully. Some call Papa a king, but he prefers not to use that title."

"A king?" I questioned, incredulous. "Your father is a king?"

"He is," Lukan affirmed.

"But if he is a king, why didn't he marry you off to the daughter of another king so he could broaden the base for peace?" I persisted.

"Papa would rather see me happy than arrange a union for the sole purpose of strengthening his position," Lukan explained. "He discerns information from many planes of existence and makes decisions accordingly. When I was born, he knew you would be following not far behind. He was aware of Mama's commitment to

81

bring you into the world so we could be together. And he has honored that intention despite demands from others that he use me for political and territorial gain."

"He made a considerable sacrifice to bring us together, then," I noted.

"He and Mama both did, as you know," Lukan noted.

"But Papa gave no indication of his stature," I commented. "He seemed perfectly content in the humble village where Mama and I lived."

"Indeed he was," Lukan confirmed. "Papa remarked after our first visit that he would love nothing more than to spend the remainder of his days in your hut."

"With Mama," I added.

"Yes, of course," Lukan agreed, "but also in that rarefied vortex. He was genuinely at home there. It's the closest thing that now exists to what he and your mother had before, in their temples of worship. Papa would willingly give up everything to live in that village and keep the vibration of the divine masculine nurtured to perfection."

"But instead he returned with you and is preparing for battle," I said ruefully.

"He does what he must," Lukan observed. "Perhaps now you can understand why I'm compelled to go with him. It's my honored duty to ride beside my father. I do this because I love and respect him, not because he insists upon it. In fact, he begs me not to accompany him. But he is an enlightened leader, a man of influence devoted to benefitting the world, and I must be with him as he pursues his intended course."

"Our life together isn't going to be simple, is it?" I asked, though I knew the answer.

"No, it won't be," he admitted. "But I hope we can make our own unique contributions somewhere, sometime. That would be worth the complications."

"When you refer to 'we' do you mean you and me or you and Papa?" I wondered.

"You and me," Lukan clarified. "I have a strong feeling the journey we took from your village to this house is only the first of many. We'll travel to distant lands and visit people who lead lives unlike ours. We'll do so not to usurp power or to gain greater wealth, but to preserve the peace and serve the good of all."

"I've come this far with you," I said, kissing him lightly. "If this is just the first step in a lifelong adventure, so be it. We'll accept whatever is presented to us and see it as a gift of destiny."

"I already have the only gift I want," whispered Lukan, "and she happens to be close to me at the moment. So close, in fact, that I may have to kiss her once or twice. And then I may need a few more kisses after that."

He lifted me into his arms and carried me to our bedroom. "Now that Papa is gone and we have the place to ourselves, perhaps we should try out our new sleeping accommodations," he suggested blithely. "Not that I intend to do much sleeping."

In the ensuing weeks I became acquainted with the people who were there to assist me. At first I was unsure how to engage with them, for I had no experience with others whose role was to make mine less arduous. I never felt burdened before with my tasks. Quite the contrary, they were sources of joy. It wasn't easy to let go of meaningful chores by asking others to accomplish them.

The cook recognized my dilemma. "If you want to help with the food preparation, or do it all by yourself, that's fine," she told me reassuringly. "There's plenty to keep me busy elsewhere."

"I love the meals you create, and I can think of nothing more pleasing than to enjoy them every day," I affirmed. "It's just that I have little else to do until I can start planting the garden."

"Then help me you will," she said, "and along the way I'll teach you my secrets."

She opened a whole new world to me with her spices from faraway lands – clove, turmeric, saffron – and creative ways of combining ingredients. I learned to appreciate the nuances of flavors and began innovating with my own herbs.

Unlike the cook, who lived alone, the caretaker had a son and a daughter. Their mother was frail and sickly, so the children were their father's constant shadow. Whenever they got in his way I invited them in for warm cider and a treat fresh from the oven.

"Papa says Lukan is about to go off to war," said the boy, trying to sound grown up. "I wish I could go, too. It would be exciting. We never get to do anything adventurous since Mama feels bad most of the time."

"Lukan will soon go to war," I replied. "But if you asked him about it, he would tell you he would rather stay here, even if there is less excitement."

"Will you be sad when he goes?" asked the girl.

"I will be very sad," I admitted. "But I have the two of you to cheer me up, and your father will be working with me in the garden. The days are getting warmer. We'll start tilling the soil soon."

"Can we help?" they shouted.

"Absolutely," I replied. "I was hoping you would assist me. I brought many young plants from where I used to live, and I would love for you to see them grow. You'll need to watch them closely and tell me about all the changes that occur."

"Will it be a garden just for food, or will we plant flowers too?" queried the girl.

"I want to have flowers near the house," I explained, "and vegetables and herbs everywhere else. Would you like some flowers around your house as well?"

"Yes, for Mama," she cheered.

I wasn't always content during my short time with Lukan before he joined his father against the Romans. Waves of panic engulfed me, and I experienced a terrible fear that Lukan might never return. The prospect was doubly difficult to bear, since we had only one moon cycle together before he would be gone.

Nonetheless, I was determined not to cloud the precious moments we did have with unnecessary hand wringing. I tried my best to maintain a grateful heart, though I failed often enough.

I had more success enticing Lukan into extended bouts of lovemaking, which were both playful and blissful. He was my perfect partner, and I craved him constantly – even more so as his departure became imminent.

The evening before Lukan was to go, we sat up late talking by the fire in the main room.

"I am gratified that you have become closer with everyone here," Lukan told me. "I couldn't bear to leave you all alone after such a short time. But you have a family of sorts to turn to now, and the children adore you."

"I've settled in quite well," I agreed. "And to dispel intermittent bouts of loneliness after tomorrow, I plan to keep expanding the garden."

I took a deep breath and asked, "Do you have any idea how long you'll be gone?"

"I have no way of predicting that," he said ruefully. "I may not return until the harvest, or possibly later. It depends."

"On what?" I pressed him further.

"On what the Roman invaders decide to do – how many soldiers they send across the water, their strategy for conquering our people, their willingness to negotiate a peace," Lukan explained. "It also depends on us – how well the tribes come together under unified leadership, the commitment of all to participate in our defense and ultimately, the courage we exhibit."

"So much uncertainty with so much at stake," I observed, revealing my worry.

"I don't disagree," Lukan replied. "But Papa prepared me well, and together we will face whatever lies ahead. I couldn't have a wiser or more adept leader at my side."

"But still," I halted, unsure of how to speak of the worst.

"My dearest Gracila," he interrupted, "let's not spend another breath anticipating what might occur and instead revel in our togetherness for one more night."

We did exactly that, with more urgency and hunger than ever.

∞ ∞ ∞

He left me. He left with melancholy regret combined with anticipation he couldn't hide. I was grateful to see the expectation in his eyes, for I knew it would shield him more effectively than remorse.

I vowed to surround him with the protection of my love, that he and Papa may be effective in their diplomacy and, if necessary, triumphant in battle. I would keep my intentions pure and use all my powers to help lead him to victory, negotiated or otherwise.

When he took his leave I didn't shed a tear. I expected to be reduced to a puddle. We had been together so briefly, and we loved each other so profoundly, how could I not be devastated with grief?

But I didn't grieve because in truth he wasn't lost to me. He was away, not gone for good. I refused to contemplate Lukan in battle, the violence of which I chose not to see for fear of compromising the powerful light around him. I wasn't prepared to lose him so soon. I wouldn't allow it.

Thus I prayed and meditated and wagged my finger at Cocidius the god of war, demanding that he keep Lukan safe and bring him back to me. Even as I did, I was aware that a larger imperative was being served. Lukan must live a long life, not for my own selfish reasons as his wife and lover, but because a new age was dawning and he would be needed to guide us through it. He and Papa could strengthen and retain the old ways despite onrushing forces intent upon obliterating them.

I expected Lukan to visit me during my sleep as he did before our marriage. But he never appeared. Not even once. I recall journeying to find him as I slumbered, but his presence was perpetually veiled to me.

One afternoon while I was digging in the soil a moon cycle after his departure, I was given an insight that brought me unexpected peace. Lukan's unavailability was his way of protecting me. It was his choice not to reveal what was occurring or how it affected him. As close as we were, I was better off not knowing.

Then a further realization dawned on me. If I was not to know Lukan's circumstances or the outcome of his struggles, I had only one responsibility. It was to love, hope and give, every moment of every day. Thus I could surround him in my love and the powerful forces of the benevolent gods who support us always.

I settled into a domestic routine of uninterrupted peace. I returned to the rhythms, phases and flows that marked my life until recently. I was able to recapture much of the fullness I knew during my years with Mama.

The only sadness I experienced was the discovery that Lukan and I had not conceived a child. I bled more than usual, as if my body were releasing my disappointment. I would not be allowed the comforting awareness that I carried his child – a means for him to live on if he did not survive the battlefield. I couldn't say to myself, "Whatever happens to Lukan, at least our child will live." There was no such recompense.

Spring burst forth in its blossoming plenty, and I threw myself into creating a splendid garden. Turnips and tulips, crocuses and cantaloupe found their special spots to grow, with fragrant herbs taking root in between. The vegetable garden was so large it would easily feed all of us the entire winter.

Flowers framed the house and were interspersed throughout the property. They gave us great pleasure, whether we were appreciating a rosebud along the path from the gate or crushing lavender leaves between our fingers for its calming scent.

One day while I was trimming a cluster of flowering vines, it occurred to me that the gardens also provided a visual feast for travelers on the road nearby. They emanated such munificence from Mother Nature one could not help feeling a bit better.

I recalled Mama's assertion that the bounty of Nature belongs to all. It cannot be held as property, stored for selfish purposes or used to gain wealth. Rather, by sharing gifts from the garden with others, with no purpose but to nurture, love and live in greater harmony, we honor our Mother. We also honor those with whom we sup or who gaze upon the glories of a blossom in the summer sunshine.

Thus I opened my home to travelers in need of nourishment.

Although I was learning to cook more elaborate meals than the soups and stews of my early years, there was a perpetual pot of one or the other simmering over the fire for wayfarers and their hungry children. I would often return from tending the garden, only to find a family seated at the long table, soothing their ravenous bellies with bowls of whatever was in the sheet-bronze cauldron in the kitchen. When they were sated, I would add fresh vegetables, herbs and spices – whatever was ripe for the picking – and after a while it would be ready for the next family in need.

The life I created was contrary to the one I knew before. I traded its simplicity, solitude and almost total inaccessibility for the opposite. It happened inadvertently and also mindfully. I never consciously said to myself, "Our home should be open to others," nor was I aware of the change that occurred over time. I simply invited people to share a meal – first those living with us, then their friends, then sojourners in need.

I wondered what Lukan would say when he returned home and found that our lives were often interrupted by the presence of a family we didn't know eating a meal by the cooking fire. Perhaps he planned for this.

A roundhouse like Mama's, composed of one circular room in which everything occurred, could never serve such a purpose. But the house Lukan designed and built for us, with its separate room for cooking and dining, anticipated this way of life. It was as if he saw it unfolding before the first stone was laid and the first thatch was in place. He built a home where we could have our privacy even when we made our harvest available to the many rather than the few.

With strangers coming and going, was I ever fearful for my own safety and that of the families who lived on our property? Didn't some who came to our doorstep have malicious intent, either to steal or to harm us? Ultimately, wasn't I taking too big a risk by being so generous? No, I never once felt vulnerable with the wayfarers in my midst.

Reflecting on my earlier comment about the difference between how I grew up and my current life, I must admit they were not really that divergent. Just as Mama had done, I established a vortex that welcomed those who were pure of heart and in genuine need of a brief respite and sustenance. Others passed by without incident. Never once did anyone take advantage of our hospitality. Quite the contrary, their gratitude and humility strengthened the vibrational frequency around our house, keeping it aligned with its original intent.

My healing work, which was accomplished with herbs I brought from Mama's garden and planted in my own soil, soon flourished. It all began with the herbal treatments I combined for the caretaker's wife, which enabled her to regain her strength and vitality. Soon it expanded to include sickly children and pregnant mothers who lived in the surrounding area. I might be living apart from the village of my childhood, but I remained my mother's daughter. Thus nearly two seasons passed after Lukan's departure. I stayed busy and worried less than I would have otherwise.

∞ ∞ ∞

I was harvesting vegetables in the autumn sun when I heard an urgent knocking at the front door. I went around the side of the house to see who it might be. A burly warrior, layered with sweat and grime from the road, was standing on the doorstep. His horse was tethered at the post by the front gate, panting and pawing at the dirt. My stomach churned with dread. Something terrible had happened to Lukan.

"What can I do for you?" I asked, summoning a modicum of composure.

"I was sent here by the king," he announced. "His son Lukan has been wounded in battle. He implores Lukan's wife to come with me immediately to tend to him in the encampment."

"I am Lukan's wife Gracila" I replied. "And you are?"

"Taranis," he responded. "The king asks that you bring your most powerful healing remedies for fever and flesh wounds."

"Can you tell me how serious Lukan's wounds are?" I pursued.

"I saw him only once, when he was covered from the neck down, so I cannot attest to the gravity of his situation," Taranis commented. "But the urgency of the king's message indicates that Lukan has sustained more than superficial cuts."

"I need only a little time to gather the required herbs and powders," I explained, astounded at the steadiness in my voice. "While I am doing that, please stop by each of the houses on the property to inform the others why I must leave. Also, would you ask them to take appropriate care of the compound in my absence?"

"Consider it done," he asserted. "Where shall I meet you?"

"You can meet me in front of the house," I suggested. "Before we depart, help yourself to the stew cooking over the fire in a room around the back. Serving bowls are on the table. Most likely you have had little nourishment since you embarked on this mission."

"Only what I could stuff in this pouch before I left and eat while I rode," he replied, holding up a small leather bag.

"How long have you been traveling?" I asked, even though I dreaded to hear the answer. The longer the ride, the less likely I could help – or save – Lukan.

"Two days," he reported. "I stopped only long enough to change horses or feed and water the one I was riding." His brow furrowed. "Are you a capable enough rider to enable us to return in roughly the same time?"

"You'll not find me lagging behind you," I assured him. "We'll get fresh mounts from the stable, which will help us travel faster in the beginning at least."

"Very well," he responded. "We'll depart as soon as you are ready and the horses are saddled."

"Don't you need to rest?" I asserted. "You can't possibly endure the ride back without some sleep."

"I am a warrior, trained for hardship in battle," he insisted. "I need no sleep when the cause is worthy and the timing critical."

I prepared for the journey with a strange clarity. My every motion was fluid and efficient, my thoughts precise. I knew exactly what healing preparations I needed: calendula, angelica, beeswax, chamomile, comfrey, red salvia and yellow yarrow. I donned a simple tunic, jacket and cloak for the journey and packed a few clean clothes along with my pouch of personal items: a comb, scissors and tweezers. My only thought was to reach Lukan as soon as possible and heal him with my love and my herbs.

When everything was ready, I sat on our bed, closed my eyes and connected my energy with Lukan's frail spirit. "Please don't go, my love," I pleaded. "I am coming to you. Soon I will be at your side."

Two fresh horses were waiting when I appeared out front carrying a hefty leather saddlebag stuffed with healing remedies and clothing, along with a smaller one containing food for the journey. Taranis strapped them to the horses as I spoke to the families who gathered to bid me farewell. I hugged each person and whispered words of assurance, though their worried glances broke my heart.

"Lukan and I will return, and he'll be thriving once again," I pledged. "Be prepared for him to chop more wood and harvest more grain than any two of you. In the meantime, please take care of yourselves and the farm."

"We will," they promised. "Goodbye, Gracila. Bring Lukan back safely."

Taranis helped me onto my horse, and we were off.

We rode through midday heat and moonlit night, pausing only to refresh ourselves and feed the horses. I barely noticed the hills and streams, forests and fields that interrupted the inner vista of my thoughts. I ate little, preferring fresh water instead. It settled my queasy stomach. After a day of relentless riding, numbness replaced my exhaustion. When I dismounted, I walked like a stiff old crone. While I was in the saddle, I could barely stay awake.

Taranis watched over me like a protective older brother. The further we went, the more frequently he suggested we stop for a rest. Just as often I declined. Arriving even an hour later than necessary could make the difference between life and death for Lukan.

We were riding hard the morning of the second day when a herd of red deer darted across the muddy cart path and spooked my tired horse. He reared suddenly to avoid them, throwing me unceremoniously into a ditch filled with grass and mud. I landed like a rag doll, flailing and uncoordinated. My clothing was smeared with sludge and soaking wet, but I was uninjured. I caught my breath and tried to get up, only to skid on the wet grass and tumble backward.

"I'm fine," I assured Taranis as he came running toward me, "just a little awkward in this slippery swamp."

Without a word he lifted me out of the ditch, placed me onto his horse, hopped on behind me, grabbed the reins of my horse, put one arm as hard as a crowbar around my waist, and we rode off.

"You didn't need to do that," I protested. "Now you'll get all muddy."

Taranis grunted in response.

"Besides, that unrepentant landing I experienced really woke me up," I continued. "I can safely ride my own horse now."

His arm tightened around my waist.

"I'll keep bothering you until you let me down," I threatened.

"No you won't," he said firmly. "You'll be asleep before we reach the top of that hill."

I forced myself to stay awake until we were descending on the other side of it. "See, I can do it," I insisted.

He loosened his grip ever so slightly, as if to indicate he had proved his point anyway. Almost immediately I fell into a meditative state. Renewing energy arose into my legs, my torso, my arms and out through the top of my head. I was being imbued with the creative power of the feminine, overflowing with love.

When I emerged from the meditation tears of joy and heartache, fatigue and unfathomable devotion spilled down my cheeks. Taranis appeared not to notice. I was cleansing and filling myself simultaneously, releasing with my tears whatever compromised my capacity as a healer and replenishing myself with revitalizing life force.

An unfamiliar chant emerged from deep within me:
Daughter of the Divine
Mother of all that is
Creator of the light
Destroyer of the dark
Fill me with your grace
That I may serve
And love eternally
I was in the Mother's hands. I could ask for no greater love and assistance.

Then something even more unexpected occurred. Rather than begging that Lukan be spared, I prayed that he be allowed to take the next step on his own divine path. If it required him to leave his earthly existence and be ushered into the realms of the spirits, so be it. We would find each other again. These words pulsed through me: "I surrender the outcome. Whether Lukan lives or dies is his choice, not mine."

There was nothing more to say or do to prepare for the ordeal that lay ahead. I dried my tears. It was time to be with my beloved.

∞ ∞ ∞

"We are nearing the encampment," Taranis declared, nudging me back to awareness. I heard a creek flowing nearby through a crop of trees. "Would you like to ready yourself?"

I was surprised by his consideration. Here was a stout warrior who had ridden beyond human endurance. And yet he was aware I might want to wash off encrusted mud from the ditch and don fresh clothes before I presented myself to my husband.

"Though I see no signs of danger here, I will keep watch while you have your privacy," he declared. "The encampment is just over that rise, or at least it was when I left to fetch you."

"Thank you," I replied. "I won't be long."

Taranis helped me off the horse we had ridden together. I dug a tunic and cloak out of my saddlebag and walked to the creek, surprisingly energized. I sat down along the edge, removed my boots and placed my feet in the water. It was warm and welcoming. I undressed and hopped into the waist-deep stream. In no time I had bathed, dried off as best I could and donned clean clothes. I was ready for whatever lay ahead.

Taranis was waiting, as lively and alert as if he had just enjoyed an uninterrupted nap on a mound of new-mown hay. A wave of thanksgiving overtook me. "Were it not for you, I might still be at home, or only halfway here," I declared. "I owe you my everlasting thanks, Taranis, and it's quite possible Lukan owes you his very life."

"You owe me nothing, and neither does Lukan," he insisted. "I serve those whose leadership I trust and respect. It's an honor to do so. I am grateful for the opportunity to bring you here to assure Lukan's recovery."

"So he will recover?" I asked apprehensively, even though I was aware there was no immediate answer to that question.

"How could it be otherwise?" Taranis replied definitively.

We arrived at the camp and were directed to a temporary thatch-roofed dwelling erected in the middle, where it could be well guarded. I scrambled off my horse, grabbed my saddlebag with healing herbs and rushed to the hut. A soldier blocked my way.

"Who goes here?" he demanded, prepared to preclude my entry.

"I am Lukan's wife Gracila," I said politely but firmly. "Please stand aside."

He cast a quick glance toward Taranis, who nodded with authority. Then a look of pity flashed across the soldier's face.

"Are you certain you wish to gain entry?" he asked. I was about to take offense when I realized he was trying to protect me as much as Lukan. "We rode two days straight to get here," I said in a low voice. I couldn't tell if I sounded imperious or desperate or both. "Please don't keep me from my husband."

"Very well," he acquiesced.

"Taranis, will you be accompanying me further?" I asked.

"No, my duties have been met," he replied. "You are delivered to Lukan."

"Before I leave you, then, I must express my gratitude to you one more time," I began. Then with no further thought, I ran to Taranis and gave him a hearty hug. "May the gods go with you always and may your life be filled with light."

"Thank you," he replied uncomfortably. "Now go to your husband. I'll help with your bags."

The guard opened the flap, and Taranis set the saddlebags inside. Then I stepped in.

It smelled of death, putrid and rotting. What if Lukan had been unable to cling to life until my arrival? I peered at him from across the room, gray and lifeless under layers of heavy wool blankets. It was late summer, much too warm for him to be so covered. Studying him carefully, I discerned that his spirit was barely in his physical form. The fetid wounds, coupled with his frailty, assaulted his body with an unyielding feverish chill.

I ran to Lukan and took his head in my hands, kissing his face and entreating him not to leave. I choked out the words, "Lukan, it's Gracila. I'm here. Don't go. Don't go. Please, let me help you."

He was barely breathing. I found his left hand, eased it from under the weight of the wool, brought it to my lips and held it to my cheek. I imagined a transfer of energy through his fingers and into his failing body. In response a slight pulsation returned from him to me, weak but reassuring.

I recalibrated my vital force to match his. Too much of a surge could shock his body. But a steady flow of vibration resonant with his, and then gradually increasing, could replenish his depleted reserves. He needed strength to heal.

Slowly, slowly, our connection escalated. Lukan received and returned my love even though he was lying near death. I gave myself over to the moment just as I had done during our oneness in love. There was no difference between the two, really.

Lukan took a slightly deeper breath, as if he were awakening from a lingering hibernation. His eyes opened just enough to verify I was really there – that he hadn't conjured my presence to gather one last spark of life before it slipped from him completely.

He smiled weakly. I affirmed, "Yes, my love, I'm here. It's not a dream. You'll be well. I'm certain of it."

His fingers moved slightly on my cheek, stroking it tenderly. I held still, eyes closed, feeling a feeble heat replace the chill of his touch. But even that small gesture expended more than he could afford to give. His hand shook from the exertion. I took it in mine and laid it at his side.

"Be still, my beloved," I whispered. "We have all the time in the world. For now, please rest and allow me to prepare my herbs and healing remedies for you."

I stood up slowly, studying Lukan with my heart as well as my mind. A hand grabbed my wrist. Startled, I turned to see who was there.

"Thank the gods and the goddesses you have come, my dear!" Papa exclaimed. "We did everything we could for Lukan after he was wounded, but he declined rapidly despite our efforts. When I sent for you I had my doubts about whether you would make it in time. But something inside me insisted your love wouldn't allow you two to be separated on this Earth after being together so short a time."

I plunged into his arms. "How bad is it?" I asked softly.

He walked me to the opposite side of the hut. "Lukan was wounded with the blow of a sword across his chest and under his right arm," he explained in measured tones. "He also received a deep dagger thrust running the length of his belly. He fought countless battles unarmored, using only his long shield for protection. But this time the Roman's sword sliced through the hide and metal ribbing on the shield as if it were made of linen and twigs.

"We have stopped the loss of blood and tried to close the wounds, but his body is becoming infested with rot around the lesions. Our efforts are nothing compared to your healing powers."

"I know so little compared to Mama," I replied, "but I'll call on it all to help Lukan recover."

"He'll mend more quickly with you here," Papa observed. "I must tell you, his injuries will prevent him from taking to the field of battle ever again. The wound in his right shoulder will leave him incapable of even holding a sword, let alone wielding it in combat. I now have a valid excuse to keep him away from the battlefield.

"Lukan refused to miss a single skirmish, even though I reminded him that such heroics weren't necessary. Each time he went into battle, I prayed that if one of us was to be taken, it would be me."

"You fought as well?" I asked in surprise.

"I did," he confirmed. "I believe that peace is preferable to war, but how could I expect others to defend us against the Romans if I was unwilling to do so myself?"

"And which side prevails?" I inquired, although I already knew the answer.

"We are valiant, but in the end the Romans will overtake us," he declared ruefully. "They have engineered a superior force of war and conquering. More importantly, they can tame the land and lead the people to accept their ways. Our future is in their hands as long as our only response is to fight."

"So defeat is inevitable," I said in despair. "Is the sacrifice of Lukan and many others worth the cost?"

"It never is. I haven't forgotten that diplomacy is the alternative to defeat," Papa affirmed. "I intend to negotiate a settlement with the Romans that will create the best possible life for our people under the circumstances. That is my singular responsibility."

"And my singular responsibility is to bring your son and my beloved husband back from the near dead," I affirmed with conviction.

"It is mine as well." I heard a familiar voice coming from the entrance to the hut.

"Mama!" I cried, turning to greet her. "You have come to heal Lukan!"

"I wouldn't have it otherwise," Papa commented.

"I didn't teach you everything I know about healing," Mama said lightly. "I have more experience than I want to recall dressing serious wounds. You can assist me and perhaps learn a thing or two, with my prayer that you will never again need to use it to counteract the depredations of war. Now, let's determine what we must do."

I hadn't yet seen Lukan's wounds, and the thought of being faced with them turned my stomach. I prepared to run out of the hut to vomit and most likely fall into a heap. But my queasiness left as quickly as it arrived, though I still felt as if a slight breeze could blow me over.

Mama and Papa approached Lukan. "His wounds are severe," Papa warned quietly. "They have grown worse, and even our best healers have been unable to alleviate the damage. As we waited for the arrival of the two of you, we prayed he would be spared. But if it is not to be, at least we'll know you used your considerable powers to help keep death from extinguishing his earthly light."

"So be it," Mama intoned. "I must now evaluate his condition. Do you wish to assist?"

"By all means," he replied. "I am your servant. Bless you, my dear, for making the rigorous journey to get here." He gave her shoulders one more squeeze before he released her to do her work.

Neither of them expected me to take part in the wretchedness that was before them. I could avoid experiencing the worst of it and wait until Mama completed her preliminary ministrations. Nonetheless, I was pulled toward Lukan by an invisible cord, his unequivocal desire to have me near. I found myself at Papa's side.

Mama whispered to Lukan, explaining what she was preparing to do and asking if he understood and agreed. He nodded slightly. Then she asked if he wanted to drink small sips of a potion to alleviate the pain. He shook his head to decline the offer.

Slowly she removed the blankets covering Lukan's upper torso, revealing a vicious gash that ran across his chest from the left side of his neck to his right armpit. Dried blood adhered to the cloths used to stop the bleeding and cover the wound.

"I need cauldrons of hot water, at least three," ordered Mama. "And bring me your sharpest knives, cleaned in boiling water, and as much cloth as you can spare, torn into strips. I also need bowls of all sizes and a clean cup. Bring fresh spring water as well."

Papa gave orders to the two soldiers in attendance. As the water was heating, Mama organized herbs and powders, oils, poultices and potions from her healing bag. I remembered my own bag and retrieved it.

"If you need any of these herbs, we can use them as well," I offered.

"They are from your garden?" she queried.

"They are," I confirmed.

"We'll use them first," she replied. "They carry the vibration of Lukan's home and more importantly, your love, which will add greatly to their healing properties."

I set about arranging my herbs for Mama. When the water was ready, so were we.

"First we'll determine which wound needs our attention most immediately," explained Mama. "We can't know that until we have removed the blood, bandages and battlefield grime. We'll cleanse both wounds. Only then can we assess the extent of the damage done and the degree of threat that each lesion represents."

When we removed the layers of rags covering Lukan's chest wound, I was appalled at what I saw. His right arm had been almost severed. The smallest shift in the angle of the legionnaire's blade would have done so. I had little hope that even if his arm could be saved, it would be useful to him. Papa was being kind when he commented that Lukan would never again wield a sword. I wondered if he would even be able to hold a spoon.

Mama cleaned the wound and covered it with warm cloths soaked in an herbal preparation she mixed in a bowl of hot water. It contained hypericum and angelica to reduce the swelling and silver to halt the decay of flesh. She suggested that I lay fresh cloths over the wound at specific intervals so Lukan could receive the healing properties of the infusion.

Lukan's body was in a state of shock, and his ability to remain alive remained fragile. Even though we both wanted to take more significant steps to counteract the severity of the wounds, she advised we go slowly. As his capacity to receive and benefit from stronger measures increased, we could make the infusions more potent.

After the first wound had been cleaned, assessed and treated, we prepared to evaluate the wound in his abdomen. Mama covered his chest with a blanket and pulled the fur off his stomach, revealing a hideous slice through his internal organs. Blood pooled and clotted. I marveled that Lukan had survived such extreme loss of blood, the damage to his organs notwithstanding.

We followed the same procedure with his abdomen, cleaning the area and alleviating the trauma. Mama's motions were delicate, as if she were attending a newborn babe.

Through the rest of the day and during the night, I changed the cloth coverings on Lukan's wounds, intensifying each infusion as Mama deemed appropriate. We added calendula salve and beeswax to soothe the open flesh. He began to breathe more easily, although he never opened his eyes. He remained in a deep restorative sleep, lacking the energy even for momentary awareness of his physical surroundings.

Papa approached us quietly the next morning. "You have been far too generous with your attentions to Lukan's needs," he said with concern. "If I allow you to continue, I will have two more people on my hands in desperate need of care. I'll take your place at Lukan's side. I've been observing your methods and believe I can do an adequate job. We prepared a private area for you in the hut. You can sleep peacefully, knowing if you are needed you'll be nearby."

"Thank you," replied Mama. "I was beginning to lose my concentration from fatigue. Come, Gracila, Lukan is resting well now, and so should we."

∞   ∞   ∞

I fell asleep at once, as much from relief as from exhaustion. No sooner had I lost my awareness of the material world than Lukan's spirit entered my consciousness. He was full of life, radiating his inimitable joy at our togetherness.

"I have missed this," I murmured.

"So have I," he replied, "My spirit stayed away from you because I didn't want you to know of the horrors I was experiencing. I was concerned that if we made contact, I would reveal more than I intended. So I chose instead to have no communication with you, even though I wanted it desperately.

"Before every battle I released my spirit to Source, then fought hard for the sake of our love and our heritage. I also fought for myself because I wasn't ready to die. I don't fear death, nor am I inordinately attached to life. But in the heat of battle I had visions of myself as an old man, with you. I was an elder statesman and a diplomat. If we fail to stop this invasion, I'll be needed to defend our ancient cultural and spiritual legacy in a different way, by creating peace derived from shared purpose. I fought to win each battle and, failing that, to prevail through alternative means."

"You'll succeed, my love," I assured him. "But first, you must thwart death and regain your vitality. You have an arduous task ahead, but you also have Mama and me and Papa, and the good wishes of the warriors who fought beside you. You'll return to full health and live to a ripe old age. Just promise me you won't become too much of a curmudgeon in your later years!"

"Never," he replied, lighthearted again, "not as long as you're with me."

"Rest assured that is in the stars," I replied.

"Then come to me, my dearest one," he said fervently. "It may be a long time before we can make love when we lie together, but that doesn't stop us from uniting in other ways."

Lukan enveloped me with his love. His body may have been damaged and tenuously holding onto life, but his spirit was as strong as ever. As I slept and he hovered between unconsciousness and death, we merged. If he was to leave the Earth plane, at least we would have this one last blessed union.

I slept for almost an entire day. During that time Lukan and I came together again and again. We held our oneness for long stretches of time. Before I awoke, Lukan made one final visit. "My fever has broken, and I'll soon be able to drink thin broths and your mother's herbal infusions," he revealed. "The worst is over. I am no longer at death's door.

"However, many hazardous procedures are required if I am to regain most of my health, my strength and my faculties. They will be almost unendurable for me and, I suspect, even more so for you. I must bear them, but your participation is not essential. If it becomes too much for you, know that I am in capable and loving hands with Mama and Papa – Mama for her proficiency as a healer and Papa for his dynamism. I draw my courage from the love of all three of you, especially from you. Your love will help me through the ordeals that lie ahead, whether you are participating in them directly or our spirits are sequestered in a serene spot outside this hut. It matters not."

"I won't leave you!" I cried out to him. "If you are to suffer, I'll be by your side."

"I'm telling you, my love, that you'll be with me whether you are holding my hand or sitting by the brook in contemplation," Lukan explained patiently. "Your love will flow through me. You needn't agonize with me to offer the strength of your love."

"I understand," I replied. "If it becomes more than I can witness, I will leave. I never want to compromise Mama's healing powers with my own fright."

"Very well," he agreed. "Then let's get on with it as soon as I am able. It challenges my soul to be so seriously wounded and incapable of advancing toward recovery. I pray that steps can be taken soon."

"As do I," I affirmed.

∞ ∞ ∞

I awoke with a start. The flap across the entrance to the hut was open, and fresh air was wafting in. The oppressive stench of putrid flesh had dissipated. More prominent was the fragrance of herbs Mama was grinding into powder, steeping in infusions and burning as incense. I looked across the room at Lukan. A linen cloth covered his body. His fever had indeed dissipated.

The aroma of Mama's stew transported me to my childhood, and for a moment I longed to return to innocence. But that didn't distract me for long. I was starving.

Seeing that I was awake, Mama asked quietly if I was hungry. "It will take at least two bowls of the magic you created in that pot to quell my appetite," I replied happily.

"When I learned you had eaten almost nothing on your journey here," she noted, "I knew exactly what would sustain you when you awoke."

"What about me?" came a weak voice from across the hut. Mama and I looked at each other with unmasked relief.

"There might be a morsel or two left for you, given that eating this stew is a family tradition," she quipped.

"Far be it from me to break with it," Lukan whispered haltingly. Even though his voice was almost inaudible, his attempt at humor was heartening.

Mama brought me a bowl of stew and another one containing a small amount of broth. "I'll feed you while Gracila enjoys her meal," Mama told Lukan. After a few spoonsful he relaxed considerably.

"We'll keep the stew pot going so Lukan can sip small amounts of broth throughout the day and night," announced Mama. "We can also share it with those assigned to guard and assist us."

Papa arrived looking grim. "We may not be able to remain here until Lukan has fully recovered," he revealed. "The Romans are advancing, and we might need to move Lukan before he is ready to travel."

"How much time do we have?" Mama asked.

"One half of a moon cycle, perhaps more," Papa responded. "What can you accomplish in that time?"

"Lukan will be able to travel by then," Mama observed. "We'll simply have to repair the damage earlier than I planned."

"How soon can this be done without risking his life again?" Papa questioned anxiously.

"He has responded exceptionally well to our care," Mama noted. "Perhaps in a day or two I can start mending what was cut or severed. Until then, we'll feed him as much broth as he can accept and prepare for the upcoming procedures. I'll take a closer look at the wounds. Then we can gather supplies and mix herbal combinations."

"How will you address his wounds?" I inquired.

"Based on what I have seen so far, there are two challenges," Mama revealed. "The first is to remove the flesh that has no chance of becoming a vital part of his body. Then I'll stitch together what was sliced through, beginning with the innermost areas that saw the blade and working my way to the skin. I brought my strongest herbs to reduce the pain. The process won't be as agonizing as it would be otherwise."

"What about the stitching?" I asked, feeling queasy again.

"I'll do it the same way I used to sew your garments," she replied. "Now, feed Lukan as much broth as he can take. More importantly, hold his hand and kiss his cheeks often. I'll select new cloths to clean and cover the wounds."

We spent the next day and a half strengthening Lukan and making final preparations to repair his wounds. We all slept soundly that night, perhaps the most important preparation of all.

From dawn to dusk Mama gently removed the fleshy debris from his shoulder wound and stitched together what was left. I worked with the herbs and prepared hot water, clean cloths and other necessities. When Mama was done, what was once a gaping slice across Lukan's chest and under his armpit was neatly closed.

Lukan was kept in a drugged stupor throughout the process, but he wasn't given so much that he might have crossed to the other side in death. Mama's ability to calibrate the precise doses of herbs needed to numb the pain was a godsend. During the most invasive procedures, when the pain became unbearable, Papa held Lukan still. I turned my head so as not to add to his agony with my own.

Mama was deeply fatigued. I brought her a bowl of stew and a thick slice of warm bread.

"Eat this, then to bed with you," I insisted. "I'll watch Lukan through the night. If he takes a turn for the worse, I'll awaken you immediately."

The next morning Lukan's fever returned with a vengeance. We did what we could to reduce the heat, to no avail. The steps required to patch up his wounds might be so traumatic, he couldn't withstand what was essentially a second assault.

Drained of my inner resources, I lay down for a nap. Lukan's spirit came to me as I slept.

"I am so sorry," he said regretfully.

"For what?" I asked.

"For putting you through this, and then getting worse instead of better," he replied.

"I know you want to live, and for all the right reasons," I assured him. "But if your body is unable to heal, your determination to stay alive will only cause you to suffer needlessly. I can't watch that happen."

"What are you suggesting?" he pursued.

"Surrender to the will of your Divine Source," I advised. "The gods and goddesses who surround you know the depth of your dedication to make a difference during this lifetime, and they cannot doubt your courage to withstand whatever is required for you to be well again. Put yourself in their hands, not mine or Mama's. I stand by their guidance and will help you regain your vitality or," I paused, "assist you in transcending to the other side. If it is the latter, I pray they take you quickly. If it is the former, I'll be your dedicated caretaker for as long as is necessary."

"Wise counsel," he affirmed. "I trust the benevolence of the gods and am turning myself over to them. Thank you for your unyielding love."

I slept soundly, experiencing no more visits from Lukan. As I was climbing back into wakefulness, I had no sense of him near or around me. This shocked me awake. I stood up with a start, running to him. But rather than being dead, he was quite alive, enjoying Mama's broth.

Eyes sparkling, albeit dimly, he said softly, "It seems I've been spared and am now recovering rapidly. At this rate I'll be back on my horse by the new moon."

Mama smiled lovingly and whispered to him, "As soon as you are able, I plan to stitch together the wound in your abdomen. That's a more troublesome lesion, and enduring the procedure will require all your strength. We'll wait until your body has stabilized, then I'll go to work. In the meantime, try to drink as much spring water and broth as you can handle."

Lukan's progress was remarkable. In three days Mama declared he was ready for the next more difficult procedure. The dagger did significant internal damage, which grew worse with time.

Watching Mama work skillfully while he shuddered in pain was more than I could withstand. I kept vigil across the hut from them, in constant prayer and meditation.

Miraculously Lukan survived the ordeal and experienced no raging fever afterward. Once he stabilized, all we had to do was keep applying compresses to the wounds and making sure he was well nourished.

The Romans were held at bay for almost a full moon cycle, long enough to enable Lukan to be evacuated in the back of a cart.

"I can't wait for you to see our house and meet the people who live around us," I told Mama.

"I am returning to my village," she confessed. "The harvest is upon us, and two babies are due to be born soon – a harvest of a different sort. I'll visit you after the spring thaw."

"And what if Lukan still requires your healing?" I questioned.

"You've learned a great deal under trying conditions," she assured me. "I'm leaving you with a generous assortment of herbs. Lukan will probably not require them, but if he does, you can put them to good use."

"Mama, you saved my husband's life," I cried. "How can I ever thank you?"

"Love him with every facet of your being," she advised.

"That I can do," I replied.

Papa remained behind. He was needed to lead the warriors against the Romans and not incidentally, identify an opportunity to offer a peace settlement. His experience with Lukan, and carnage from too many battles, convinced him that a solution beyond war must be found.

∞ ∞ ∞

Lukan was lying in the back of a long cart with layers of fox furs underneath to cushion the inevitable jarring and jostling. We were on our way home. Taranis rode guard alongside the cart. Other soldiers escorted us as well. We made slow progress, but it was steady enough. Lukan fared well, thanks to the fresh air and sunshine. Taranis kept Lukan's spirits high with constant reminders that he was prepared to challenge him in a training match as soon as he was fit enough to take him on.

After two days we were out of range of the Roman invaders and had to watch out instead for thieves and bandits. But the warriors who rode with us were so ferocious everyone we passed cut us a wide swath. Men hiding in the woods waiting to surprise an unsuspecting, poorly armed sojourner remained there until we passed.

The weather was growing more autumnal as we approached our home. The harvest was upon us, and I

Love, 24 AD

prayed our homestead and gardens had been well tended in my absence. If not, it would be a long, lean winter.

"We're almost there," chirped Lukan despite his weariness. "I can hardly wait to experience the world from a different vantage point than looking up at the clouds, birds and trees from the back of this cart."

"It has served you well," I reminded him. "We may have to construct a shrine around this impressive carriage to commemorate its service, complete with a sign that says, 'This cart brought our beloved Lukan home from the battlefield, never again to go to war.'"

"It will be put to better use hauling corn and cabbages," he retorted with a grin. "Essentially the same purpose it has been serving this past week."

We rounded a curve in the cart path, and our home came into view. We pulled up outside the gate. Before I had a chance to dismount my horse, the caretaker, the gardener, the cook, their children, and a few others I didn't recognize hurried to help.

"You are alive, my lord!" cheered the gardener. "We grew increasingly concerned as time passed and you didn't return. But we kept telling ourselves that perhaps it was a good sign. If you hadn't survived, Gracila would have arrived sooner. Please let us help you into the house."

The daughter of the caretaker thrust her tiny hand upward, saying softly, "Here, Lukan. I picked these flowers so you would know how happy we are to have you home at last."

Lukan tried to raise himself to accept the bouquet, but he faltered and fell back into his makeshift bed in the back of the cart. When everyone saw how fragile he was, it was clear how badly he had been wounded.

114

"Don't be concerned, my lord," the cook assured him, "we'll take care of everything while you get well and Gracila tends to your needs. By spring I fully expect you to help us enlarge the garden. I have plans for even more delicious meals, but I need to grow the ingredients for them first."

Lukan pulled his strength together, eager to respond to this outpouring of welcoming and affection. "Thank you for caring for our homestead and my dear Gracila in my absence. I have returned, wounded and weak. But with your continued support and cook's robust roasts, I have no doubt my recovery will be rapid and complete."

The soldiers took the flat planks they used during our journey to move Lukan in and out of the cart, and one last time eased his body onto them. Our welcoming group watched intently. They stood by silently as I led the men into our bedroom, where they lay Lukan on our bed.

"Ah, now I know I'm home," he sighed. "I can't remember another time in my life when I've been happier to sink into a mattress."

"Oh, really?" I asked jokingly. "Some of those occasions were quite memorable to me!"

The men laughed heartily, Taranis included. Lukan emitted a weak chuckle, which seemed to pain him inordinately. He smiled at me, took my hand and kissed it.

"That kiss will have to do for now," he said to me despite our audience. "Though I must admit, I suddenly acquired an additional motivation to get well as soon as possible."

More laughter ensued, as much from relief that Lukan was safely home as from his remark. Then he looked around the room at the men who accompanied us and cared for him with diligence and determination, addressing them solemnly: "I deeply appreciate your steadfast commitment to defending our land, serving my father, and helping me step away from the edge of death and back into life. I have come to know and respect each of you in our training ground and on the battlefield. Your hearts are as big as your bodies are strong. That is your legacy. May you live long and see our beloved homeland safe, secure and thriving with new possibilities. I am forever in your debt."

Imposing warriors more brawny than tender were clearly moved. I had witnessed a moment emblematic of the deep bonds shared by men defending what they value and depending on each other for their success and survival. Finally I understood why Lukan insisted on going into battle with them.

∞ ∞ ∞

Our house was buzzing for the next week with the soldiers preparing for their return journey, resting and eating more than I thought was humanly possible. Children and adults alike sat with them in the evening, listening to their stories and reveling in the adventures they shared.

I spent most of my time caring for Lukan. He was able to eat and drink more than before, and he slept long and soundly. Each day he grew stronger.

After the soldiers left, the household settled into a comfortable routine. I helped with the last phases of the harvest and the storage of our food supplies for winter. We had more than ample provisions. Even though Lukan couldn't hunt, I could count on the caretaker and the gardener for fresh meat as we needed it.

At night Lukan and I slept curled up together. Feeling his warm body next to mine was beyond reassuring. I awakened with no need other than to experience his presence next to me.

One morning as I was waking up slowly, I felt Lukan's lips on my cheek. "Good morning, my love," he whispered. "It seems I've recovered in at least one significant way."

"If your recovery can be measured in kisses, I'm ecstatic at the news," I replied happily.

"Something other than kisses can be measured," he said, smiling broadly. Then he took my hand and brought it slowly down his torso.

"You are recovering quite nicely there," I murmured. "But how can we enjoy ourselves without harming the mending occurring elsewhere?"

"Somehow I don't think that will be a problem," he chuckled. "We can go slowly . . . and carefully."

Slow and careful became our preferred approach to making love, not just while Lukan was healing from his injuries but frequently thereafter. We were so much more together that way, taking our time and luxuriating in the sensuousness of our bodies and spirits coming together. We savored the subtle ways we responded physically to each other. This new way to love may not have included the total abandon we experienced before, but it was exquisite nonetheless.

We made love twice that morning, moving only slightly but still irrefutably one. Afterwards Lukan needed a lengthy rest. He slept more peacefully than he had since he was wounded. I lay with him, listening to his even breathing and grateful for every beat of his heart. Then I slept, nestled next to my precious one.

∞ ∞ ∞

With support from the gardener Lukan was able to walk cautiously around the house. Although he was gaining strength and movement in his right arm, his fingers were limp and atrophied. "What is the use of my arm if I can't get my hand to work?" he bellowed one day in frustration after multiple failed attempts to add kindling to the fire.

I put down the blanket I was weaving for the caretaker's wife, who was newly pregnant. "Give your hand more time to discover its former capacities," I suggested. "You are healing rapidly and without complications everywhere else. Your hand will mend as well, though it may take a bit longer."

"And what will I do in the meantime?" he complained. "I can't write or wield an ax or help enlarge the cellar."

"You'll fetch water with your left hand, and build a fire with your left hand and hold logs for the cellar in place with your left hand," I replied.

"But I am so uncoordinated when I do that," he resisted.

"You'll soon be as proficient with your left hand as you were with your right," I assured him. "And when all your faculties have returned, you'll have to choose whether you want to use your right hand or your left one, both being equal."

"Some things I can already do proficiently with my left hand," he admitted, encircling my hand in his left one and bringing it to his lips. "I'll have to practice with my right hand as well to gain confidence and competence."

"Use me as your training ground as long and as often as you want," I parried back. "I'm at your service." He did and I was.

Over time Lukan became more active around the farm, insisting on taking as much responsibility as the other men. The more he demanded of himself, the more thorough his recovery.

"This is one fine piece of fruit," he commented one day as he walked into the kitchen holding an apple, "crisp and delicious." He took another bite of it.

"The apples this year are the best," I replied, not bothering to look up from the bread dough I was kneading.

"This is one fine piece of fruit," he remarked again, uncharacteristically redundant. That gave me pause. Something was different. Then I noticed the obvious.

"Lukan, you've done it!" I exclaimed. "Your right hand! How much agility has returned?"

Taking the apple in his left hand he showed me. His fingers moved slowly, like those of a very old man. They could neither clutch tightly nor close completely. But there was enough movement to indicate that eventually he might regain the full use of his hand.

"Did this happen quickly, or have you been seeing gradual improvement?" I asked.

"A little of both," he replied. "I've been willing my fingers to grab this apple ever since it was harvested. At first it just sat in my open hand. Little by little my fingers began to curl around it. I told myself I would eat the apple as soon as I could hold it, and that had to happen before it became rotten. Fortunately, I am able to enjoy it today with nary a brown spot."

"I'm thrilled you have come this far," I cheered. "When I first entered the encampment and saw you barely alive, I had little hope you would survive. And now here you are, back to your old self, eating a piece of fruit with a hand that was once useless."

"That is behind us, and I can now enjoy unlimited apples," he quipped.

"And unlimited massages on that newly activated hand of yours," I replied, reaching for the rosemary scented oil I used on his hand.

He finished his apple with a flourish. I took his right hand in mine and massaged each finger, his palm, his wrist, warming every part with the pressure of my touch and the healing herbal oil. Ministering to that hand was a daily ritual, and I intended to keep it up until he regained full use of it.

Children from the families on our farm visited Lukan throughout his recovery, regaling him with their fantastic stories and jubilant laughter. I worried at first that he was using too much energy engaging with them, but invariably he was refreshed afterwards.

"I'm surprised you are not yet with child," he commented one winter evening as we sat by the fire. "All we have done lately is make love. And yet no child has been conceived."

"It concerns me as well," I admitted. "I fully expected to be pregnant before you left for the battlefield. We had spent most of our days loving each other. And yet nothing happened. Now it is the same again."

"Don't fret, we have all the time in the world," he said to console me.

"I have a sense that no child will be forthcoming," I revealed. "In our earlier life together, I was incapable of having children."

"But you didn't necessarily carry that condition forward," he objected.

"Perhaps not," I replied tentatively. "If it's meant to be, we'll have a family. If not, we can enjoy everyone else's children. Either way, we have each other and our days and nights together. That is more than enough."

"It is indeed," he said, reaching over to take me in his arms and hold me tenderly.

∞ ∞ ∞

"How's my son doing?" A bellowing voice interrupted the silence from just inside the gate. I ran to open the door.

"Papa! You are home from the battlefield!" I cried, immensely relieved. "Come in and warm yourself. I'll fetch you a tankard of mead and a bowl of stew."

"I seem to recall your Mama offering the same sustenance to a man and his son, lost in the snow," he replied laughing. "That was the beginning of great things for the son."

"And the continuation of them for you and Mama," I laughed, taking his heavy plaid cloak.

"Papa, I was wondering when you would find your way home," Lukan effused, crossing the room rapidly.

"So was I," Papa acknowledged. "My leadership on the battlefield lagged somewhat after you were carted off, since I was still worried about you. But as time went by and I heard not a word of your demise, I engaged again in the battles in earnest. Now I see why there was no word of your demise. Obviously you are thriving."

"Yes, I am almost completely back to normal," Lukan reported, "although I do have some mean looking scars to remind me of what I came through."

"And to remind me never to allow you to go into battle again," Papa observed. "You are not as strong as you once were, especially with your sword arm."

"I'll accept that, except for the part about your allowing me," replied Lukan. "Tell me, Papa, aren't I beyond the 'allowing' phase of our father-son relationship?"

"Perhaps you are," admitted Papa, "in all matters but this one. You may have forgotten that I am the king, and as such I have full jurisdiction over who goes to war and who doesn't. I'm declaring unequivocally that your warrior days are over."

"At such an early age?" refuted Lukan humorously.

"At an age when you are fully ready for the role you'll play for the rest of your life," Papa announced without offering specifics.

"Which involves," Lukan encouraged.

"Negotiation and diplomacy," replied Papa.

"But I know nothing about either," Lukan objected.

"You'll learn at my side," Papa declared. "Meanwhile, I plan to remain with you until spring."

"When Mama arrives," I noted, not allowing this fact to go unnoticed.

"She will be on her way here after the spring thaw," Papa affirmed. "Then after she departs, the three of us will embark on the first of what I hope will be many diplomatic missions."

"I am to go as well?" I asked incredulously.

"I would never take my son away from you again," Papa commented. "Besides, you'll be a considerable asset."

"In what way?" I asked.

"There is ample time to explain," answered Papa. "But first, I want to enjoy a hearty meal and a good night's sleep on something softer and warmer than the frozen ground."

"That we can provide," I said, taking my leave to attend to Papa's requests. Looking back at father and son, I saw them already in deep conversation. What lay ahead for us?

∞ ∞ ∞

Dinner was late that evening, since we didn't want to wake Papa from his nap until he had rested sufficiently. When he did arise, he was in rare form. He talked, we listened.

"There are some things you need to know," he commenced, after eating his first bowl of stew thick with vegetables and venison. "I've been contemplating what I am about to tell you ever since we learned of the impending Roman invasion. Now it's time to share my thoughts with you both. I ask only that you consider them as you chart a course for your lives."

Lukan's expression was noncommittal. I paid rapt attention.

"As you know, I've always been a contrarian," Papa continued, having been served a second bowl of stew and another generous slice of bread. "Many of the tribes in this land pride themselves in doing battle above all else. Going to war is a badge of honor to be gained in no other way. To die in battle is thought to be a direct route to the highest realms of the netherworld. And to die a courageous hero, even off the battlefield, is exalted. Our warriors don't fear death, which is what makes them so fierce. It's an obvious advantage when we must defend ourselves. Unfortunately this island has been forever at the mercy of predatory forces from abroad.

Love, 24 AD

"It is my duty to defend our people and their way of life. I see them not as vassals whose sole purpose is to do my bidding, enrich my coffers and expand my holdings. Rather, we have a mutual responsibility. I owe them protection, opportunity and a good life, just as they owe the kingdom a share of their gain in exchange for the communal good.

"At issue is how to ensure this for the long term when a powerful force is landing on our shores with troops and horses, weapons and tools, training and experience that far surpass our own. Of course, we need to try with all our might to defend our land, our people and our heritage, and send them packing. But if it becomes evident we cannot win, no matter how many warriors are willing to die in battle, then are we not wasting the promise of their lives? Aren't they dying for naught? Isn't it wiser at that point to enter into a negotiated treaty while we are still relatively strong?

"To fight to the bitter end and still be defeated would result in the destruction of our culture, our families and our lineage. It makes no sense to be devastated on the path to defeat. It is preferable to halt the fighting while we still have our country intact."

"I couldn't agree more," Lukan affirmed. "Devastation can be averted, even if defeat cannot."

"Spoken like a true leader of the people," Papa declared. "With that in mind, I've sent word to Vespasian, the commander of the Roman II Augusta. His legion is annexing our land to the south with ruthless efficiency, step-by-step and warrior-by-warrior. I have informed him that I would like to enter into discussions with him. I hear he is a good man from a humble background. And I know for a fact that he is a credible leader. If he is willing to meet with me, and if we can agree upon terms that suit us both, I am willing to lay down the sword and the shield, and officially allow the Romans to occupy our homeland."

Lukan was looking steadily at Papa, nodding his head slightly. How fascinating, I thought, that a man who was mortally wounded in battle might be supportive of such a path. Didn't that nullify all he had fought for?

Papa saw the questioning on my eyes and addressed me directly. "Gracila, this may seem to be a cowardly course, one that betrays considerable blood spilled by those who fought to keep our land free of outsiders. Any hesitation you may feel to support this idea is fair and reasonable.

"The central question is whether our defeat is guaranteed. Initially I didn't know the answer, but now I do, unequivocally. If we keep fighting, we'll be rendered helpless. Our men will be dead, our families will be starving, our towns will be burned, and our countryside will be nothing but one big graveyard. In the end, despite our heroic resistance, this land will belong to the Romans. We'll have no resources with which we can preserve our way of life. Nor can we partner with them from a position of relative strength to create a future together."

"Partner?" Lukan couldn't help himself. "You expect to partner with the Romans? Isn't that naïve, or at least overly optimistic?"

"Perhaps it is, but it's better to envision an optimal future than to surrender to its opposite," Papa asserted. "If we approach the Roman commander while we still have reserves and capacity, and before either side has lost so much it is impossible to create common ground, we might be able to communicate as equals."

"But you just acknowledged we aren't equals and are certain to be overcome by the Romans' superior numbers, resources and capabilities," Lukan pursued. "Vespasian must be aware of this. How can you expect him to treat you as a partner, even if you do happen to be a king?"

"You forget one critical factor. The Romans aren't here just to win a war," Papa asserted. "This is an economically driven expansion of the Empire. It is as much about commerce and profits as it is about victory on the battlefield.

"This isn't a contest of philosophy or spiritual beliefs, although if the Romans are victorious they will attempt to establish their own views and suffocate ours. Rather, it is driven by the desire to expand dominance and trade, power and wealth. The means to that end is acquisition at the end of the sword. I believe there is still time to lay down the sword and come to the table with the Romans to determine the parameters within which we can live together peacefully on this land."

"But they will rule," protested Lukan.

"They are going to rule anyway," Papa shot back, not from despair but from realism.

"You would give up your kingdom to the Romans, without further resistance?" Lukan challenged.

"That's not my purpose," responded Papa thoughtfully. "My intention is precisely not to give up the kingdom, but to help us retain our strength in collaboration with a dominant new presence in the land."

"What makes you certain that in the end your goodwill won't be betrayed and we'll not be violently defeated anyway?" Lukan asked pointedly.

"Self-interest is stronger than the desire to vanquish," Papa observed. "It serves the best interests of the Romans to keep this country whole and vital. The sooner their engineers can build roads and infrastructure for trade, the more quickly the Emperor can profit from their occupation. Protracted war runs against their interests as much as it does ours. I know this and so does Vespasian. Thus we can meet and talk, man to man, without pretense."

"You make a strong case for partnering with the enemy," Lukan admitted.

"I didn't hesitate to resist the Roman threat, or to send my son and many others' sons into battle in order to drive them back," Papa noted. "The only responsible path was one of violent, valiant resistance, and resist we did. But as I saw the Romans' apparently endless supply of men and materials coming ashore, I had to face the fact that they were fully prepared to expend unlimited military capacity to conquer our land. We don't have such infinite resources. Once I came to terms with that, I began to ponder the possibility of a negotiated peace. And the time to lay the groundwork for that is now."

"I understand," Lukan replied. "More importantly, I agree with your assessment of the situation and the most advantageous course of action."

"I was hoping you would," Papa commented, relieved to hear this declaration from Lukan. "To be quite frank, I was concerned that the sacrifice you made in battle reinforced your conviction that we should fight until the last man standing was struck down."

"My experience as a warrior birthed within me the heart of a pacifist," Lukan stated. "One can't comprehend the implications of going to war without experiencing hand-to-hand combat. Just before I was

127

wounded I peered into the eyes of the Roman soldier attacking me. I was fully aware of what was about to happen.

"In that moment I saw him for exactly who he was: a young man trained to do his job and save his life by killing another. And in that moment I forgave him. He had no vendetta against me, just as I had none against him. We were both pawns in a bloody game being played by the Emperor of Rome.

"He seemed to sense my connection with him, and perhaps even my forgiveness. He hesitated for an instant then everything began to occur in slow motion. I saw his sword starting its downward arc, ripping through my shield and into my chest. I witnessed the glint of his dagger in the sunlight before it entered my belly. The next thing I knew I was being taken away and Papa was urgently summoned.

"One of our warriors reported later that he was coming up behind the soldier but didn't make it in time to save me. He saw the sword and dagger go into me, and just after the damage was done, he sliced off the man's head. I felt dreadful when I heard that. It was bad enough that I might be sacrificed in battle, but to have both of us lose our lives was a needless waste. If I was to die, he should have lived."

I was stunned at this revelation. Lukan's unwavering character, even at the point of his own sacrifice, was staggering. I appreciated him in a new way. It's not that I loved him more. Rather, I respected his unconditional compassion, which extended even toward the man who would slay him. Lukan was a warrior for the light.

"Gracila," Papa interrupted my thoughts, "what do you make of all this?"

Myriad responses crossed my mind, about Lukan's capacity to forgive, Papa's foresight, the conflict between war and peace. I replied, "I admire your wisdom, selflessness and leadership. Lukan shares your lineage and will work with you to create the future you envision. My life has already been transformed twice: once when I met you and Lukan and again when I almost lost him. I can think of nothing more satisfying or inspiring than to spend my days in service to you both, as you pursue the path of peace."

"I have big plans for you, my dear, and they don't involve your standing, walking or sitting behind us," Papa revealed. "You have learned the ways of the divine feminine. Your Mama taught you well. We will harness the communal power of the feminine to help create a fertile context for our discussions. Without it we would most certainly fail. With it we have a far better chance of succeeding."

"Will you ask Mama to assist us from afar?" I suggested, already intuiting the answer.

"Before I visit Vespasian this spring, the four of us will establish a secure vortex within which the negotiations can occur," Papa explained. "Just before Lukan was wounded, I knew to my bones that compromise would be necessary. Your Mama confirmed it after she arrived at the encampment. We engaged in long discussions about how to proceed and finally agreed to meet in the spring. She will bring all the elements of her ritual worship. We will invoke the assistance of the feminine. After she returns to her village she will support our efforts from afar."

"So it won't be a friendly family visit to see how my healing has progressed," Lukan chuckled.

"Obviously not," Papa replied in good humor, "although she and I have both been looking forward to our reunion."

"With each other, most especially," I chided him lovingly.

We chatted about more ordinary topics – the copious harvest, Lukan's recovery of the use of his right hand, the children whose joy helped him heal. Lukan swept me into his lap, and I nestled into him unabashedly. Papa took it all in, smiling broadly.

"I see you two are no less smitten for the ordeal you have been through," he commented wryly.

"My biggest regret about being up and about now is that I am spending less time lying prone with Gracila," Lukan quipped, kissing me on the cheek.

"And my biggest regret is that Lukan has still not learned when enough is enough!" I teased.

∞ ∞ ∞

I insisted that Papa retire to his room early to sleep as long as he needed. He did so without protest. Lukan and I went to our quarters soon afterward. It had been a long day, and dark circles were growing under his eyes. He still tired easily, though he was reluctant to admit it.

I was lying quietly in Lukan's arms, listening to the winter winds outside and his breathing beside me. As I offered a prayer of gratitude that Papa was with us and Mama would be on her way in the spring, he whispered, "It's incredible that we might contribute to the peaceful resolution of our conflict with the Romans. Even though I fought alongside warriors who gave their all to attain victory, I see no weakness in Papa's approach."

"Nor do I," I agreed. "The two of you might well be successful in your endeavors."

"I certainly hope so," replied Lukan. "If we aren't, we face conflict to no worthwhile end. We must avoid that."

"You will, my love," I whispered. "You will." With that Lukan was fast asleep.

We settled into a new routine with Papa around. The soldiers who protected him built temporary quarters for themselves a short distance from our house. With so little to do, they kept busy training and chopping wood, repairing thatching and hauling water from the nearby stream. The place was beginning to look like a small fort, full of activity and marked by efficiency.

The children followed the soldiers around, asking questions and mimicking their every move. The boys decided they would be fierce warriors when they grew up, and the girls declared only an equally fierce warrior would qualify as their mate.

The weather was beginning to turn. Green stalks appeared out of the previously frozen earth. I started planning our new garden, thankful that the one we planted a year ago yielded a harvest plentiful enough to keep us in food all winter. Everyone was healthy and happy, and the caretaker's wife was due to give birth soon. When I counted our blessings, there were many.

One night during our evening meal Papa revealed, "I sensed today that your Mama is on her way. Then it occurred to me why she might be getting such an early start. She wants to be here in time for the spring equinox, the first anniversary of your sacred union. A year later you two are even more in love than you were four seasons ago. Now that's something to celebrate!"

"We could plan a feast for everyone here," I proposed.

"Or the four of us could have a quiet celebration, followed by a pot of ceremonial stew," Papa suggested.

"A much better idea," I confessed. "We'll forever be serving stew on special occasions, and for good reason."

"Will Mama be safe on her journey?" Lukan asked, less interested in our plans for a celebration. "She isn't traveling alone is she?"

"I've already sent word to have an escort of soldiers waiting for her when she emerges from the forest surrounding her village," Papa assured him. "You know as well as I that none of them could find her village. They couldn't even see it! So I arranged for the next best thing. She'll be in safe hands the rest of the way here."

A week later I was busy in the garden, paying little attention to the travelers along the road, when I heard, "This place is lovelier than what I saw in my meditations." It was Mama!

I dropped what I was doing and ran to her. My hands were caked with dirt, my face was smudged, and my hair was so tangled from the work and the wind, it resembled the nests the birds were building. But none of that mattered. Mama had arrived on her first visit to my home.

She climbed off her horse and opened her arms to me. I flew into them, practically knocking the wind out of her. She was temporarily speechless.

"My darling Gracila," she said finally, "Lukan built you a beautiful home, substantial and with generous proportions. And you have made it even lovelier with your gardens."

"You inspired me," I replied, "and I had assistance from many others. Here, let me help you get settled inside".

I addressed the soldiers escorting her. "Lukan and his father are felling trees on the edge of the forest. You might want to let them know you are here and request their further instructions. Meanwhile, I'll ask the cook to prepare a substantial meal for you. Thank you for bringing Mama here safely. I'm in your debt."

"No, we are in her debt," the group leader countered. "She regaled us with stories and prepared herbal potions that gave us more vitality than we've had in a long time. We arrived rejuvenated and invigorated, all because of her."

"Nonetheless, Mama has nary a scratch nor, I am certain, a tale of a single altercation. That's your doing," I replied emphatically.

"There was one altercation," reminisced Mama mischievously. "We came upon a herd of sheep that refused to make way for us. We were forced by their sheer number to stop for a mid-afternoon break, which caused everyone great consternation. As you can imagine, my stalwart escorts prefer forward movement to interludes in the spring sunshine."

"It wasn't a very peaceful interlude," contended one soldier, "with the sheep bleating for no apparent reason and incapable of moving in any direction. We had no intention of giving the upper hand to a confused bunch of farm animals, except that we had no choice in the matter."

"Spoken like a true warrior," laughed Mama, giving him an affectionate hug. Clearly she had disarmed them all by adopting them as her surrogate sons. "Thank you for your delightful company on my journey here, and for your protection. Now, take a pause. I look forward to sharing a robust evening meal with you."

Mama surveyed the quarters prepared for her. "This one room is about the size of my entire hut," she observed. "I'll be comfortable here. But if I try to prepare a pot of stew in the fireplace, remind me you have a separate room for that."

"I have a different life from before," I acknowledged, "but I've also maintained aspects of the years spent with you. Lukan may have more resources at his disposal, but our community shares a spirit similar to that of your village."

"I felt peaceful energy emanating from this beautiful spot long before we arrived," Mama replied. "I knew you had taken the best of what you learned from me and created your own unique version of it. And Lukan, how is he faring these days?"

"He is almost completely healed," I reported. "How is that possible? You saw him after the battle."

"It is possible, my dear, because he has every motivation to live," Mama observed. "He has you and the infinite love you share. In addition, he and his father have an essential purpose to pursue together, one that you and Lukan will continue long after we both are gone."

"You've seen this?" I asked.

"I have, and Lukan's father confirmed it," Mama assured me. "I am here for more than a visit, although the visit will be a joy. My purpose is to align the three of you with each other and the mission that lies ahead. You'll be representing the divine feminine, emanating her capacity to enhance the potential for unity around a shared intention. This calming, collaborative presence is essential to balance the potent forces of the masculine. I'll be involved as well, but from a distance."

Without hesitating to knock, Lukan and Papa surged into the room with the energy of five warriors. Such escalation of male exuberance occurred often lately. In the absence of a battle to fight, Lukan and Papa fairly erupted with boundless vigor.

Papa got to Mama first, giving her a hug so fierce I feared he might break a few bones in the process. Then he pulled away just far enough to gaze upon her with unmistakable love.

"You fared the winter well, I see," Papa noted. "And your escorts obviously took good care of you on the journey here."

"They did indeed," replied Mama. "But then, their loyalty to you knows no bounds, even on an assignment to accompany a lone woman for a family visit."

"It's my turn," asserted Lukan, tapping his father on the shoulder and embracing Mama decisively with both arms.

"A perfectly balanced hug!" she noted happily. "What a blessing that your arm has healed!"

Lukan kissed her on both cheeks and replied, "I have you to thank on two counts. One, for pulling me from the brink of death, and two, for teaching your daughter well so she could continue to nurse me back to health."

"I suppose Gracila's nursing took many forms," Mama laughed delightedly.

Without missing a beat, Lukan replied, "She applied the power of the feminine in all her manifestations."

I intervened so Mama could rest while I rounded up help in preparing a bountiful meal for additional hungry soldiers.

"It means a great deal to me to have the four of us back together under more auspicious circumstances than the last time," Papa commented to Lukan and me. "And we are in your home, no less. What a pleasure!"

He hugged us both in his great big arms. The wave of love emanating from him moved me deeply. Like his soldiers, I would follow him anywhere and serve however he requested. Such was the power of his capacity to lead and love in equal measure.

That night Lukan and I were lying together after a sumptuous dinner spiced with considerable conversation. I was aware of impending change. "We are about to become wayfarers, traveling far afield and staying away for long periods of time," I thought to myself.

"What occupies your mind?" asked Lukan gently. "You were far away. Was it a pleasant reverie?"

"I was thinking that although we are all together now, such occasions will be the exception," I replied. "We'll make our home in a distant land although we always have this farm to come back to."

"That may indeed result from the diplomatic course Papa wants to follow with the Romans," Lukan noted.

Then I received a lucid image. "We'll be in Rome, not just as visitors but as a part of the community," I revealed.

"Perhaps then Papa's diplomacy will be successful," Lukan suggested, pulling me closer to him. "I trust your ability to glimpse what lies ahead. I also trust Papa's wisdom and integrity."

"What do you trust about yourself?" I asked.

"I trust that as my father's son, I have the benefit of his lineage and his tutelage," Lukan replied. "I trust my honesty and ability to empathize with others – two essential qualities of a diplomat. And finally, I trust I can create solutions that serve the common good and transcend petty politics and corrupt power plays. That may be my greatest strength except, of course, my infinite love for you."

We made love tenderly that night, sealing our understanding and acceptance of an unprecedented future together. The only known aspects would be our love and our shared commitment to a cause. That was more than enough.

∞ ∞ ∞

We feasted and talked, dug in the garden and stayed up late sharing stories. Life meandered, a luxury all four of us relished. Then one evening the tone of the conversation shifted. Mama led the way.

"Tomorrow is the spring equinox," she reminded us. "We will be preoccupied with our celebration of the sacred union that occurred one year ago. Tonight as we prepare for the introduction of new energies for rebirth, I suggest we invoke the support of the divine feminine and the divine masculine in the endeavor you are about to undertake. We can do so in a ritual that releases limitations and brings forth sacred powers vibrating in perfect alignment with our highest good."

"No more frivolous family chatter?" Papa quipped.

"Not tonight," Mama replied lightly. "The energies this evening feel particularly suited to this work. After we accomplish what I have in mind, we can return to abject frivolity."

"How shall we begin, then?" asked Papa.

"I've prepared a fire with the appropriate wood and herbs. We'll honor the masculine and feminine with our gifts to the fire, then allow messages to come through us that clarify and ground the divine intention of your mission," Mama explained.

She led us to the room in front of the house. A lively fire was crackling away, emitting a mystical fragrance.

"What sublime combination have you used this time?" I asked.

"Sandalwood, juniper and sage, with a touch of cedar," Mama replied, handing each of us golden crystals of dried resin.

"Frankincense never fails to remind me of our lifetime in the temples, when our incense burners perpetually emanated this intoxicating fragrance," Papa commented.

"Traders from distant lands bring it now, and through luck and conscious design, some of it finds its way to me," Mama observed. "I save it for special rituals like this one."

"You burned this for our sacred union," I recalled. "What is its power precisely?"

"Frankincense has the capacity to make a direct connection between earthly reality and the higher realms," explained Mama. "It establishes a vibratory vortex that enables contact, communication and travel between the two frequencies. Within that vortex we can affirm the larger objective of your diplomatic endeavors, which is sustained peace, and call on additional support as appropriate.

"Follow along as I lead the chanting. When the vibration reaches the appropriate frequency, I will sprinkle the incense in the fire, wait for it to burn and smoke, then speak the words I am called upon to say. You may do so as well."

Mama began a familiar chant in her melodic voice and we joined in. Soon my body was buzzing with an exceedingly high vibration. Just when it seemed we could hold the frequency no longer, Mama raised both arms and phased out the chanting. The voice that came from her lips reverberated with the resonance of the ages. Another presence was speaking through her. As she sprinkled frankincense into the fire, I closed my eyes and surrendered to the transcendent fullness of the moment.

Mama intoned these words: "In the name of the Source of all life, I come to you with the love and oneness that reside at the core of my being. From this oneness flows an eternal river of divine consequence, which demands that all live by the principles of the Unified Oversoul. These principles are to love without condition, forgive without hesitation and recognize divinity everywhere. This creates perfect complementarity between masculine and feminine impulses, which invariably move toward oneness. Everything derives from Divine Source and returns to oneness with each other and with Source. We devote our lives to this principle, that we may serve humbly with all that we are, all that we do and all that we have."

"May it be so," we affirmed.

Papa was next. Adding incense to the flames, he said, "Behold, we are your servants, without capacity, resources or function were it not for the gifts you so generously bestow upon us and that we so gratefully receive. May we make the world a peaceful place where children can grow up with full bellies and stable families, where shared purpose takes precedence over disputes and unnecessary wars, and where the infinite divine potential inherent in all peoples comes to fruition in each individual's thoughts and deeds, hopes and desires. May we create community with inhabitants of many cultures and traditions, that we may strengthen our similarities and honor our differences. May we breathe life into the spark of spirit residing in us all, that we may join in a common vision of mutual benefit."

"May it be so," we said in unison.

A surge of energy pulsed through me as I added frankincense to the fire. Then I heard myself say, "In the name of the divine feminine, I beseech that the wisdom of the ages be accessible to us. May we imbibe the profound knowledge that derives from past, present and future as they exist simultaneously. May we never hesitate to hear your guidance and speak the truth that emanates from your font of knowledge. May we recognize the power that resides within us to create a blessed world for all, a world of pervasive joy and perpetual peace. May love lead us to oneness, and may oneness affirm our lineage of eternal love."

"May it be so," we vowed.

Lukan shifted position, preparing to participate. He added frankincense to the fire and waited for inspiration. Drawing a deep breath, he began, "In the name of the masculine aspect of being, I present myself in my humility. May war become the last alternative after all others have failed rather than the first. May peace become so palpable and precious it will not willingly be sacrificed. As I help transform this potential into reality, may doors open to me freely and without conflict. May love light every step of my journey and inspire every word I utter. May I remain a worthy servant always and in all ways."

"May it be so," we prayed.

We sat for a long while in silence, in a room infused with the potent essence of frankincense. I was neither on Earth nor anywhere else. I existed in a void of nothingness, experiencing blissful detachment.

Eventually we returned to our bodies and slowly opened our eyes. We were each smiling broadly at the others, drunk on divine love.

"I sealed the intention – a critical final step," Mama revealed. "I invited the beings participating with us to come forward with objections or observations. All were affirming without hesitation. Then together we surrounded the proceedings with the highest vibration associated with earthly activity and surrendered it to divine will. Our task now is to find the flow and remain in it."

"Something shifted within me," Lukan observed. "I have no need to know how the future will unfold. I released the plans, goals and viewpoints that formerly gave me a false sense of control. Something much larger is working through me now. My primary responsibility is to stay out of the way and let it emerge. It feels completely natural and unforced – remarkable!"

"Congratulations, my son. You are resonating with Source," Papa declared. "The most effective statesmen embody the capabilities you just described. Beyond that, you might have noticed that during the invocation the language shifted from a broadly defined 'we' to a singularly individual 'I'. When you spoke last, you made a deeply personal statement. The beings working with us went from the general to the specific, from the expansiveness of Creation to the spirit manifest within you. It takes both. One is ineffective without the other."

"I experienced that happening, though I wouldn't have described it that way," Lukan commented.

"The commitment you made was yours alone," Papa continued. "It was also a representation of what anyone can do at any time. By focusing the energy from the universal to the individual, we were able to merge both aspects of the human condition and increase the potential for humankind to evolve toward our highest and best purpose, collectively and one person at a time. All is well. All is perfect, in fact."

"How can we make the most of this gift?" Lukan inquired.

"We will begin by seeking an audience with the Roman Vespasian," Papa advised.

"What do you know of him?" I wondered.

"He is more reasonable and less arrogant than most," replied Papa. "That should be enough to convince him to meet with us initially. Then it will be a matter of listening carefully, acting astutely and identifying shared objectives and long-term interests."

"Is he in a position to make a binding agreement with us?" queried Lukan.

"He is far from the seat of power in Rome, charged with leading one of the conquering legions," Papa explained. "He has the authority to determine the most appropriate, effective and intelligent approach to achieving his goal. I intend to enlighten him regarding alternatives worth considering. And you, Lukan, will charm him with your earnestness and quick wit. He will judge my integrity based not on my words, but on the son who grew up at my side. You are my secret weapon, since you will convince him of my honor and credibility just by being yourself."

"I am up to that task," chuckled Lukan, "and relieved you aren't expecting me to negotiate a peace treaty with a sly Roman military leader."

"One sly old fox deserves another one to tangle with," Papa replied sardonically. "I have a few tricks up my sleeve, but they are reflective of the intention we stated and sealed this evening. There will be no misrepresentation or underhandedness."

"Then we must pray he is equally trustworthy," Lukan commented.

"He is our best hope," Papa confirmed. "We have everything to gain and little to lose by approaching him as I am prepared to do."

"May it happen soon, before scores more are needlessly slaughtered defending their conflicting causes," Mama pledged.

"So be it," declared Papa firmly.

The fire had burned down to glimmering embers, and the room was growing chilly.

"I'll fetch some mulled wine to warm our bones and celebrate yet another evening we'll remember always," I offered.

We shared the wine and equally warm conversation, then retired to our rooms and slept peacefully all the night.

∞ ∞ ∞

"Good morning, my love," Lukan whispered, nuzzling me awake with a kiss. "I wanted to be the first to offer my congratulations."

"For what?" I asked, half asleep. I had obviously forgotten what day it was.

"For managing to survive an entire year as my sacred partner," he said, only half in jest. "The day of our union you had no idea what a challenge it would be to share your life with me."

"I had no idea what a challenge it would be to keep you alive!" I exclaimed. "Had I known you were about to go off to do battle as soon as you had me safely ensconced in our new home, I might have declined to go through with the ceremony."

"Which is precisely why I didn't tell you until the knot had been tied and you were obligated to stick with me," he laughed.

"And stick with you I have," I retorted, "through thick and thin and everything in between. You've made your point, that I'm no longer living in the sanctuary of Mama's village."

Lukan grew serious. "I speak too lightly about what I pray will have been the most difficult year you spend with me," he whispered, pulling me closer.

"Ours is a sacred union," I replied. "It endures the vagaries of our earthly experience and is nurtured by our infinite love. As long as I have your love, nothing is difficult or even impossible."

"That you have, my dearest," replied Lukan. "Our love transcends separation, mortal wounds and even lifetimes."

"But for the moment you are lying next to me, just as you did the night of our union," I murmured as I tucked myself into him. "Do you have the same stamina you exhibited a year ago? I recall endless hours of lovemaking."

"My stamina may be diminished," he admitted, "but fervent desire still flames within me."

"A welcome declaration," I said, kissing him softly, "because I intend to fan that flame with all my womanly wiles."

"I'll take them one at a time," he teased. "If you thrust them upon me all at once, I'm likely to expire from overexertion. And you wouldn't want that."

When we finally appeared from our room, it was almost midday. Papa was enjoying a light meal, along with Mama.

"I see you two have been celebrating your first anniversary," Papa observed wryly, "leaving the two of us to fend for ourselves. It took everything in my power to convince your Mama that you were not sick from the frankincense and in need of her healing interventions."

Mama slapped his hand lightly, her eyes sparkling. "Actually, we were just commenting on what an exceptional match occurred on the equinox one year ago," she informed us. "We are both quite proud of ourselves for bringing you two into the world and making sure you met at the perfect time."

"Making sure?" I asked, pretending incredulity. "I thought it was an accident, a man and his son who got lost and just happened to wander into our village."

"Oh, that's right," Mama amended. "That's the story, isn't it?"

"Unless it was a well defined strategy," I quipped.

"As you know, the four of us planned it before we were born," Mama replied. "We agreed upon the circumstances of our lifetimes, how we would come together, and the opportunities and free will choices that would present themselves."

"So far it's progressing as anticipated," added Papa.

"How much do you know exactly?" queried Lukan.

"Only the broadest aspects of what lies ahead," replied Papa. "Knowing more than that blunts my ability to live in the moment."

"You'll celebrate many more anniversaries, I promise you," Mama assured us, "long after Papa and I have taken our leave. You'll both be old and gray, and as much in love as you were the first time you laid eyes on each other. Perhaps more so, for your love can only grow stronger and more devoted with time."

It was a beautiful day, infused with intimations of spring. We walked together around the property, blessing the buds on the trees and the early blossoms just beginning their moment of glory in the sun. The afternoon was so sweetly reassuring I wished momentarily that nothing would change. What would be the harm in living a quiet, simple life surrounded by those I loved? I knew the answer, but it was a tempting thought nonetheless.

Mama hosted a surprise party for us that evening, inviting the families who worked the farm. Somehow she and the cook managed to prepare a feast, complete with honey cakes and second helpings of everything. It was a genial gathering commemorating the life we created together on this spot, in this home.

In the ensuing days I purposefully left Mama and Papa to themselves. They were like young lovers, attentive and solicitous of each other. I grew so accustomed to seeing them together I couldn't picture them apart.

But the time did come for Mama to leave. Papa sent for escorts a few days earlier, and we all knew that once they galloped through the gate they would be impatient to be on their way. Mama gathered her traveling items and sorted through her healing herbs, selecting ones to leave with me.

I was watching her pack when she said gently, "It's been a year, and even though Lukan was gone or disabled much of that time, you should have conceived by now. That hasn't yet occurred, has it?"

"No, unfortunately," I replied, despondent. "With each lunar cycle my hopes rise, only to be dashed once again. So I stay busy and try not to think about it."

"How is Lukan dealing with it?" Mama asked.

"He is more concerned for me than anything else," I commented. "He says he'll be as happy without children as he would be with them. He tells me that as long as he has my love, he is amply blessed and needs nothing more. I believe he truly means it."

"And you?" Mama pursued. "Do you need more?"

"Not really," I revealed, surprising myself with a previously hidden truth. "If I don't bear children, will it displease the Mother terribly?"

"Whatever happens or doesn't pleases the Mother," Mama assured me. "When love such as what you and Lukan share is involved, the result is always perfect. Your love produces outcomes aligned with the divine intention for your lives. Rejecting that disrespects your love. Celebrate your togetherness and continue to embrace whatever unfolds before you."

"I'm comforted by that," I told Mama, hugging her with all my might.

"Even if you bear no children of your own, you'll be surrounded by many of them," Mama assured me. "Look at what you created here already, an extended family with the joyful laughter of little ones all around."

"Just like the village where I grew up," I noted appreciatively.

"Just like where you grew up," Mama concluded.

She left a few days later, amidst a profusion of tears on my part, multiple embraces from the three of us, and the impatient snorts of horses ready to take to the road. I watched her until her entourage rounded a bend in the path and was out of sight. Then I began digging in the soil again, the better to let go of her one more time.

∞ ∞ ∞

That evening Papa approached me. "Lukan and I have completed the arrangements for our journey to meet with the Roman commander. We want you to accompany us. We need to discuss the details so you and Lukan can prepare the families here to manage the household, gardens, livestock, and crops while you are gone.

"Vespasian has agreed to meet with me, although no date has been set. I sent a return message suggesting a neutral place for us to come together. It is distant enough from the battles to enable us to talk at length without alarming those in our command, who would rather we fight to the death than converse civilly or show any sign of weakness. I have set out additional terms for his consideration: how many soldiers we will each bring with us, how long we might prepare to meet, where we could set up camp. As soon as I hear back from him, the three of us can depart."

"Please remind me why I am going," I requested, hoping to quell my insecurity.

"You are from an imposing feminine lineage," Papa replied. "I want Vespasian to experience what our women are made of, which is pluck and intelligence, self-confidence and significant capability. That's not what he is accustomed to in Rome."

"What are the women like in Rome?" I pursued.

"They are powerless and therefore relentlessly manipulative," Papa declared.

"How will we approach Vespasian?" Lukan asked for my benefit. No doubt he and Papa had already planned their encounter in detail.

"I will outline our purpose, which is to negotiate an arrangement that limits the casualties and destruction of war and serves the interests of both sides," Papa explained. "I will also admit I am at a double negotiating disadvantage. First, we have fewer warriors to lead into battle and second, the conflict is being fought on our land. We have more to lose in the course of endless warfare than they do, even if we were confident we could sustain it."

"Why would you admit weakness so early in the negotiations?" I questioned.

"It establishes that I am a man of integrity," Papa replied. "If he is as well, he will continue the discussion to see where it leads. If he isn't, he will ridicule me, declare me a foolish old buzzard, remind me of his superiority, and exit with his feathers flying high. In that case I will have taken the measure of the man and done my best to preclude the destruction I want to avoid. Then we will be on our way."

"So it will either be an abbreviated conversation or a much longer one," noted Lukan.

"Exactly," Papa agreed. "Of course, I am hoping it lasts for days."

"If it does, what do you want to accomplish?" I asked.

"I don't command the stronger forces," Papa observed. "But if I remain resilient and responsive, we may reach an agreement that benefits our people at least slightly, and perhaps a great deal more than that."

"So you trust the process, with some help from Mama and our prior invocations," I summarized.

"If I weren't confident of the support I'm receiving from the seen and the unseen, I wouldn't be as anxious to encourage a confrontation," Papa admitted.

"Confrontation?" Lukan challenged. "I thought it was to be a negotiation."

"One must first confront the person he is meeting at the negotiating table," Papa explained. "You challenge your opponent first, see how he responds, then realign your strategy accordingly."

"I am learning from the best," Lukan observed, smiling broadly.

"As you must," confirmed Papa. "Soon you will be doing this as well, but without me to guide you."

The unknown before us was when a meeting with Vespasian would occur. There were numerous delays – so many, in fact, that we despaired of ever hearing from him.

The days were growing warm, and I was tending my flowers and plants with the care of a young mother toward her first child. When I saw the king's messenger arrive, it took all my willpower not to approach him first to hear the news. Instead I continued my gardening and waited until Papa called Lukan and me indoors.

"We depart in the morning to meet with Vespasian immediately," announced Papa. "We have just enough time to arrive at the appointed location when he does. Prepare at once."

I asked no questions, nor did Lukan. I fed the messenger and helped him settle down for a much needed rest. Then I gathered the families to review what was to be done in our absence. We had planned so thoroughly for this moment, there was little left to do except pack clothing and food, bless our home and be on our way.

It was a grueling journey despite the temperate weather. Warriors are trained to endure hardship and demand continuous service from their bodies day and night. We traveled at an unremitting pace, with limited time to eat and sleep. This was routine for Lukan, Papa and the others. I wasn't quite so predisposed. Just as I was about to suggest that Lukan hold me against him on his horse so I could sleep, Papa informed us we were nearing our destination. I perked up and kept going.

We entered an open field where tents had been erected. The Roman commander had already arrived, how much earlier we couldn't ascertain. I hoped we would precede him so I could clean up in a nearby stream and a take a nap, in that order.

A Roman soldier greeted us and showed us to our accommodations. Papa, Lukan and I would share one tent and our warrior escorts another, when they were not on guard duty. We were arranging our few possessions in our tent when a Roman courier arrived.

"My commander requests a meeting over the evening meal in his tent, just after sunset," he announced. Papa sent word gratefully accepting the invitation.

"He wants us to be rested," noted Papa. "If he were manipulative or impatient, he would insist we commence immediately. This bodes well."

"It also means I can wash off the travel grime and make myself presentable," I remarked with relief. "I may even have time to sleep a wink or two."

"I'll go with you," offered Lukan. "Better I than one of our warriors guard you while you are swimming naked!"

"I was about to suggest more swimming and less guarding," I replied.

"That, too," laughed Lukan, selecting a change of clothes for himself before we headed to the river.

∞ ∞ ∞

The Roman Vespasian was imposing but surprisingly not fierce. He was wearing a red and black knee-length tunic embroidered with an intricate band of gold. His leather boots were laced to the ankle, and a red cape was fastened carelessly at the shoulder with a large gold pin in the shape of a lion's head. He didn't seem to take the vestments of his rank all that seriously.

Then again, his aim was to overthrow those whose families, tribes and clans had ruled our land for generations. And so I was wary.

"I would welcome you, but I am an unwelcome trespasser on your land," he began. "I shall not pretend to offer my hospitality as if it were mine to give."

This was an unexpected beginning to the evening, an auspicious portent. He sounded more than minimally like Papa.

"Nor shall I presume to welcome you," responded Papa, "given that you clearly have the upper hand and are showing no sign of backing down."

The two men smiled faintly in acknowledgment of the first round of positioning.

"Who are your two escorts?" asked the Roman.

"This is my son Lukan and his wife Gracila," Papa replied. "I asked Lukan to accompany me and suggested it would be unwise for him to decline. Then I invited Gracila along as well. Lukan was severely wounded in battle and only recently has regained the use of his right arm. I couldn't bear to watch Gracila let him go one more time, so I insisted she join us."

"A family outing of sorts," chuckled the Roman. "I would do the same if I could. How shall we begin?"

Papa followed the plan we discussed earlier. Vespasian seemed as intrigued with Papa as he was with his proposal of a negotiated peace. The leaders talked congenially, as if they were on anything other than opposing sides. Then Vespasian suggested the conversation continue the following day. It was past time for a meal.

During our repast – partridge rubbed with coriander and baked with leeks, turnips and carrots, followed by dates, apricots and nuts – the talk took an informal turn. The Roman wanted to know about our daily lives, when the men were not off fighting invaders. Eventually the topic turned to my life before marriage and the village where I grew up.

"It's a community comprised of only women and children?" he asked incredulously.

"It is," I affirmed. "Its inhabitants are entirely self sufficient and quite happy as well."

The Roman laughed heartily. I was relieved he didn't deem me impertinent.

"There must be some men around on occasion," he ventured. "Otherwise there would be no children."

"Men are invited to festivals and commemorations of the seasons," I explained. "Plus we see errant wanderers on occasion who happen upon our simple circle of huts quite by accident." The irony in my voice wasn't lost on him.

"Let me guess," he intervened. "Lukan and his imposing father?"

"How astute of you!" I acknowledged.

"And just in time for Lukan to reserve you for himself before any other suitors might stumble upon your community," guessed the Roman.

"Correct again," I replied.

"So it was by design after all," noted Vespasian.

"If you believe in a grand design for all things, then I would agree," I qualified. "If not, then perhaps it was indeed a chance meeting."

"Knowing the particular king involved, as I'm just commencing to do, I suspect little is ever left to chance," he observed.

"You suspect correctly, sir," I validated. "And so we have created a bit of a conundrum."

"If not a conundrum, then certainly a labyrinthine puzzle," he replied.

Papa beamed as he witnessed our banter. Lukan was thoroughly relaxed, enjoying the exchange as well. I recalled Papa's earlier statement of why he wanted me to accompany them. I wasn't negotiating anything, nor would I, but I was playing a balancing role in the proceedings simply by being myself.

Turning to Papa and Lukan, Vespasian remarked, "I like strong, smart women who aren't afraid to speak their mind. The world has far too few of them, not because they don't exist, but because most men want their women to be superficial and tongue-tied. I never understood it."

"Obviously, tongue-tied is not something we value either," Papa replied casually.

The meal progressed cordially. After Papa and Vespasian agreed on the next day's meeting time, we retired to our tent, guards at the ready.

We had just dined and conversed comfortably with the enemy. So far the line differentiating friend and foe had proven to be malleable and surprisingly arbitrary. I felt calm, as if I had begun a lifelong friendship. Strange as it seemed, I suspected that just might come to pass.

Papa attended the meeting alone the following day so he could communicate his position and his proposition clearly. He and the Roman met in private until mid-afternoon, refusing food and forestalling all interruptions.

The longer the meeting lasted, the more hopeful Lukan and I became that the result might be beneficial. Anything preventing the horrific devastation that lay ahead would constitute a success. Beyond that, if Papa could negotiate a partnership, even one blatantly in favor of the Romans, it would be a victory.

Papa looked relieved and not a little pleased when he returned to our tent. We asked nothing and waited for him to speak.

"It went well," he said simply. "Vespasian is a tough commander, but then, I expected nothing less. The outcome remains uncertain – we have many more talks ahead – but I believe there is a chance he'll be open enough to consider my proposal. We'll see.

"Vespasian asked about you," Papa mentioned to Lukan. "You were quiet last night. He wanted to know about the extent of your wounds. He was concerned you may still be experiencing side effects from them. You can expect a few questions from him when we dine this evening."

"I am ready to answer them all," asserted Lukan. "I may even have a question or two for him."

"He would welcome that," affirmed Papa. "This Roman is no brute. He is intelligent and considered in his opinions. Given his rise in the military, one would expect him to be somewhat insufferable. But so far I see none of that."

"Given that you are a king, one would expect you to be somewhat insufferable as well," I inserted. "But I see none of that, either."

If Papa had any residual tension, it melted away with his hearty laughter.

"Did I ever tell you how much I love you?" he asked unexpectedly. "Not as much as Lukan does, of course, but you can count me as one of your ardent admirers."

"That's good to know," I said at once. "If Lukan and I ever have an altercation which, by the way, has yet to occur, I'll know whom to turn to for solace and support."

"That you will have," he responded happily. "Knowing this, Lukan will probably be more reluctant than ever to pick a fight with you."

"My fighting days are over," Lukan declared. "I'm capable of only loving now."

"That I can well imagine," Papa quipped. "But I'll ask for neither details nor proof in that regard."

"As always, your sagacity and statesmanship have won you two loyal hearts," Lukan observed wryly.

Papa settled down for a nap, and Lukan and I explored the countryside.

"I'm intrigued by the dynamics so far, not because of Papa's interactions with the Roman but because of who you are with him," Lukan observed.

"How so?" I ventured.

"Obviously, you are comfortable around powerful men," he noted. "Whereas I grew up with them in my midst, you were isolated and protected. And yet you are confidently yourself around Papa and Vespasian. You relish sparring verbally with them."

"Yes I do," I admitted. "As much as I love our home and the life we have there, I would happily go elsewhere with you if your service required it."

"And you would sit at banquets going toe-to-toe with the most influential power brokers in attendance," Lukan predicted.

"Most likely I would," I admitted, "unless to do so would cause problems for you. I'm well aware, as Vespasian observed last night, that Romans prefer their women ignorant and inarticulate."

"They may prefer their own woman that way, but they'd appreciate your forthright nature," countered Lukan. "Especially since you're married and wouldn't threaten their masculine prerogatives."

"What an odd way to live, wanting one's partner to be silly and stupid, even if she has to pretend to be so, but valuing the opposite in others," I remarked. "Does it bother you that I am so outspoken?"

"Let's see, would I want you to be mindlessly boring and interested only in manipulating me to acquire another bangle for your arm, or am I satisfied with a woman who is my equal in all ways?" mused Lukan. "That's a tough choice. But since your mother involved so many spirits in our sacred union, I'd best not anger them by wishing otherwise."

He drew me to him and into a fierce embrace. We kissed, grateful to be together in these unlikely circumstances. Lukan began to pull me to the ground, his intentions evident, but I shook my head in refusal.

"The guards," I reminded him. "They've been keeping their distance, but we're still in their line of sight. We have no privacy. Or have you forgotten?"

"I was well aware of distant observers," Lukan admitted. "But I tossed that consideration aside."

"And I put it right in front of us again," I replied merrily.

"I think I'll amend my earlier declaration," chuckled Lukan. "Give me a woman who is slow, mindless and accommodates my every whim."

"I'm in trouble now," I laughed, kissing him quickly then taking his hand and heading back for our evening with the Roman.

∞ ∞ ∞

Papa was correct in predicting Vespasian would be assessing Lukan. He began doing so almost immediately.

"So tell me, Lukan, how does it sit with you to be involved in negotiating with an enemy at whose hand you were mortally wounded?" he asked.

"It pleases me to no end," Lukan responded. "I see no value, or valor, in warfare. Brute force impresses me far less than intellectual honesty and heartfelt compassion."

I glanced at Papa, who was suppressing a smile.

"But you learned to fight with brute force," tested the Roman, "and you did so, no doubt valiantly, for an extended period of time."

"That I did," Lukan affirmed. "My time on the battlefield was invaluable. It caused me to consider more deeply what I wanted to do with my life besides ward off invaders."

"Still you fought," continued Vespasian, ceding Lukan no ground whatsoever.

Unfazed, Lukan replied, "I fought, and I killed or wounded many of your men. I never shrank from the heat of battle. Quite the contrary, I usually ran right into the thick of it."

"I expected nothing less," noted the Roman.

"My father taught me well," Lukan recalled. "He personally instructed me in the art of swordsmanship and archery. He made this body of mine as solid as a rock. It had to be, so I could keep up with him.

"Beyond that, he urged me to ponder the implications of my actions, to assess their larger, unintended impact. He guided me to think like a leader who cares as much about people and cultural heritage as he does about victory and power."

"The world is a vicious place," Vespasian persisted, "full of those who would see such behavior as weakness and take advantage of it."

"I am no innocent, sir," Lukan shot back. "I am aware that empathy might be perceived as vulnerability and concern for the powerless as exhibiting powerlessness. I believe one must influence through the appropriate use of power and serve the greater good by being willing to give a little or, if necessary, a lot. This can be done with shrewd awareness, calm forethought and not a shred of weakness."

"You sound like your esteemed father," observed the Roman.

"That's the highest compliment you could pay me," Lukan replied.

"You also sound like some of the more liberal, freethinking senators in Rome, who argue for the republic," continued the commander. "They want government to be in the hands of the people more than the Emperor. They make their case passionately despite opposition from many quarters, including the Caesar himself. But still they persist in asserting that the only sustainable way of organizing a society is through self-governance. Would you agree?"

"I don't know enough to agree or disagree," Lukan responded honestly. "But I'd be pleased to learn more and then offer my viewpoints."

"The only way for you to do that is to come to Rome. Perhaps some day that will be possible," Vespasian suggested.

"It is my fervent hope that we might meet peacefully in your land, with nothing to debate but whether the common people should be granted the privilege of self-governance," Lukan concluded.

"It is mine as well," affirmed the Roman.

We shared stories about our homes and families, and once again the gathering concluded later than it seemed.

A similar rhythm followed in the ensuing days, with Papa and Vespasian engaging in private conversations followed by the four of us at dinner in the evening.

We were nearing the end of the negotiations, or so Papa hoped, when Vespasian asked during dinner, "Do you believe in love?" He directed the query at no one in particular. In fact he was looking at a half eaten slice of roast meat when he posed the question. I wondered if that was deliberate.

His inquiry was followed by an awkward silence. I was waiting for Lukan or Papa to speak first and, as they explained to me later, they were each considering how to respond. Lukan jumped in first.

"Absolutely. Love may be the only thing I have any faith in because it produces more good for more people. Beyond that, can one love and be loved irrevocably? Yes, I believe in that kind of love, for I have it in my life."

"How do you know it is not a fleeting infatuation?" asked Vespasian, adopting the role of interrogator.

"It exists without conditions," Lukan continued. "Gracila and I recognized each other the moment we met, and we have loved each other ever since."

"How can you be sure your love is reciprocated?" asked Vespasian, more curious than challenging.

"I leave that to Gracila to answer," replied Lukan. "I wouldn't presume to represent her perspective on the subject."

"I love Lukan with the ease of a river flowing to the sea and the inevitability of the seasons," I ventured. "I love him with the same certainty that causes the stars to twinkle in the sky at night and lose their glow to the morning sun.

"With that said, the answer to whether one's love is reciprocated – and how to tell – is more complicated. No definitive response exists, really. The world is replete with protestations of love that in truth come from a hollow heart. I would assert, however, that to love without concern for reciprocity is a gift so great, it needs nothing in return to be worthy."

"Spoken like a true romantic," asserted the Roman.

"Spoken like one who is capable of loving," I retorted. "And you?"

"Are you asking if I am capable of loving? What does it matter, if I am capable of killing?" Vespasian challenged.

"It matters all the more, in your case especially," I replied. "And of the two, loving is more important to you."

"What makes you so uniquely prescient?" he questioned.

"For one, I am my mother's daughter," I replied. "More to the point, I have witnessed you during our nightly conversations."

"Do I love someone in particular?" He was testing me now.

"Yes, you love your children," I replied.

"An easy answer," he declared. "You'll have to dig deeper."

"You love another," I stated. "She is remarkable despite her lowly station. You gave your heart to her even though you knew you would never be allowed to marry."

"Under the circumstances, why continue loving?" he queried, as if consulting an oracle.

"You love her still, perhaps more than ever now that she is lost from you," I observed. "But wait, she is not lost after all – only temporarily set aside."

"You imply a possible reconciliation," he commented, admitting the essential truth of my statements. "That's not likely."

"You didn't marry for love," I remarked, taking the not insignificant risk of offending him. I couldn't help myself.

"That is a luxury afforded the very few, especially if they have any wealth or power," Vespasian declared as if he were reciting the law. "I married as appropriate."

"Then perhaps you don't believe in love?" I asked, risking I might provoke him.

"I believe in doing one's duty to country and family," he asserted decisively, every bit the military commander.

"But not to oneself." I made an attempt at having the last word, if such a thing was possible with this man.

Papa shifted uncomfortably, doubtlessly wondering if in one brief round of give-and-take with Vespasian I managed to destroy his carefully tended negotiating strategy. Lukan looked ever like a man who regretted relinquishing the conversation to his overly assertive wife.

The Roman sat quietly, looking within. We were sharing a rare moment of intimacy with the enemy. I thought to myself, "If the tide turns against us, it will be my doing. How could I have been so rash?"

"You do me the honor of speaking truthfully," Vespasian said at last. "That is the highest form of respect. You also cause me, painfully and reluctantly, to see my life not as a series of predetermined choices made from obligation, but as how it might have been.

"What might have been is a humble existence in the country with my true love, a former slave now freed, and perhaps a few happy, well fed urchins of our own, celebrating our good fortune and teasing each other about our impending old age. Instead I am in a faithful but loveless marriage, commanding legions for the purpose of expanding the Empire, living the legacy of my ancestral privilege, or so it is labeled. It is a travesty, to be sure."

Papa intervened. "Don't despair. I could tell you the same tale. My love lives apart from me because of destiny's purpose as much as the demands of my kingly heritage. Like you I long to trade simplicity with her for the complexities of my rule. But somehow I found my way here, with you, accompanied by my beloved son and his equally beloved partner. We are exploring possibilities with far-reaching implications, all of them good. Yes, you and I have sacrificed a great deal to be here. But we *are* here, and that is what matters most."

"You speak like a man who has made peace with his choices," noted Vespasian.

"And you have not?" asked Papa, going to the nub of the issue.

"Most of the time I would argue I have," replied Vespasian. "But watching Lukan and Gracila reminded me of when I was their age and in love with another. I couldn't hide from what I sacrificed to get here."

"But you are here, as I said," Papa asserted once again.

"I am, and we are, and this is far preferable to the battlefield," confirmed the Roman.

"It's more subtle, but it's a battle nonetheless," noted Papa.

"If it were otherwise, I would have departed long ago," conceded Vespasian.

With that we switched to the casual conversation that wove our evenings together. Nothing was lost.

∞ ∞ ∞

Not long after that an agreement was reached. It would be written later that Papa relented and gave up too much due to cowardice and weakness. But we knew better. He had averted the inevitable, the future destruction of his people and their livelihood.

We were about to gather for our last meal together, more a commemoration than a celebration. Neither Vespasian nor Papa felt the need to boast or gloat. A workable accord had been reached through their mutual determination. Humility was more in evidence than pride.

We were preparing to conclude when Vespasian offered us an unprecedented invitation. "We are about to put our stamp on your way of life with everything from our roads to our deities," he observed. "Of course, you'll try to keep from being overwhelmed by these forces that threaten your heritage and your cultural identity. That is understandable.

"Still, a blending of the two is inevitable. Eventually one will dominate. And long afterward another power unknown to either of us now, will overtake whatever survives your efforts and mine. We have accomplished a great deal and, over the longer term, perhaps nothing at all. That remains to be seen.

"I have found three friends in you, quite unexpectedly I might add. I predicted you would be a worthy adversary, which alone would have provided a reasonable distraction from my usual duties. I have enjoyed our evenings together immensely, and I would like them to continue. As long as I am here, you are welcome in my quarters. I am giving each of you a document with my official seal that allows access to me.

"Eventually I will return to Rome and then be assigned to legions located in other parts of the Empire. When I am in Rome, you are welcome to visit or meet with me at any time. It is a sign of my deep respect that I offer you this open invitation. I hope you recognize its heartfelt sincerity."

He handed us each an impressive document, written in Latin, with the seal of his military rank below. I assumed I would never use it; rather, it seemed more like a precious piece of memorabilia.

"You do us great honor with your invitation, and I would like to reciprocate," Papa replied. "What we have agreed upon will become real in the context of our shared respect and ongoing communication. It will be worth little, and perhaps nothing at all, if we assume others will act in accordance with our agreement. We can ensure greater success if our most trusted staff are fully engaged, with our continuing involvement."

"Agreed. I must comment, however, on our distinctive perspectives," Vespasian continued. "I appeal to our emerging friendship, and you emphasize the impact of our collaboration. Both are relevant and mutually reinforcing. I am far away from home and appreciate finding a family of sorts, and you strive to assure the longevity and lineage of the families under your rule."

"I am grateful you take no offense," noted Papa. "More importantly, I am glad you recognize the imperative of assuring our agreements are acknowledged as valid by both sides, who are in a position either to strengthen or nullify them."

I listened intently to these two leaders, each expressing his views and priorities. I had come a long way from Mama's village. Or had I? What larger forces had Mama brought to bear on these proceedings? No doubt she had a great deal to do with the outcome of the talks between Papa and Vespasian, though she was not physically present.

"Lukan, what are your plans when you return home?" the Roman asked.

"I will grow the best garden in the region and stay fit by hunting for deer," he replied. "Other than that, I may be in danger of becoming a man with too much leisure."

"As I predicted," Vespasian divulged, a smile punctuating his broad face. "I've been thinking. Your father has an entire kingdom to concern himself with, and I will be busy making sure my soldiers refrain from sacking and pillaging everything they come across. We need an emissary. Are you interested in serving in that capacity?"

"I would consider it, especially if it offered a more rewarding challenge than chasing chickens around the yard," Lukan responded wryly.

"So you might give up the pleasures of a more settled life for that of a peripatetic diplomat?" clarified the Roman.

"Under one condition, that Gracila be allowed to accompany me," he stated.

"Why else do you think I provided all three of you with official documents?" Vespasian crowed, having anticipated where the conversation might proceed.

"And you believe Lukan can remain an unbiased messenger for us both?" Papa asked, requesting verification.

"I do," affirmed the Roman. "He is more suited to that role than any of my own men. I wouldn't have suggested this were it otherwise. Gracila, what say you regarding this proposition?"

"I am at the service of the three of you," I replied. "My life took on greater proportions when I met Lukan and his father. Yet another formidable individual has been added to the stewpot. I'll assist you however I can."

"Then it is done, and we are in the stew together," Vespasian declared. "Let us drink to a satisfactory new beginning."

He poured wine into four silver cups, each engraved with the eagle standard. Raising mine, I had the aberrant thought that I was about to participate in either a most enlightened or compromising ritual. Silently I appealed to Mama to help me cleanse from our toast any aspect that did not serve the highest and best good.

We departed the next morning, having agreed to a plan for Lukan's further involvement. I was relieved to be heading home, our purpose having been achieved.

That night around a campfire Papa was in a particularly contemplative mood. "I'll be either lauded or damned for what I have done," he observed. "But that matters not in the context of what I hope to have preserved for the present and the future. And I daresay, I couldn't have accomplished it without you both."

"You give us too much credit, as always," I commented. "It was your doing entirely. I am thankful to have had a chance to see you in action."

"I wondered if I was thoughtless inviting you two to accompany me," he admitted. "If the negotiations had failed, you would bear part of the burden even though you weren't responsible for the result. If they succeeded, you'd have been drawn into a different life from the one you were creating together."

"So you anticipated that if you succeeded, I might have a role in keeping the peace," Lukan posited.

"I was prepared to suggest precisely what the Roman proposed," confirmed Papa. "He did so instead, expressing his confidence in you. That's essential to your effectiveness.

"My son, you have been groomed for this responsibility from the beginning, although I didn't identify it until recently. You have the qualities that are needed: integrity, perceptiveness, candor and patience. Most critical of all, you have the confidence of the two men at the center of the agreement you are responsible for maintaining. Ultimately your contribution will be more impactful than mine."

I watched Lukan as he opened and closed the fingers of his right hand, exercising them to keep them strong and flexible. He stared at his hand for a long moment. "So it was all meant to be," he said slowly. "I had to face my own death and choose life to prepare for what was about to occur. My training as a warrior, my tenure on the battlefield, my desperate wounding, my tentative hold on life and my eventual recovery created the person I am today. The two of you had a major role in that as well. But that particular sequence of events was essential to my readiness for what lies ahead. I see that now."

"When you insisted on joining the others in battle, I made a halfhearted attempt to stop you, for I anticipated the outcome," Papa recalled. "It wasn't fatherly fear that caused me to try to protect you. It was the certainty that your life would be hanging by a thread. I prayed for guidance then let you go. Later I recognized the larger wisdom in what you had undergone as well as the grace inherent in your being allowed to live. That's when I knew if the negotiations were even somewhat successful, you'd be the one to make them real across the land."

I watched the two men I loved most dearly as they revealed their intimate truths to each other. In more ways than one Lukan was the man he had become because of his father.

That night I lay awake looking at the stars and wondering what was ahead. Rather than being anxious, I was surprisingly content. I prayed, "Thank you for this sublime fullness. Please hold Lukan, Mama and Papa in your loving embrace."

Love, 24 AD

PART THREE
ROME

As straightforward as Papa's negotiations with Vespasian were, the actions required to ensure the effective implementation of their accord were quite the opposite. Both men faced hostile constituencies upon their return, Papa with tribal leaders and Vespasian with officers in his legion.

Vespasian was seen as having needlessly given away too much, defined as anything at all. There existed within military ranks no sentiment in favor of compromise. The prevailing perspective was one of entitlement by the conquering forces – access to everything, either to own it or destroy it, through dominant force.

The Romans saw their victory as inevitable and were anxious to appropriate the property and people they felt were their due. To skip the pleasures of victory along with the aftermath of plunder was absurd. How could their commander even entertain the idea of a treaty with the Britons, let alone agreed to it?

Papa faced similar resistance. Tribal leaders asserted he capitulated too soon. They were convinced that given adequate time the invaders could be forced to retreat. Negotiating a treaty so precipitously was proof of abject weakness, the last quality anyone expected Papa to exhibit.

Many thought the prospect of losing his son in battle had slain his appetite for war. They underestimated his capacity to assess the current and future situation with ruthless objectivity. Instead they presumed the contrary had occurred.

Thus both men faced strong opposition when they returned to their respective jurisdictions and outlined the parameters of the negotiated peace. Despite their positions of authority, they were challenged almost exclusively and praised only rarely. They anticipated this reaction, though not its severity. Later both leaders avowed that even if they had known the resistance they would encounter, it would not have affected the course they chose.

Lukan's role would not begin in earnest until the loudest complaints and contrarian voices on both sides died down. Vespasian and Papa remained in their respective locations taming the opposition and smoothing ruffled feathers. Papa kept Lukan informed of progress, or more typically lack thereof, while we enjoyed our time at home with no major initiatives or emergencies to attend to.

When Lukan and I weren't planting additional rows of vegetables, we escaped to the nearby creek for a picnic or an afternoon snooze. Not since the moon cycle following our union had we shared such unobstructed time together. I savored every moment of it, privately aware of how fleeting it would likely be.

"Have you experienced a change of heart?" Lukan asked me one afternoon as we lay in the sun, listening to the water dance over the rocks.

"About what?" I wondered.

"About my accepting the mission Papa and Vespasian proposed," he replied. "There's nothing I would rather be doing right now than lying here with you."

"Have you experienced misgivings?" I asked, wondering if his question was an indication of his own ambivalence.

"Perhaps I have," he conceded. "The incessant wrangling since the peace agreement was announced is disappointing. If people can't see the value in it, if all they can do is accuse two forward thinking men of stupidity and capitulation, then why do they deserve my involvement? Why should I sacrifice the life we have now for the benefit of unappreciative obstructionists?"

"I've had similar thoughts," I admitted.

"Of course, disengaging from the settlement has never been an option, nor, I suppose, would I want it to be," Lukan declared. "My father is a king. I am as responsible for those in his tribe as he is. It is both a blessing and a burden that the life I lead can never be separated from that of everyone under his rule."

"Since the agreement was initiated by your father and not a chieftain from another clan whom you neither trust nor respect, it's your duty to make it a reality whatever the opposition," I observed.

"True," Lukan agreed. "But I entertain a fantasy now and again that you and I settle more permanently into a simple little life like the one we have now. That's not meant to be, but I dream about it anyway."

"Perhaps we'll be afforded peaceful intervals such as this one, which are all the more delicious for being rare and temporary," I suggested. "Were we to live in perpetual routine and ease, we'd become bored. As it is, we'll never tire of our lives. And when we are here, with little drama and nothing to accomplish, we can celebrate the slower pace."

Lukan took my hand in his, brought it to his lips and kissed it with a soft caress. "I don't suppose you might like to enjoy a slow paced, private celebration right now," he proposed.

Turning to him and wrapping my legs around his, I asked with feigned innocence, "What exactly did you have in mind?"

"Something unhurried, indulgent and delicious," he responded.

"Sounds like I need to create a pot of mulled wine for us to sip leisurely this evening," I offered, pretending to leave.

He grabbed my arm and pulled me on top of him. I settled into my favorite spot and began kissing him. "On the other hand, this is beyond delicious," I murmured.

I felt his arousal beneath me. "How quickly you set aside the troubles of being the son of a king in a land full of recalcitrant tribal leaders," I noted. "You just slipped comfortably into your life as a country farmer with nothing to do but plow fields."

"Including yours," he laughed.

"That's what was hoping you would say," I teased, nibbling on his ear.

We made love all afternoon in the soft grasses by the creek. I was about to drift off to sleep when Lukan stirred. "Do you believe we'll always find each other, however many lifetimes we live?" he asked.

"Yes I do," I replied, nestling into him.

"And do you think we'll be lovers every time?" he pursued.

"We'll love each other," I answered. "It's impossible for us not to. But lovers? I'm not sure. We may make other arrangements."

"What other arrangements?" he asked, frowning.

"Such as the one Mama and Papa made before this lifetime," I noted. "They love each other as deeply as any two people could, yet they're not lovers."

"I couldn't bear it," Lukan declared.

"You may have to at some point," I replied. "We're together now despite your brush with death. I must remind you, though, that you came very close to abandoning me to a lonely life of gardening and stew making."

"Never!" he roared, embracing me in the vise grip of his arms.

I closed my eyes and allowed myself to sink into him. Our togetherness in this lifetime would be lasting. In that reassuring security I slept, as did he.

∞ ∞ ∞

Papa's messenger kept us informed of the progress being made toward an actual peace following the negotiated one. After their initial resistance, denial and hesitation, the opposition on both sides receded. Papa and Vespasian shared a commitment to achieve this objective, and eventually their authority prevailed. It was time for Lukan to become engaged in the process of keeping the peace.

We made arrangements for the long-term care of our home and farm. Then we waited for word to depart.

Within days Papa asked us to join him at his residence, where he would debrief Lukan regarding what had occurred since the meeting with Vespasian. Then we would be given our assignment.

We arrived at Papa's holdings without complication. I had visited his sprawling hilltop enclosure only once before, briefly overnight. We expected this to be an extended visit, and I was looking forward to being with Papa in the context of his daily life.

What struck me this time was his relative wealth. Papa owned items of superb craftsmanship, everything from engraved silver dishes and serving pieces to beautifully carved furniture, sumptuous weavings and lively wall paintings. His rambling stone home surrounded by an imposing fortress wall bespoke of supremacy handed down through many generations.

I noticed earlier that his tunics and capes were of the finest fabrics, with adornments handcrafted in gold rather than being molded in bronze. But he was unaffected by it all. He may as well have been wearing homespun. His natural authority, on the other hand, and the degree to which he was comfortable in his power, were something else altogether.

I remembered Mama's humble hut and how Papa was so at ease there, without a hint of condescension. His lack of arrogance was extraordinary given his power and prosperity.

Lukan and I settled into our quarters, which included a sitting room with a hearth, cushioned oak furniture and a doorway leading onto a garden. Our bedroom featured an outsized bed along with exquisite trunks, tables and linens.

Papa had taken extra care to include special items for my comfort: hair combs inlaid with silver, a polished bronze mirror decorated with Damara the queen of the fairies, gold scrollwork pins and glass bottles with scented oils. I was touched by his thoughtfulness, such caring from a man so imposing.

Walking in the garden one sunny afternoon, I came across an ornate Celtic emblem of interwoven knots carved in a round, flat pink and grey stone the size of a shield. It featured the words, "Walk with the Mother, talk with the Mother, for She resides here." No doubt Lukan's mother had placed it there. This was the first evidence I encountered of her earlier presence in the household.

Lukan revealed little about her to me. I knew only that she entered into an arranged marriage with Papa and died when Lukan was four years of age, soon after his younger brother was born. He had scarce recollection of her.

"Tell me about your mother," I ventured that evening.

"She played only a minor role in my life," Lukan recalled. "She was rarely present, and even if she had been, I was so young when she died.

"Wet nurses raised me until I was a toddler, then I spent most of my time with boys my age. I was tutored and trained, in equal measure, by men. Papa was the most influential person in my life. He was generous and kind – quite tender, actually – except when I was training in the art of war. Then he was a ruthless, unforgiving opponent. Bless him for that."

"Did he love her?" I wondered.

"Their relationship was more tolerant than affectionate," Lukan observed. "After she died he rarely mentioned her, and when he did he spoke as if she were a distant relative rather than his wife."

"The two of you differ significantly there," I commented.

"I have him to thank for that," Lukan acknowledged. "When I was old enough to understand the implications, he assured me that I could marry for love. He was adamant I wouldn't be constrained as he was, even if we missed an opportunity to merge our holdings with those of another chieftain."

"You received no additional holdings when you entered into a union with me, that's for sure," I laughed.

"Which is precisely the point," Lukan replied. "I was free to marry for love, with no consideration whatsoever for the consolidation of land and influence. I recall when Papa and I were returning home after our first meeting with you and Mama. He exclaimed, 'Now you see, what are power and wealth when such love is available to you?' He was exuberant."

"Papa is a wise man," I declared, "and we are the beneficiaries of his intelligence and understanding."

It goes without saying, Papa's wisdom extended well beyond matters of the heart. The next day he provided a tutorial in advanced diplomacy.

"Here is what I want us to accomplish, separately and together," Papa commenced. "I'll continue to meet with kings and chieftains throughout the land, those who agree with my position with regard to the Romans and those who oppose it. I can talk with them as equals. Whether I convince them to support a negotiated peace will be a function of my persuasive abilities and their openness to new thinking.

"While I'm occupied with that, you'll be establishing a deeper and hopefully more enduring relationship with Vespasian. In this regard the future is more in your hands than mine. Our ability to sustain our way of life in the context of the Roman presence will reflect our ongoing credibility with them. And that will depend on how well we retain Vespasian's trust and respect.

"Your role, Lukan, is to develop such a strong relationship with him that he naturally, and perhaps even unconsciously, represents our best interests along with those the Empire. We need to be seen as partners, not enemies, and collaborators, not competitors. You can solidify that viewpoint and assure that our actions align with those expectations.

"The minute you pursue an agenda that compromises our partnership, you lose credibility. I doubt you'd do so, but things can go astray when disagreement from elsewhere surrounds good intentions. Do nothing to sacrifice Vespasian's confidence in your goodwill. Stay the course and have the courage to remain authentic throughout. I am counting on it, as is he."

"You do me great honor in affording me such trust and responsibility," Lucan said with sincere humility.

"It's an honor you well deserve," Papa assured him. "I am ever grateful that you are my son. Remember that always."

Lukan and I were to travel to Vespasian's encampment and remain there until an update needed to be delivered in person to Papa or an issue occurred that could be resolved by none other than him. Beyond that, we had free rein to engage with the Roman and address situations as they arose. Although those parameters seemed vague to me, they were all Lukan needed.

On the journey to Vespasian's military quarters, we passed through fields of battle that showed signs of havoc and destruction. The heartbreaking heaviness of needless slaughter remained. To die violently was not synonymous with dying valiantly. Many would argue otherwise, but not I. Sensing the loss each spirit experienced when it was cruelly separated from the powerful but not invincible physical body where it resided, I understood more acutely the imperative of our mission.

I spoke with Lukan about this one evening during a pause in our journey. "Whenever we pass a battlefield, I feel the sadness of lives being cut short despite bravery and fervent commitment to a cause. I can't reconcile the cost of such violence with the purported benefits. It makes no sense to sacrifice thousands, or tens of thousands, of lives in order to expand an empire and make its ruler all the richer. That's the furthest thing I can imagine from living a life guided by Source."

"That's why Papa gave us our current assignment," Lukan stated. "We haven't been seduced by the heroics of warriors, and we're not impressed by battle scars."

"I am quite impressed with yours," I teased. "They make you so much more rough-and-tumble masculine, and thus worthy of my attentions."

"I'm glad someone sees a long-term benefit in them," replied Lukan, "because I creak and move more like a man three times my age, thanks to those rough-and-tumble markings."

"The fact that you are creaking and moving at all is a great joy to me, however aggravating it might be to you," I teased. "Tell me, do you feel prepared for the unpredictability that lies ahead?"

"As prepared for the unpredictable as anyone can be," Lukan observed. "Papa believes that as Vespasian's appreciation for our way of life grows, he'll be more willing to make the necessary accommodations to keep things as they are to some extent, at least. As he gets to know us he might develop a deeper understanding of this country's values and culture. Papa wants me to adopt a stance of service toward the Roman, but from a steady center of personal power. I can do that, and I am confident you can as well."

"What form might this service take?" I asked.

"I am to participate in whatever helps keep the peace," Lukan stated. "Papa's only requirement is that I not divulge secrets unnecessarily. As for my ability to discern what is to be kept secret and what is not, that is yet to be tested. You and I both know how wily the Roman is. I'll need to be wary, but not to the point of being ineffective."

"I am more worried about myself than I am about you," I admitted. "I tend to reveal what's on my mind without pausing to consider the need for secrecy."

"You may believe you are speaking without forethought, but your mind works so quickly, that is far from the case," Lukan observed. "You have uncanny acumen."

"I do sense what I should and should not say," I allowed. "It happens in an instant."

"There you have it," Lukan said. "That's your answer on how to prepare for unpredictability. Own your discernment, trust your instincts, and all will be well."

∞ ∞ ∞

A few days later three Roman soldiers met us on the road and said they were to take us directly to Vespasian. They informed us that our quarters were near his dwelling in a relatively permanent Roman encampment. Apparently we were to be welcomed rather than spurned or shunted aside by our host.

When we arrived I was amazed at the size and organization of the fort. A complex temporary community was established with blacksmiths, weapons makers, stone carvers, training grounds, cooking facilities, an infirmary – every conceivable skill and service the legion might require.

One thing was clear to me. If Roman military might didn't overtake our land, their capacity for planning and order would do so. Whereas we were spirited and impetuous, they were disciplined and specialized. Those first impressions only solidified with time.

Lukan and I were shown to a provisional structure built in the rectangular Roman style, which would serve as our home. Two spacious rooms, one for meeting and dining and one for sleeping, were well appointed with oil lamps molded in the shape of animals, silver tableware, fine bedding and other necessities of excellent quality. Thick red carpets covered the wooden floors, and cushions in green wool and gold silk were arranged on the bed, chairs and sofa. A portable dining table with iron legs and four matching chairs were at one end of the main room.

I expected something more austere and rustic. We were in a military fort, after all, but Vespasian's arrangements for our stay were generous and thoughtful. Somehow this made me more cautious than comfortable.

I poured water from a terra cotta pitcher with an intricate hunting scene painted in glaze on the outside. Studying the design as I drank the refreshing liquid, I commented to Lukan, "Are we the hunters or the hunted?"

"We are neither pillagers nor prey," he replied. "Rather, I like to think of us as bees that go about their work unobtrusively while others are engaged in more important activities. Then in the end their honey soothes the soul and sweetens the more acrid aspects of life."

"We are to make honey, then, and find ways to share it with Vespasian," I acknowledged. "I can do that."

"You have done so already," Lukan declared. "Our only requirement is to stay the course we established earlier."

That evening we were welcomed into Vespasian's quarters, which were appointed similarly to our own. He could have created a noticeable discrepancy as a statement of his rank and superiority, but he chose a more egalitarian approach. Perhaps that gesture portended how our stay might unfold.

"I hope your accommodations are adequate and to your liking," he stated. "This is to be your home for quite a while, and I wanted you to be comfortable."

"You've been most considerate in your preparations for our arrival. Gracila and I couldn't be more pleased," Lukan assured him.

"Splendid!" Vespasian effused. "Then you two can settle into our community, though I have my doubts you will ever become Romans."

"Just as you are not likely to become a Celt," responded Lukan jovially, "even though you are currently living in a pool of Celtic culture, history and lore."

"I'm too stubborn to change my ways that drastically," laughed the Roman, "but I have to say, much of what I learned since I arrived impresses me greatly. You're not the barbarians you were alleged to be by those who knew nothing about your traditions or way of life."

"Confirming we are not barbarians, Papa sends his greetings and offers this gift to you," Lukan stated. "He counts you as a true friend and trustworthy partner. With that in mind, he had this made for you by our most accomplished craftsman."

Lukan handed Vespasian an intricately carved wooden box, about three hands wide and two hands high. Ivy wound across the top and sides of the box, symbolizing the vitality of friendship. The Roman admired the workmanship. "This is an impressive piece of artistry," he commented.

"That is only the container," Lukan informed him. "Please open it."

Vespasian studied the box, which was crafted so expertly it appeared to have no opening. Then he noticed a small ivy leaf carving that could be pushed to the right, unlocking the lid. As he peered inside the box, he looked more like a youth at a festival than a military commander.

Lifting a solid gold goblet from its carrying case, he declared, "This is a gift of immense generosity and great regard." Four intertwining bands forming Celtic knots were engraved on the bowl. They represented the connection of our four spirits, with no beginning and no end.

"Extraordinary!" Vespasian exclaimed. "Given your predisposition to magic, if I drink from this, I may be in danger of becoming a Celt after all."

"There are worse things," Lukan quipped.

"There are indeed, as I have witnessed on military campaigns and, I regret to say, even in Rome herself," Vespasian admitted. "I accept your father's gift with deep appreciation and will use it always. Speaking of that, I had honeyed wine and honey cakes prepared for you. After all, one can never enjoy too much honey."

Bees and honey! I shot Lukan a quick glance of recognition. His comments about our role were already being borne out by the Roman himself.

"So Gracila," Vespasian began after quaffing the wine from his new goblet and taking a generous bite of cake, "what have you been doing lately, besides keeping your husband happy?"

"I have been creating new combinations of healing herbs, powders, oils, potions and poultices," I revealed. "Mama taught me a great deal when I was with her, but we had little call to apply her wisdom and skills to the needs of the battlefield."

"That's a blessing," Vespasian commented.

"I grew up protected from the darker aspects of the world. The subtle approach to healing that I learned from Mama involved fine tuning to keep the body and spirit healthy and strong," I explained.

"An optimal circumstance," the Roman observed.

"It was optimal in its own way," I noted. "But when Lukan was wounded I followed a different approach to healing – one I had been developing at our home. When travelers stopped for a meal, I saw even young children with horrible ailments and disabilities. To help them I experimented with a more potent combination of medicinal herbs and prayer."

"Prayer?" queried the Roman.

"Prayer is an essential factor in the healing process," I asserted. "One doesn't pray for the healing to occur, but rather for the intentions of the individual to be honored. If the person is committed to returning to health and maintaining it, I pray the herbs will help make it so. The power to heal is in the afflicted individual, not in the healer or her herbs."

"What have you discovered?" pressed Vespasian.

"Many people actually want to remain infirm or weak," I ventured, wondering if I should be stepping into such controversial terrain. "When I access the energy around them and ask their spirit if they want to be healed, I discover that sometimes they do not."

"But who would answer negatively to a question like that?" asked the Roman. "It seems preposterous."

"I also thought so initially," I replied. "I wondered if it was an illusion I created so I wouldn't feel guilty when my healing was ineffective. Whenever I sensed the person didn't want to be healed, I asked the spirits why.

"The answers I intuited were stunning. Some people were reluctant to take on the additional responsibilities that good health and a strong body would introduce. Others were confused about who they might become if they no longer defined themselves as victims of a burdensome ailment or handicap. Still others didn't believe they could be healed. I understood and accepted their reluctance. Even so, if they wanted me to help them, I gladly did what I could.

"It was striking to witness the progress made by those who fervently desired to transcend physical limitation. My herbal combinations worked wonders with them."

"You have proof of that sitting beside you," Vespasian remarked, nodding toward Lukan.

"I do," I replied. "Soon after I saw how mortally wounded Lukan was, I released him to make his own choice whether to live or die. I committed to honoring his decision. At the time we had no idea whether he would be anything but an invalid, if he survived at all."

"He must have been unconscious," noted the Roman. "I've seen many mortally wounded men, and they're rarely awake or conversant."

"It happened in the sleep state," I explained. "We came together in full, alert consciousness and had the discussion then."

"And you trusted your recollection afterward?" challenged the Roman.

"Absolutely," I declared.

"What did Lukan say to you that made his decision so credible?" Vespasian pursued.

"He said he would be needed," I began then hesitated.

"Needed to do what?" Vespasian queried.

"Needed to do exactly what he is here to accomplish with you," I responded.

"Well, one thing is for sure. Your approach to healing is truly remarkable," Vespasian declared. "Lukan is the picture of health, though no doubt he has some ugly scars as evidence of what he endured to be here today."

"With you," I clarified.

"And with you," Vespasian added.

"With you both. I would have it no other way," Lukan affirmed.

Thus we began what turned out to be a long and fulfilling chapter in our lives.

∞ ∞ ∞

Our initial stay with Vespasian lasted almost three seasons. During that time we became acquainted with a number of his officers and many others in the encampment. I learned enough of their language to converse with relative ease. Most importantly, I assisted in their infirmary, treating wounded soldiers and those who had been stricken with serious ailments. After a while they sent for me whenever a particularly difficult case presented itself. I was developing a reputation as an effective healer, due in equal measure to the results of my ministrations and Vespasian's confidence in me.

Lukan had more difficulty during the transition because the Roman soldiers persisted in treating him as the enemy. His presence was a thorn in their side, a constant reminder that their commander had gone soft or worse, lost his good sense. They saw no positive purpose for his being among them.

"How's the honey making going?" I asked Lukan one afternoon when he seemed particularly discouraged.

"Not so well," he admitted. "I'm here to build bridges between the Celts and the Romans, but the only one who seems even remotely interested in that is Vespasian. Everyone else tolerates me because they've been ordered to do so. But they don't respect me, nor are they interested in accomplishing anything collaboratively.

"Instead they tenaciously maintain that there are two classes of people, the victors and the vanquished. Our peace treaty sidestepped the clear victory to which they feel entitled, and they resent it. Few soldiers give me more than a cursory greeting, and it's a surly one at that."

"What if you literally helped them build bridges?" I asked. "Their biggest projects involve road construction and bridge building so Rome can expand trade routes. Why not serve as their ambassador with the villagers and farmers being impacted?"

Lukan was silent for a moment. "Of course!" he exclaimed. "I just declared that I am here to build bridges, but I've been so frustrated and disillusioned I missed seeing the obvious. Luckily, you didn't.

"I will introduce myself to the officers in charge of road and bridge construction and offer to go with them in advance of their work. I can visit everyone living on the land along the way and ask for their cooperation and support. The Romans will see how partnership with us makes the going easier. And we'll benefit as well."

That is what Lukan did, to great effect. Word spread that his intervention with the locals made large-scale construction projects less troublesome. People in the countryside began to invite the Romans into their roundhouses to share a meal, not as an occupying force of soldiers but as engineers with capabilities that were improving their way of life. By the end of our first stay with Vespasian, Lukan had made himself indispensible to the Roman engineers and construction crews.

"I've been hearing good things about you from the officers," reported Vespasian one afternoon as he came upon us taking a stroll. "You've tamed the wild beast in the heart of soldiers that demands victory, and transformed our warriors into advocates of Celtic hospitality."

"You're generous with your acknowledgment," responded Lukan. "But your men value my role more than I deserve. All I do is stay a step or two ahead of them and convince our people that it is better to welcome the Romans than to pelt them with rotten apples."

"What you are accomplishing can be done by none other," observed Vespasian. "Everyone knows you are the king's son. And yet you neither boast nor belittle. People trust you, and for good reason. Because of that trust, you've given both sides a different experience of those they might otherwise consider their enemy. You have a remarkable capacity to create commonality of purpose, something I rarely see."

"Papa told me at an early age that I was a born diplomat, but I wanted nothing of it," Lukan recalled. "The more he insisted on it, the harder I trained to become a warrior."

"What changed your mind?" Vespasian asked.

"I grew up," replied Lukan. "My heroes were no longer the ones with the biggest muscles or the most adroit men on the training field. I began to spend more time with Papa and his peers, listening to them debate everything from the true test of courage to whether we should trade with the Phoenicians. Eventually I began to join in the debates, although I didn't forget entirely about my training."

"A judicious blend of competencies," remarked Vespasian. "I've been thinking. When I return to Rome, would the two of you consider joining me? I have no idea how long I might remain there, since I'll inevitably be needed elsewhere. But when I do go back, would you be willing to make the trip with me?"

"We'd be honored," Lukan responded immediately. "If Papa can spare me for a lengthy sojourn, consider your invitation accepted."

"I want to establish you in the capacity of emissary between Britannia and the Empire," explained Vespasian. "Many misperceptions exist regarding Britannia and its peoples. I want those in power in Rome to get to know you so they can take a more thoughtful approach to dealing with what they label a conquered territory."

"And I am to represent the conquered?" asked Lukan, taken aback.

"No, you are to represent the Celts," corrected the Roman. "I'll have considerably more influence when I return to Rome than I did when I left, due to the annexation of Britannia into the Empire. That can be either a blessing or curse for your people and for Rome. We would all be better off if the Caesar and the senators saw this as an opportunity to work with you peacefully in partnership rather than reaping short-term riches at the cost of longer-term stability. That is your father's vision, and he couldn't be more correct."

"It is his vision and my mission," Lukan declared.

"As for you, Gracila, you are far from an afterthought," noted Vespasian with a sparkle in his eyes. "I'd appreciate the presence of an additional gutsy woman in Rome. You'll win the hearts of many a Roman, male and female alike, with your resolute independence and exceptional capacities as a healer."

"I'd better expand my herb garden, then," I laughed. "If we are going to make such a long journey, we'll most likely be staying a while. I'll need an ample supply of healing ingredients and perhaps quite a few cuttings as well."

"Have you received word that you are to leave soon?" Lukan inquired.

"I expect to remain until all resistance in the south has been subdued and we've established an unassailable presence," the Roman indicated. "I invited you to Rome well in advance of my departure because your response affects how we work together going forward.

"If you had declined to leave your homeland, I would have doubted either your commitment or your perseverance," Vespasian revealed. "For all I knew, your father might have thrust you into a position you prefer to conclude at the earliest opportunity. If your desire had been to return home with Gracila, I would applaud your choice. But your role as a diplomat and partner would diminish.

"If, instead, you were to respond as you did, then I was prepared to take every advantage of your presence and participation here. Yes, I will share you with your Papa. But if I have anything to say about your tour of duty, you will remain integrally involved in key projects as long as I am assigned to this post. Have I been too presumptuous?"

"Not at all," Lukan assured him. "You are every bit the man I've grown to appreciate and admire, one who is both pragmatic and preemptory. If you aren't careful, you'll become as much a role model for me as my father has been."

"If you see the difference between being preemptive and presumptuous, and you consider my thoughts to be the former but not the latter, then perhaps I can play a small part after all," noted the Roman. "Now, let's identify your next initiative after you return from your visit with your father and your brief homecoming."

Later people would say that the Roman occupation of Britannia destroyed the Celtic way of life. I wouldn't disagree, which would then argue that Lukan and I were unsuccessful in our efforts to preserve the culture through peaceful means. But that isn't altogether true. We succeeded in establishing a more equal footing between the forces of the Empire and the Celtic tribes, which I deem a considerable accomplishment.

The primary reason our efforts seemed in hindsight to be ineffective was that the Romans were unprecedented in their ability to exert dominant power. They amassed the largest empire of its day for a reason: they were extremely adept at invading, subduing rebellion and imprinting their way of life wherever they went. We did eventually become the conquered, not so much by brute force as by the Romans' superior capability to create and sustain change.

∞ ∞ ∞

We traveled between Papa's holdings, our home and Vespasian's various dwellings during the duration of the Roman's stay in our land – well over two years. I came to see myself as rather like an itinerant seller of pots. I journeyed with few personal belongings and a large supply of healing herbs. When I was at our house, I focused more on the herb garden than anything else.

Home was wherever I was with Lukan. That was as settled as I needed to be.

Over time I accepted the probability that I was not to bear children. If I had been able to become pregnant it would have occurred, perhaps many times over. But no child was conceived. I gave up anticipating that one would make its presence known, and when I bled with each moon cycle, I no longer felt a sense of loss.

Considering the life we led, having no children may well have been for the best. Being constantly uprooted, shunted between various temporary dwellings and thrown into contexts where few children existed, would have been challenging to even the most self-confident young ones.

I could call forth endless stories about our interactions with Vespasian, our visits with Papa and our interludes at home. One vignette in particular expresses more about Vespasian than I could describe in an entire volume.

Papa sent a messenger inviting Vespasian to attend a celebration of the autumn equinox at his compound. Lukan and I were at the Roman encampment when the messenger arrived, anxious to return with a positive response for the king.

Lukan and I were enjoying the golden light and warm breezes of late summer. Papa's messenger stretched out in the grass, dozing off.

Vespasian appeared unexpectedly and without fanfare. "It must be nice having nothing to do but while away your days sunning yourselves like fat cats," he barked at us.

Lukan and I were preparing an equally snappy response when the messenger jerked awake, stood up, faced Vespasian and said, "I regret you have taken offense. Most surely I should have been tending to my horse, which is overtired, or helping Lukan chop wood."

"Or instigating a fight with the enemy, perhaps?" asked the Roman.

"No, sir," responded the messenger. "I wouldn't consider such a thing away from the battlefield."

"And on the battlefield?" prompted Vespasian

"Well, that's a different matter," stated the messenger. "On the battlefield I'd pursue your men in earnest, doing my best to slay as many as possible. Mind you, I don't mistake a foe for a friend."

"And we are foes?" continued the Roman.

Realizing his error, the messenger looked to Lukan to save the situation, then to me. Neither of us responded. Vespasian waited for someone to say something.

"I fear I just stepped in a considerable pile of horse manure," the messenger said haltingly. He entreated us silently for affirmation, but we were united in our resolve to remain noncommittal.

"Or worse, I may have caused you to take such offense at my effrontery, you'll decline the king's invitation to teach me a lesson," the messenger continued.

Still we were silent.

"I offer my humble apologies and request that you allow me to make amends," he continued meekly. "I'll do whatever is required to return the king to your good graces. I had no intention of tarnishing his friendship with you."

"Then we are friends after all," noted Vespasian, his eyes dancing.

"Yes we are," stated the messenger gravely.

"Friendship can't be vanquished with one small mishap," Vespasian observed, "horse manure notwithstanding. Shall we all dine together this evening and make the necessary arrangements for me to attend the king's harvest feast?"

He slapped the messenger on the back and gave Lukan and me a quick wink. "Friendship is a hard-won luxury," Vespasian declared. "Once it has been forged by two or more people with goodwill, it cannot be rendered absent at the hands of others, especially if they are misguided but well-meaning. I am honored to accept the invitation."

∞ ∞ ∞

Lukan and I arrived at Papa's holdings well in advance of the celebration. I was eager to assist with harvesting and drying the many herbs I planted there. He was constantly teasing me that if he went to sleep for a year or two, he would wake up to discover that every plot of land had been turned into an herb garden. He wasn't incorrect. Since I believed I could never have too abundant a supply of remedies, I appropriated all available space.

While I worked in the garden, Lukan provided his father with background information on progress with the Romans. They were intent on sharing ideas and comparing perspectives before Vespasian arrived. Papa was pleased to have such a capable son to assist with his objectives, and Lukan was gratified that his father valued his efforts.

Vespasian was to stay in the best guest quarters. We made the suite more welcoming and comfortable with objects showcasing Celtic craftsmanship. New weavings were hung on the walls, and the best wool blankets were removed from storage trunks and aired in the fresh breeze outside. A gold bowl and platter were set on a table, ready to be filled with dried fruits and fresh berries. A drinking horn inlaid with silver was ready for Papa's special mead.

There were the inevitable rumblings from neighboring kings and chieftains, who complained that they were treated with less care and honor when they visited, but Papa laughed them off. "Why go to all that trouble for someone who would as happily sleep in a stable or under the stars?" was his rejoinder. They continued to grumble, albeit surreptitiously.

Although we were well prepared when Vespasian arrived, we were taken aback at the size of his entourage. We expected perhaps six or eight soldiers to be traveling with him. Instead there were four dozen. Everyone available was pressed into service to hunt and roast boar and venison, harvest every last stem and root in the vegetable garden and improvise additional sleeping accommodations.

Papa met Vespasian as he was alighting from his horse. "Welcome to my home," he said, clasping the Roman's hand and giving him a vigorous embrace. "It's an honor to have you here for one of my favorite celebrations."

"I am pleased to be sharing it with you," replied Vespasian. "Just so you know, I considered adopting

Lukan and Gracila as my own, but I thought better of it. I was concerned that such action would invalidate the progress you and I made so far, since you would be loath to give them up."

Smiling, he approached us both and gave us an affectionate hug. "I see your Papa hasn't been working you too hard since your return," he quipped. "By the way, I decided to bring a few additional soldiers with me."

"One or two, I'd say," Papa joked.

"Your women have a reputation for being great beauties," explained Vespasian, "and since your feast days are noted in particular for their frolicking and free flowing honey mead, I thought my men would enjoy all aspects of the celebration."

Dumbfounded at Vespasian's audacity, I nudged Lukan slightly with my elbow.

"Our women are gifts of Nature," replied Papa smoothly, "but then, so is that patch of pumpkins over there."

"And how are their personalities?" asked the Roman.

"Are you referring to the pumpkins or the pretty females?" Papa retorted with impeccable timing.

"The pumpkins, of course," Vespasian bantered back. "We all know that celebrations can become so raucous, you can't have a decent conversation. Therefore, the personality accompanying a pretty face is irrelevant."

Papa and Vespasian laughed with gusto, having effortlessly returned to their inimitable good cheer and quick wit. They enjoyed verbal combat, and there were few with whom either of them was so equally matched. Vespasian's visit was off to a splendid start.

When we escorted him to his quarters, he acknowledged the measures we had taken in anticipation of his arrival. "These accommodations are preferable to sleeping on the hard ground at night and using my cupped hand to drink water from a stream," he said appreciatively. "But just in case, I brought this." He took a familiar wooden box from his traveling pack and retrieved the golden goblet Papa had given him. "I drink from this every night, toasting our friendship with good wine.

"I've brought something for each of you as well." Vespasian pulled out a bag of supple purple leather and handed it to Papa ceremoniously saying, "For someone who shares my vision of the possible. May we live to see it come to pass."

Papa accepted the gift with a smile, dipped his huge hand inside the bag and retrieved an object, round with a spout, obviously made of gold. It was a miniature oil lamp carved with intertwining vines like the ones on the wooden box containing the goblet he gave Vespasian.

"May your vision of peace and harmony for all be held in eternal light, and may the vines of our shared intention become so intermingled, it is impossible to tell where yours ends and mine begins," Vespasian vowed.

Papa was deeply moved. "We are brothers in spirit if not in lineage," he replied. "We are also former enemies who chose to chart a different course, one based on common objectives and mutual trust. We are creating the potential for a new heritage for all people. May the vines of our shared respect and the light of our goodwill remain vital and ever expanding."

He raised the oil lamp in his hands and invoked the support of spirit. A flash of brilliant white light sparked from the center of the lamp, even though it had no oil, wick or source for a flame. Papa's invocation had been heard.

"If I witness nothing more on this visit, I will depart with a deeper respect for your resonance with the spirit world," Vespasian declared. "That was remarkable!" Then Vespasian offered me a small pouch of bright green leather, saying, "Gracila, for your deep communion with the Goddess of Nature and your ability to heal with her abundant harvests, I offer you this gift."

I accepted the bag gratefully. Inside was a delicate gold brooch in an oval shape, filigreed with flowers, stems and leaves. The workmanship was exquisite, and its symbolism delighted me even more.

"It's gorgeous!" I said appreciatively. "I'll wear it always, with the deepest appreciation for the spirit in which it was given and the man who embodies it. Would you please adorn me with it?" I handed it to Vespasian and touched a spot on my shoulder where it was to be fastened. Given his size and perpetually commanding presence, he handled the situation with ease, smiling all the while.

"And finally, for Lukan," Vespasian announced, revealing a leather pouch in an arresting color of ochre. "This is a tribute to your great skill as a diplomat and builder of roads, literal and symbolic, through uncharted terrain."

I wondered what was in the pouch. A folded map of the territory the Romans called Britannia? A small horseshoe in tribute to the interminable months Lukan spent on horseback ahead of soldiers constructing roads?

Lukan's face broke out in a knowing smile when he saw what the pouch contained. "It's a replica of the surveyor's chain that engineers use to measure distance, worked in gold, no less!" he exclaimed. "Thank you."

"Although your ability to span a distance applies to your diplomacy more than road building, your gift is an apt memento," noted Vespasian. "You have an uncanny capacity to lessen the space between two opposing positions until it becomes inconsequential. We wouldn't have achieved the progress we made without you."

"You do me great honor," replied Lukan. "But in truth, the credit falls solely at the feet of you and my father."

"Ah, yes, then there is your humility, an essential ingredient in effective statesmanship," Vespasian observed. "May you never lose that unique advantage."

We talked for the rest of the evening, grateful to be together once again. As we prepared to take our leave, Vespasian raised his goblet and suggested a final toast. "Here's to family, ancestral and otherwise, and to the bonds of enduring friendship that unite us. May they remain unassailable, whatever twists and turns lie ahead."

Vespasian proved to be an astute diplomat himself during his visit. On his last evening with us he revealed his strategy. "Have you determined why I brought such an excessive number of soldiers with me?" he asked.

"To ogle and perhaps succeed in seducing our comely damsels?" replied Lukan.

"That wasn't my main purpose. But from the satisfied looks I saw the morning after, on men and women alike, I can venture that the revelry continued in private after the party was over," the Roman noted.

"You wanted your men to experience an aspect of our tradition and culture that they couldn't access otherwise," Papa observed. "You were also hoping they, too, would come to see us as potential allies, if not friends, and no longer foes to be obliterated."

"That's true," replied Vespasian. "But why did I invite these particular men?"

"They're not your top officers, nor are they all of the same rank," Lukan remarked.

"Right again," confirmed Vespasian. "But why this group?"

"Because they have the most influence over others," I submitted. "Perhaps they are the most respected by the soldiers of their rank, or maybe they have a broader range of acquaintances. Or it could be they are the most outspoken, and you wanted them to bring back a credible, positive message about who we are."

"Lukan, you may be the diplomat, but your beloved is the strategist," observed Vespasian. "Every man I invited to accompany me was hand-picked for his stature among a large group of peers. I also selected those who evidenced open-mindedness to back up their intelligence and influence. It would have done no good to bring fifty oblivious, intransigent soldiers ready to dismiss their experiences or twist their stories to prove their superiority. You seem to have won over most of them. They will spread much good news upon their return. And I won't have said a word."

"Well done," replied Papa. "From another perspective, I observed their impact on our people, satisfied smiles notwithstanding, and they fared well. The next thing we know, a few of them will be asking you for leave so they can return here instead of Rome, to visit a certain someone they can't seem to forget."

I grew nostalgic thinking about the first time the four of us met and the uncertain outcome of our intended conversations. So much occurred since then, all of it because Papa and Vespasian had the temerity to explore a new way of moving into the future as partners instead of opponents. And incredibly, I had been witness to it all.

∞ ∞ ∞

In the few years that passed since our union, Lukan and I matured. He evolved into a leader and a trailblazer, taking to both roles easily and with his characteristic understatement. The more accomplished he became, the more unassuming was his nature.

I developed into a woman of the world, given the myriad multicultural situations in which I was engaged. The further afield I ranged, the more convinced I became that people are more similar than different. We are one community if not one family.

I approached my healing work from that perspective. I valued no one individual more than another, nor did I modify my interventions in accordance with the status, beliefs or homeland of the person in need. Everyone deserved equal treatment, Roman and Celt alike, which meant they received the best care I had to offer.

Beyond that, Lukan and I changed as a couple. From the beginning we faced so many interruptions and surprises, we gave up trying to plan our lives. Given the lack of routine and the elusive nature of our time together, every moment was precious to us. Even in our later years, we never took our relationship for granted. There always seemed to be a look, a touch, a smile that brought us together, whether we were packing for another journey or sitting by the fire on a cold winter's eve.

My views are those of a woman who has loved long and well, and who recognizes the larger blessings of that love. It gave us the courage to imagine the impossible and believe it could be made real. Such is the power, and quite honestly the audacity, of love.

If you have experienced this story so far, you know our love was profoundly sexual. We gave ourselves over to oneness, slipping into the ecstatic void in which the other dwelled. There we merged, not to escape our separate existences but to affirm our divine union. Our lovemaking provided perpetual wonder for us both and thus was something we shared often and sometimes all night.

Such intimacy provides security amidst the uncertainties and turbulence of human existence. But we didn't come together to feel safe. We did so to lose ourselves in an alternate state of being. Thus we found our way to joys that were unavailable otherwise.

I've come to believe that when love is so pervasive, as it was with us, it is possible to step into – or swim in – a divine flow that guides right action. Not once did we oppose the tide that carried us through our days. And because we resonated with each other so easily, we rarely argued. Our uncanny agreement existed not because we suppressed or denied divergent viewpoints but because we were constantly returning to our oneness. And from that place our lives flowed, together.

With that said, I recall one of our rare misunderstandings. We returned home from a difficult overland journey during which I felt a particularly deep longing for my hearth and gardens. I spent most of my time visiting with those who cared for our place, playing with their children, tilling the soil, helping the cook – all the pleasures of being home. I interacted with Lukan less than usual, at meals and briefly before I fell asleep at night exhausted from the day's work. He said nothing and simply tucked in behind me in bed, his arm around my waist, the way we usually slept.

After a few weeks of this he approached me while I was pulling weeds. "I've been thinking that perhaps we should cease our vagabond life and tell Papa we desire nothing more than to spend our days here," he suggested.

The sun was sparkling behind him. From my vantage point, on my knees in the soil, he looked like a blonde Norse god, temporarily in our midst to slay a dragon or right a wrong.

"You are too effective, and your work is too important, for us to remain here," I responded matter-of-factly.

"But it requires so much sacrifice," he continued. "I've been doubting lately whether it is worth it."

"What sacrifice, and by whom?" I asked.

"Well, you are constantly being uprooted, and you can never enjoy for long what you are doing now, digging in the dirt," he replied. "A plant can't thrive if it is perpetually being relocated. This place nurtures you, and you it. We may have gotten our priorities backward."

"I love it here more than anywhere. How could I not?" I admitted. "As long as we have this place come back to, I can go wherever you need to be."

"I've seen your resilience and adaptability," Lukan noted. "But over time, in five or ten years, wouldn't you begin to resent never being home for long? Wouldn't you grow angry with me for causing constant disorientation? Wouldn't you eventually insist on settling here for good, perhaps when it would be impossible for me to do so? And then where would we be?"

I saw the concern on his face. He perceived us to be at a crossroads, and he wanted me to know I could choose a different path from the one we were pursuing. More importantly, and very much like him, he would agree to it.

I stood up, brushed the dust from my clothes and approached him. When he stood straight and tall as he was then, he looked as if he reached halfway to the heavens. I needed to hear what I was about to say as much as he did.

"Please don't mistake my joy at returning home for a desire to remain here," I declared. "That's not how I feel. I've come to love our vagabond life, and I have no doubt that given a full cycle of seasons here I would become restless. The garden would need no more tending, the children would have tired of my adventure stories, the cook would want her hearth back, and you would be ready to start a conflict with the Romans just to have a problem to solve.

"Our home is wherever we are; my home is wherever you are. I can dig in the dirt anywhere, except perhaps in Rome, where I hear the overcrowding makes gardens miniscule if not nonexistent."

Lukan swept me into an embrace and held me tightly. "I've been watching you since we returned," he revealed. "You immerse yourself in your life here as you do nowhere else. It seemed wrong to ask you to give that up, no matter how valid the cause. But if you are truly happy on the path we are pursuing, and if you are sure you'll be content wherever you find yourself in ten or twenty or thirty years, I'll be your most solicitous traveling companion. And when we do return home, I'll be happy to see you flourish once again."

"And you?" I asked. "When you are here, do you flourish?"

"For about as long as you do," he mused. "In truth, I seem to be ready for a change just slightly before you are, but that matters not. It gives me a chance to build relationships with those who live in the surrounding villages. They'll experience a predominant Roman presence eventually, and I can prepare them for it."

"Then we're agreed that our peripatetic lives are configured perfectly," I replied, my cheek on his chest. "Something else is configured perfectly, for I know nothing but bliss right now with your arms around me."

We kissed, one of those long, deep, soulful kisses that speak of a new recognition, a more profound understanding of our togetherness. We could be standing anywhere, kissing as we were, in the warmth of our love, and we would be equally content.

"It occurs to me," I whispered during an interlude between kisses, "that there is one particular pastime I have been neglecting in my excitement about being home again. I intend to do something about it immediately, to celebrate us wherever we are."

We walked side-by-side, arms around each other, to our room, where we made love all afternoon, then slept, then made more love that night. The best part of being home was loving him, in our own room, in our marriage bed, where we made love the night we arrived after our sacred union; where we made love during his recovery from the battlefield; and where we would make love, hopefully, until the end of our days. To be home and miss that point was to make the biggest sacrifice of all.

∞ ∞ ∞

When we first met Vespasian we didn't know if he would consider our proposal, nor could we predict how long he would remain in our country.   Once our collaboration was underway, we set about grounding our agreement solidly in practice so a change in Roman leadership wouldn't tear it asunder. Blessedly, we were given more than enough time to build a foundation for long-term success.

We redefined our life in those few years. Our world expanded to include the Roman Empire, just as the Empire expanded to include our world.   Our lives became inextricably linked with the Romans.   We supported the best of both cultures, Celtic and Roman, and nurtured co-existence based on relative peace and harmony.   Along the way we set the stage for another significant shift in our own lives.

Lukan and I were relaxing one afternoon at the encampment where he was working with Roman engineers and I was serving as their healer. He had just returned from a journey to launch the building of an extraordinary feat of engineering, a Roman road later named Fosse Way, when Vespasian popped his head through the open door.

"I've received word that there will be a change in command here within the year, and I asked for ample time to prepare for this transition," he announced. "My superiors assumed I was referring to the need to quiet potential rebellion. But I am focused on the opposite, making sure that what we built together is so sturdy and undeniably successful, the next commander would be a fool to mess with it."

"What do you anticipate will be our biggest challenge once you are gone?" Lukan asked.

"Monotony," Vespasian replied jovially. "I'm less concerned about what will happen among the ranks than I am about how glum you'll be with nothing to do."

"A measure of monotony would be welcome," Lukan parried back, "if for no other reason than it would prove our unequivocal success."

"Vespasian, I sense you have something in mind besides tying up a few loose ends," I interjected. "No doubt you are already contemplating your next campaign elsewhere."

"Actually, I've been contemplating *your* next campaign, and it just happens to be elsewhere," he admitted. "As always, you are a step ahead of me Gracila."

"It's impossible to be a step ahead of you," I said. "But every now and then I can anticipate where you might be headed."

"I've been considering how to use your experience to best advantage," Vespasian revealed, "and I believe you would be better positioned to represent the shared interests of Britannia and the Empire if you lived in Rome."

"You mentioned our going there before," I recalled, "but what could we accomplish so far from home? No one there knows us and would have little reason to trust us."

"I agree, which is why I'm proposing you leave with me so we can arrive in Rome together," Vespasian replied. "I should have a brief period of time there before I am reassigned. That would give me an opportunity to introduce you around, starting with the Emperor Claudius."

"Impressive! You plan to start at the top," commented Lukan.

"Of course," Vespasian retorted. "That way you can serve the same purpose your Papa had in mind when he brought you to our first meeting."

"How do you know that?" I wondered.

"He told me," Vespasian revealed. "When we were talking recently, I questioned why he didn't come alone to meet me initially. He divulged his strategy, and I assured him it was supremely effective. Not being one to walk away from a proven approach, I'm suggesting you accompany me to Rome.

"Your father and I discussed this at length. We both agree you would be of greater use in Rome than here. Rome is riddled with misconceptions about Britannia. People think you are giants who paint yourselves blue to go into battle with the protection of spirits. Well, you do go into battle with the protection of spirits, but not all of you paint yourselves blue.

"You and I are fully aware that trade is the key to keeping the Empire stable economically and providing families and communities in Britannia with resources they will need in the future. When certain people in Rome understand and value what we have created here, we'll have taken a critical step forward in assuring it is maintained."

"Still, you'll be the conquering hero, returning with great credibility and visibility," I observed. "Why are we needed when you can make the same point effectively?"

"Most likely I'll be in Rome only a short period of time," Vespasian reiterated. "After all, a conquering hero must necessarily be sent out to conquer yet another dissident group and return a hero once again. When I leave, you two will be well situated to carry on without me."

When Lukan glanced at me, I nodded in approval.

"Gracila and I will do this," he declared. "I assure you we'll live up to your highest regard and maintain the greatest respect for your stature."

"Thank you," Vespasian replied. "I know you to be a man of your word. I also know you and Gracila to be an inspiring, intelligent, insightful couple. I have invited both of you because together you are a force to be reckoned with."

"Actually, she's the force. I am merely one who benefits from her virtues," Lukan observed.

"We all will benefit when you get to Rome, just as we have benefited here," noted Vespasian. "I look forward to our continued collaboration and growing friendship. You will realize when you are in Rome what a refreshing addition you have been to my life, one I intend to maintain."

Thus we changed course in an instant, even though moving to Rome represented a monumental shift for us. I could neither fathom what life would be like in the heart of the Empire nor predict how utterly transformative it would be.

∞ ∞ ∞

Lukan and I returned home, and I immersed myself in preparing our household for our indefinite absence. I released two new workers who were stealing from the garden and selling the produce. Not a hint of untrustworthiness could be tolerated among those responsible for maintaining our home while we were abroad. When we made the final preparations for our journey to Rome, reliable stewards were in place.

The thought of leaving Papa for an extended period made my heart ache. We were dining with him one evening when he revealed to me, "I will miss you sorely after you have gone, perhaps even more than I will miss Lukan.

"I asked myself why I love you so much. Then it occurred to me: You are your mother's daughter, but you are also your own person. I see her in you, without a doubt, and when that happens I am both amused and melancholy.

"You differ from her in notable ways, however. For instance, she is fiercely protective of her privacy, and you are willing to be in the world. She is ever the priestess worshiping the divine feminine. You embody the feminine while you bring out the divine masculine in the men around you. You have become my daughter as completely as you are your mother's. I daresay, you exhibit aspects of my character as if you were my very own flesh and blood."

"Papa, it is a privilege to have you in my life as a mentor, protector and friend," I replied softly. "No woman could ask for more than that from a father. But the love we share is most important of all. We need not collaborate on grand strategies or entertain Roman commanders to have a loving relationship. You could be a peasant farmer, and I would love you just as dearly."

"But I am a king, and there is a Roman commander in your life," Papa replied.

"Which brings me to a question I've wanted to ask," I ventured. "You and Mama, Lukan and I all knew each other in our prior existence. Were we also acquainted with Vespasian?"

"Yes, we were," Papa verified. "After you and Lukan came together in that lifetime, you became the guardians of a young boy and girl to save them from a terrible fate. You raised them as your own. After the fall we lived together not far from your Mama's village."

"Let me guess," I continued. "The boy was reborn as Vespasian."

"Correct," Papa confirmed. "He was destined to return to this land, but not in the way of most conquering commanders. On some level he remembers having resided here before, though he is not conscious of it. He also remembers me – the three of us, actually. That is why our initial negotiations went so smoothly. He knew he could trust us. Over the years we earned his deepening respect, and he ours.

"Vespasian is taking you and Lukan with him to Rome in gratitude for your having been his guardians in your earlier lifetime. He is also doing so to honor the new homeland we sailed to in our previous incarnation, though he believes his homeland is in Italy. It is, but it is also here."

"And the girl?" I prodded, impatient to fit the pieces together.

"He referred to her the first evening we were together," Papa recalled. "She is his true love, as she inevitably would be, and not his wife."

"Will she and I meet?" I asked Papa.

"No doubt you will," he assured me.

"One more thing if you don't mind," I continued. "Will you and Mama end up together?"

"That depends on what you mean by 'end up'," he replied. "Eventually, after many lifetimes, she and I will indeed become one again. We will often be lovers. More importantly, we will love each other in all of them, and in between as well. But during this lifetime, I cannot say."

"Will you and I be together in other lifetimes after this?" I wondered.

"I can't fathom agreeing to further incarnations if you didn't delight me in at least some of them," Papa assured me.

"Thank you for revealing this to me," I told him. "Anything is achievable with all of us working together, and not just in this lifetime."

∞ ∞ ∞

I had one more journey to make before we left for Rome. It was to see Mama. I visited her every spring to help with the planting and participate in the ceremonies welcoming the season of renewal. My interludes with Mama were precious to me. It is a privilege to live separate from the power struggles and tactics of conquest that inevitably occur when two cultures vie for supremacy. Such darkness never entered Mama's village.

One morning we were tending the herbs, enjoying the sun on our backs and our hands in the soil. We expected Lukan to arrive any day for a short visit before our departure from our homeland.

"I've asked the Mother Matres to be with you always," Mama said softly, "not so much to protect you, but to enable you to emanate her love and wisdom to help others. I have her assurance that it is already so. Thus I can bid you farewell and let you go one more time, knowing you will be serving spirit as you were meant to do."

"Do you see anything specific in store for me?" I asked.

"You will be the confidant of men in power, as will Lukan," replied Mama without hesitation. "Living in Rome will become so comfortable, at times you will forget you ever were a Celt. You and Lukan will lead a full life, mostly in Rome but also here as time permits.

"Decades will pass, and when you both are old and gray, you will realize you have become a blend of the Roman and the Celtic, the best of both. You will represent us well and enable us to live in peace. Over time those who reside here will find they too have adopted Roman ways and begun to forget their Celtic heritage. It is unfortunate but inevitable. You, my love, will make the most of the situation, for yourself and for the people and communities in your homeland."

Our departure was heartbreaking. As we crossed the channel and the coastline of Britannia disappeared, I sobbed with a terrible sense of loss. Lukan held me securely, a gentle reminder that I wasn't leaving everyone I loved behind. By the time we stepped ashore on the other side, I was ready for whatever lay ahead. I never looked back.

∞ ∞ ∞

As we traveled with Vespasian across the unfamiliar territory of Gaul, I was at once reassured and disturbed. I witnessed the extent to which communities were sacrificing their prior way of life to that of Roman rule. The closer we got to Italy, the more reflective of Roman standards everything became. Given enough time, I sensed, parts of Celtic life would look as much like Rome as the city itself.

Vespasian entered the city ahead of us. A special escort took him directly for an audience with the emperor. He had been accorded the *triumphalia ornamenta* two years earlier but had not returned to Rome for the parade or the honors. Something less obtrusive and more to his liking was planned to commemorate his success in Britannia.

When we arrived in Rome we were taken to our temporary residence, an apartment consisting of a living room, bedroom, bath and small kitchen, along with running water and an ingenious heating system. (Clearly I was no longer in Mama's village.) Care had been taken to make the place welcoming, probably at Vespasian's insistence.

I arranged our clothes and meager belongings and prepared to make a new home. That was easier said than done. The cacophony of the city filled my ears everywhere I went. Unfamiliar cooking smells assaulted my senses, along with the overwhelming stench of masses of humanity packed into tight spaces.

I discovered all too quickly that since upper floor apartments had no running water, waste was summarily dumped out the window. It covered the streets, if not also unfortunate passersby. I longed for the countryside I had taken for granted earlier, with the fresh fragrances of trees and herbs and bread baking in the oven.

Lukan and I were confident we learned quite a bit of the language from Vespasian. But once we arrived and realized how much we depended on him to communicate with us in our own tongue, we set out to find a tutor who could teach us to converse in Latin.

A week after our arrival we received an invitation to visit Vespasian and his family in their home. He arrived to escort us there, declaring we would never find our way in Rome's labyrinthine streets. Besides, he wanted to inspect our new quarters to make sure we were comfortable.

I was so pleased to see him I threw my arms around his neck and kissed him on both cheeks. "I see you are happy to lay eyes on a familiar face," he quipped.

We descended the stairs to the street, where four soldiers were waiting to escort us.

"Here's your first lesson in Roman culture: Your escort requires escorts," Vespasian remarked with no little irony. "I have made it unscathed through countless battles, but you never know what dangers lurk in the alleyways of Rome. I need substantial protection."

We walked quite a distance, chatting the whole way. To my surprise, we were entering a neighborhood even more crowded and significantly more dilapidated than ours. I assumed we were taking a shortcut, since I envisioned Vespasian living in more upper class accommodations. After all, he was a successful legionary commander, a national hero. Certainly he would be compensated accordingly.

"We're here," he announced. I looked at the apartment building he called home. It appeared to be on the verge of collapse. I worried it might not withstand the introduction of three additional people, two of whom were exceptionally large.

We followed Vespasian up the narrow stairs. I could hear children crying. Strange cooking smells filled the hallway. He opened the door of what I took to be his apartment.

A boy about five years of age came racing up to him, grabbing him around the legs. "Papa, Papa!" he said, followed by chattering I couldn't understand.

Then his wife came out of a room I thought must be the kitchen and stood in front of us smiling. He introduced us with words spoken slowly, hoping we could understand them. Lukan and I responded with a phrase we practiced in advance. We must have gotten it right, because his wife began speaking excitedly to us, too rapidly for me to comprehend.

A daughter, slightly older than the boy, arrived dressed in a tunic she had obviously been sleeping in. Dark circles were under her eyes. She looked as if she had been ill for some time. I felt her forehead, which was hot with fever.

"I must help her," I said to her mother, trying my best to recall the words I needed. "Where are your cooking herbs?" She knitted her eyebrows in question. When Vespasian explained to her what I wanted, she showed me her limited assortment.

That evening I did what I could for the girl and offered to return the next day with my own supply of herbs to alleviate her symptoms. She was sleeping peacefully when we left.

In our own quarters afterwards I commented to Lukan, "Were you surprised at the modest apartment Vespasian has for his family?"

"I was," he admitted. "It's strange that a man with so much responsibility and stature would have such limited means. But then, I can't pretend to understand how this society works. We saw only the military and engineering side of it, which might well be more egalitarian than what exists at the center of the Empire. Vespasian was second in command in Britannia. But here he is just another army officer in a city teeming with people who have significantly more power and wealth."

"I find him all the more credible as a result," I responded. "He's the same man we knew at home. The only difference is that he seems less of a commander around his wife and children."

"He's not caught up in the games people play here," Lukan replied. "If the only change we see in him is the ability to adjust to being with his family after a long absence, I'd say we have a friend we can count on."

And indeed we did. Although we didn't see Vespasian as often as we had in the past, he connected us with people who could teach us about the city, the language, the culture, the social structure and the politics of the Empire.

After six moon cycles we were conversant and comfortable in Rome. We leased an unpretentious but beautifully proportioned domus, a single family dwelling in a good neighborhood. It had a large living and dining room, a bedroom suite for us, a guest room, and equally important, a sizeable kitchen. The marble bath, mosaics on the walls and floors, and serene courtyard added touches of luxury I must admit I loved.

We were ready to begin our diplomacy.

∞ ∞ ∞

It is difficult to recall details of our first year in Rome. Much of it has faded with the years, like the color of my hair. But I remember a few incidents as if they occurred only yesterday.

The cramped and crowded city of Rome was a long way from the hidden circle of huts of my youth. What defined Rome most uniquely and intrigued me endlessly was its position at the center of an expansive, ever expanding empire. The city was both a crossroads and a hub of power. Thus it attracted people from the far reaches of explored territory. Some of them came willingly; others did not.

The heterogeneity I encountered became my lifeblood. I thrived on the constantly shifting complexion of the neighborhoods, which were small subcultures unto themselves. In contrast to the simple stews Mama and I made, I had access to exotic spices and fruits, oils and vegetables, nuts and sweets.

I loved exploring market stalls with foreigners offering a variety of cuisines and the ingredients to create them. I experimented with eclectic combinations of flavors, most of which turned out quite well.

My renewed interest in cooking served an additional purpose. Lukan was spending his days pursuing diplomatic ends, and after I learned the language and the layout of the city, I was at a loss as to how to occupy my time. I would never be content languishing in the baths with friends or having a new silk tunic and matching wool cloak custom made. Instead, I became an avid student of the ethnicities represented by the common people throughout Rome, learning about their food along the way.

Once my avocation as an inventive cook took hold, I realized it was ludicrous to prepare elaborate meals just for Lukan and me. I suggested he invite others to join us so the food wouldn't go to waste. He agreed, and the next night he showed up with three hungry senators in tow. Thus began our many years of entertaining.

One thing led to another, and we decided to hire a cook to help prepare for our larger dinner parties and gatherings. Based on my growing interest in inventive cuisine, I wanted someone as passionate about cooking as I was.

Vivendi's eyes sparkled with every canister of powdered herbs she opened in my kitchen. She swooned over the flavors and fragrances in the marketplace. After our first shopping excursion, which was my foolproof way of evaluating prospective cooks, I hired her on the spot.

Vespasian's initial efforts to introduce Lukan to the influential people he knew in Rome paid off handsomely. We came to Rome to strengthen relations between our homeland and Roman power brokers – senators, military commanders and patricians alike. And we did indeed build relationships at those levels.

In addition, Lukan drew to him diverse individuals from far and wide who ended up being invited to dinner. Soon enough, Romans and others throughout the Empire counted him among their friends.

Vivendi worked in the kitchen almost daily, helping me cook meals for groups of all sizes. I ceased asking Lukan for advance warning about additional dinner guests. He rarely gave me timely notice, since his invitations were often spontaneous. Instead I made sure we were amply prepared.

It didn't take long for word to spread throughout the top circles in Rome that dining with us was a unique treat. People even offered to do Lukan a special favor in exchange for dinner with an assortment of guests in our home. Lukan's sphere of influence was expanding, as were our culinary innovations.

I planned the meals so that when Lukan arrived, I could join him and our guests. As much as I loved creating delectable dinners for a constantly changing group of people, most of whom were male, I was also drawn to the conversations that occurred before, during and after we dined. Lukan never once suggested I leave the men to themselves. I was welcome to participate in their discussions, which never failed to captivate me.

Thus I developed a reputation for being an accomplished cook and an equally facile conversationalist. Even so, I was struck by the intrigues that were openly discussed and the attention given to gossip. Apparent rumors were invariably reported as fact.

These gatherings, which occurred four or five evenings a week, increased our influence. What started out as a way for me to experiment with my cooking and avoid throwing most of it away, turned out to be an effective venue for diplomacy. We became known as the engaging foreigner and his talented wife, recently transplanted from Britannia, who were surprisingly lively hosts.

Others with more wealth and influence gave lavish dinner parties with preposterous amounts of food and drink, music, dancing and women to entertain male guests. Our gatherings consisted of a meal spiced with exotic herbs and stimulating conversation. They became the preferred venue for a defined segment of the Roman elite.

Sometimes after an evening with dinner guests, Lukan and I would piece together a comment here, an indiscretion there, and be stunned by what we learned. During these get-togethers we came to understand the inner workings of the Empire, all of which we kept to ourselves.

One evening after a particularly provocative exchange with two sea merchants, Lukan was helping me clean up before we started to bed.

"Do you feel at times that we are leading someone else's life?" he wondered.

"Here in Rome?" I asked.

"Yes, here, especially when we are entertaining," he clarified. "I think of how our lives began, you learning the ways of the divine feminine as a healer and me training to do battle with the inevitable invaders, and I wonder how we got here.

"Then again, I know full well how we got here. Still, there are moments when I'm in awe of the guests who come to dinner regularly, the ideas we share, the information that is exchanged and the potential impact of it all. Not incidentally, but for your superb cooking we'd be dining alone each evening."

"They trust you," I asserted, "and they know if they tag along with you for dinner they'll be treated to exotic fare. With that said, I too experience moments of abject disbelief. They usually arrive when I'm doing something routine that would have been unimaginable not long ago. I find this cluttered, discordant city to be stimulating and unconstrained."

"By the way, I encountered Vespasian today," Lukan segued. "He looks well and is keeping busy, but he says he'd rather be in Britannia making peace with the locals than swimming in the shark infested waters of Roman politics. That is an exact quote, by the way."

"I do miss our conversations with him," I commented, "especially since they invariably resulted in a match of wits."

"He sends his best to you and wants you to know that word of your magic in the kitchen has reached his discerning ears," Lukan reported. "He considers it unforgivable that you kept this talent under wraps in Britannia, when he was our sole dinner guest."

"I hope you offered to make amends by inviting him and his wife for a private dinner," I continued.

"I did, but he told me she can't abide social evenings," Lucan observed. "Apparently she becomes much aggrieved when the conversation turns away from children and toward the latest scandals and infidelities."

"Well, there is not a hint of scandal or infidelity in this household," I retorted, patting him on his rear end, "even if we have been known to enjoy a few scandalous things in bed on occasion."

"Now that you mention it, we've been so busy keeping others entertained, we almost entirely forgot about entertaining each other," Lukan mused. "Shall we invent a new scandal, my sweet?"

"I thought you'd never ask," I whispered seductively, leading him to our bedroom. That night we enjoyed such extended and creative lovemaking, it most surely would have set tongues wagging throughout Rome had anyone known about it.

∞ ∞ ∞

During our first stay in Rome, which lasted almost three years, Lukan succeeded in negotiating trade arrangements with a number of seafaring countries, in addition to keeping the Romans thoroughly satisfied with their mutually beneficial agreements with Britannia. We were preparing to return home to spend time with our parents and verify information we were receiving about conditions there. During one of our last dinner parties a prominent senator spoke candidly with Lukan.

"Are you returning in order to replace your father as king?" he inquired with his characteristic forthrightness. He had become a close acquaintance, which made this question all the more surprising.

"Absolutely not," Lukan replied. "My father's leadership goes unquestioned, and his people are devoted to him. He is in his prime."

"I didn't mean to offend you with this question," explained the senator. "My purpose was only to discredit the rumors I have been hearing ever since you announced your impending departure. Such hearsay proves the Roman predisposition to inflate one's importance through association. After all, it is better to know a future king than the son of one, brilliant though he may be."

"I hadn't heard the rumor. Apparently in this rare instance people chose discretion over disclosure," Lukan commented wryly. "It is telling that my standing in the family of a tribal chieftain in an unassuming corner of the Empire could escalate expectations so considerably. The next thing you know, the citizens of Rome will be reporting that I have plotted against my father and, after a stunning example of patricide, will seize what is rightfully mine. Please don't repeat this, by the way."

"Someone already beat you to that juicy tidbit of gossip," replied our guest. "I heard that rumor only yesterday."

"Then let us be gone as soon as possible," Lukan declared jovially. "Once we are absent for a day or two, people will forget we were ever here. I am constantly amazed at how abbreviated the average Roman's memory is."

"Our stomachs, however, have memories as long as an elephant's," noted the senator, looking in my direction. "We will be counting the days until your return, for there is no better food in all of Rome than the inspired creations constantly emerging from your kitchen."

"I knew it all along," Lukan quipped. "Every agreement I successfully achieved is a direct reflection of Gracila's artistry, not my shrewd cunning as a negotiator."

"Your artistry is equal to hers," the senator affirmed. "You two have a remarkable partnership. I envy you that."

Lukan took my hand in his. "I would be a miserable wretch without this fantastic woman, even if she never found her way into the kitchen."

"How did you to manage to marry for what so obviously is love and an abiding appreciation for each other?" asked the senator. "Such unions are rare in this emotionally corrupt city, where marriage occurs to consolidate power instead of celebrating deep devotion."

"Our parents wanted nothing less than a love-based union for each of us," I explained. "They set up the circumstances in which we met."

"Was it love at first sight?" asked our guest.

"It was, and we have been in love ever since," replied Lukan. "If anything happened to Gracila, I couldn't go on. It is my hope that we die at an advanced age, when our shared adventures are over and our bodies are frail. In the same moment we both know it is time to leave, together. Thus we would never be apart."

"May it be so," declared our guest.

∞ ∞ ∞

Our first homecoming was a celebration of progress. Lukan had accomplished a great deal in Rome with is trade agreements, and Papa had kept the peace. Nonetheless, not long after our arrival, we acknowledged that as much as we loved our homeland and our family, our lives had grown beyond them.

I felt like a stranger in my own home. The children who had been babies when we left didn't remember us, and the adults had established their own sense of purpose apart from us. Unsettling as this was, everything had been well tended in our absence. Our home was in capable, trustworthy hands.

A few days after our arrival, I was walking alone near the edge of the forest. I wanted to plant my feet firmly on the ground in hopes of reconnecting with life there instead of feeling like a stranger.

I was also experiencing an uncharacteristic misalignment with Lukan. We seemed to look and talk past each other. We were both preoccupied, sorting through something private and not sharing it with one another.

I retreated to my favorite spot by the creek where Lukan and I used to spend pleasant times together. Those recollections felt bittersweet in this new context.

As I was approaching an opening between the trees that led to the banks of the stream, I heard something stir and proceeded cautiously. A familiar rust colored tunic came into view. It was Lukan's.

"What could have drawn us both here at the same moment?" I asked by way of greeting.

"It couldn't possibly be that we want to get away from it all, because there is nothing to get away from here," Lukan observed. "The loudest noise is the chirping of the birds in the morning. And as for teeming masses of people, they are neither massive nor teeming. What brought you here, my dear?"

"I am feeling unsettled and a bit disappointed," I revealed. "I was looking forward to our return home.

But now that we're here, I feel like a foreigner. Although I appreciate everything that has been done in our absence, this doesn't feel like home anymore."

"That's because it isn't home anymore," Lukan declared. "I have been experiencing a similar sense of loss and letdown, so I came here to figure out why. Just before you arrived I realized that while this is our homeland, a place we visit on occasion, our home is in Rome now. We planted our hearts there, together. If we were asked to choose one place or the other to live full time, it would be Rome."

"That would be my choice," I agreed. "But if it weren't yours as well, I would reconsider. Home is wherever you are. My happiness is unalterably with you."

"Then Rome it is," Lukan confirmed. "We left here three years ago thinking we would make a brief sojourn to a distant city. Neither of us expected to settle in as easily we did or remain so long before coming back.

"More importantly, I have no calling here. Papa is leading with his characteristic vision, resilience and acumen. He doesn't need my assistance, and I am not cut out to tend the garden and go hunting every day. I would be paralyzed by the tedium."

"I would be as well," I affirmed.

"Now that I know how you feel, the solution is straightforward. We will give a portion of this property to those who tend it, under the condition it not be sold and they remain here as caretakers," Lukan proposed. "That will motivate and reward them for treating it as their own, which it will be to some extent. We can stay in the house whenever we return, but we won't expect it to feel like home. That way we will enjoy it more.

"Beyond that, I have been discussing our future in Rome with Papa, and there are a few possible changes I would like to discuss with you."

"Go on," I encouraged.

"Papa has been supporting our activities in Rome, and his investment has paid off many times over. It is time to set myself up formally in business," Lukan explained. "I have made many valuable contacts and built my credibility. Based on that, I am in a unique position to represent those who want to engage in commerce between the Empire and Britannia. I can negotiate the necessary approvals and introduce opportunities for more expansive trade.

"We could take the money I earn and buy a home of our own, establishing a permanent, self-sufficient life in Rome. A semi-permanent life here no longer suits us. That has been clear to me the past few weeks."

"What a relief!" I exclaimed. "I assumed that because we spent the early days of our marriage here, and you had recuperated from your wounds here, and Mama and Papa celebrated our first anniversary with us here, it must necessarily be home to us."

"We have wonderful memories," Lukan observed, "but they represent the past, not who we are now."

"So it's time to move on and create a lasting home in Rome," I concluded.

"Exactly," Lukan effused, giving me a hearty embrace.

"I do have a few requests regarding our new residence," I interjected. "It must have a bigger kitchen, larger rooms for entertaining, and guest rooms for Mama and Papa."

"Guest rooms?" Lukan shot back in mock astonishment. "I hope at this point they would insist on sharing a room, so as not to put us out, of course."

"Perhaps we could tell them that since homes with ample guest accommodations are too expensive, they will have to accept our apologies and sleep together," I suggested.

"That should take care of the economics of our home purchase," Lukan noted, "especially since the lion's share of our funds will be going into your kitchen!"

We relaxed after that. Even so, our sense of being visitors in what was formerly our home didn't vanish completely. A phase of our lives was over, and an extraordinary new one was about to begin.

∞ ∞ ∞

We extracted promises from Papa and Mama to visit us in Rome, though they were unwilling to specify when. We may have made our home there, but it was still a foreign place located an arduous journey away. We understood from their hesitant responses to our repeated invitations that we would be doing most of the traveling back and forth. That was acceptable, but still we hoped that once they got acclimated on their first visit, they would be more eager to return to Rome.

Mama seemed to be evolving further into what I was later to call her high priestess phase. She was living beyond the material world as much as she was in it. I recognized this change the first time I visited her upon our return. Lukan and I traveled to her village, and when she greeted us on the periphery of the circle of huts, she had changed. I sensed myriad subtle realignments and a deeper detachment. She was happy to see us, but her former effusiveness wasn't as evident.

She hadn't forgotten us or grown to love us less. Rather, her spiritual evolution was more predominant. When I was living with her I kept her grounded in the material world. After my union with Lukan, she was free to commune with the wood nymphs and compelling energies of the feminine. Although both had been available all along, she gave so much of herself raising me and preparing me for the world, she had little left for her own unfolding.

Mama taught me a great deal. But on this visit I questioned whether I was applying it to help others as much as I should. I recalled the months after Lukan left for battle, when I welcomed wayfarers into our home for food, warmth and a respite. I wondered if I was so caught up in Roman politics and exotic cuisines, I had lost my way.

Mama could teach me even more now, given her enhanced capacity to flow with the magnetic frequencies of the feminine. I wanted to learn all I could before we left. Given her reluctance to travel, I assumed our next separation would be lengthy.

"How much teaching can you fit into our visit?" I asked her one morning.

"Are you looking for something you can apply in Rome?" she asked.

"Yes, but mostly I want to know more about how you align with the feminine," I replied.

"You grew up having your spiritual life fully integrated into your daily existence," Mama explained. "Because the two were not separate, you learned from me naturally. It was a joy to watch your own spirit unfold as you matured.

"In truth you have little left to learn. But due to the demands and dynamics of your new life, you may have lost touch with what you already know."

"I lost touch with something," I admitted.

"You reside in an urban area full of people who vibrate at the lower frequencies of human consciousness," Mama observed. "It is difficult to maintain the high vibration you were imbued with when you lived here. Growing up as my daughter, it was inevitable you would become a spiritual adept. Perhaps that capacity has been compromised in the downward spiraling vortices of Rome."

"What can I do about it?" I asked. "I don't want to sacrifice myself to the grasping gods of the Roman Empire."

"Of course not," Mama agreed. "Your spirit is longing to be realigned with the passion and purpose of the feminine. I can help you do that."

"Does it require me to make big changes in our life in Rome?" I worried.

"Not at all," Mama replied reassuringly. "Few adjustments are needed. But the ones you do make will greatly impact the perspectives and opinions of those who flock to your home for your well spiced cooking and conversation."

"How can I do that?" I pursued.

"Integrate your spiritual practice into your daily routine," Mama suggested. "We do that naturally here. Make a conscious choice to do so when you are back in Rome."

Hearing that, I experienced both relief and regret – relief that I wasn't failing spiritually after all and regret that I hadn't recognized this earlier.

Mama took my hands in hers. "Gracila, you are an amazing woman," she assured me. "If you changed nothing at all, your life would be worthwhile. But like me you are about to enter a new phase of your spiritual existence."

Mama's eyes exhibited the faraway look that accompanied moments when she accessed the realms of timelessness. She was seeing what lay ahead for me. I waited for her to continue.

"You came into this life to benefit the world as Lukan's partner," she declared. "The two of you work in perfect harmony, strengthening each other with your love and your expansive belief in the possible. Just as his Papa and I are equals, so are you.

"Nonetheless, your gender difference affects the way you interact with others. The masculine is catalytic, energizing change, be it incremental or transformative. The feminine is creative, expanding the presence of love and destroying the limitation of lovelessness. I speak, of course, of the divine masculine and divine feminine, not the fallen consciousness that has a stranglehold on so many."

"How can I bring more of the divine feminine into my life in Rome?" I asked.

"First, create a simple altar in your home where you place talismans of the divine masculine and the divine feminine, then pray to them in thanksgiving each day," Mama explained. "I made both talismans for you and imbued them with a pristine vibration.

"Next, hold three inviolable intensions in your heart: to love, to be compassionate and to forgive. Commit to maintaining them at the center of your beliefs, thoughts and actions."

"I can do that," I vowed.

"First, love always," Mama advised. "See Source in all and reflect it back with your love. Few people do that, you know.

"Related to that is compassion. When you acknowledge others in the context of their divinity, you are being compassionate. Recognize their eternal reality, the spark of spirit that lies within them, and their earthly reality as well.

"Finally, forgive instantly and completely," Mama exhorted. "Forgiveness frees the forgiver and the forgiven from the bondage of any transgression, perceived or real. It is a gift to both."

"Love, be compassionate, forgive," I repeated. "Those are the most exalted intentions."

"And they should constitute your daily practice," Mama urged. "If you take this advice to heart, you will serve the divine feminine joyfully. That is my wish for you."

I was compelled to ask one more question, even though it was embarrassingly mundane. "What about my cooking?"

"How could I have forgotten that?" Mama replied. "Your cooking is at the center of it all. When you prepare food with love and imbue every morsel with a blessing, those who eat it fill their bodies and consciousness with love. That alone can transform attitudes, values, choices and purpose.

"When you and Lukan entertain, people of power and influence are immersed in a vortex of love. Your conversation engenders openness and expansiveness, not control and conflict. And your cuisine infuses them with goodwill. That is a formidable combination disguised as an informal evening with delicious food and lighthearted banter."

"I see how it all comes together," I acknowledged. "It's a great way to strengthen the power of the divine masculine and the divine feminine in Rome. Now I am prepared for our return."

"My love, I have been preparing you for this from the moment you were born," Mama replied.

Of course she had.

The remainder of our visit was delightful. I allowed myself the luxury of just being, in that enchanted setting with two people I loved the most.

∞ ∞ ∞

Lukan and I arrived in Rome with a shared sense of coming home. We belonged there.

Vivendi maintained our residence responsibly while we were away and in the process managed to build a prosperous business of her own. After we left she was deluged with requests to cook for special occasions hosted by others. Those who enjoyed her creations at our house wanted to make them available to their guests.

"I withheld our best recipes," Vivendi assured me. "No way was I willing to share everything we created together. I made dishes that were just exotic enough to keep everyone fat and happy. Our most unique combinations remained locked in my head."

"In that case, we must get to work and unlock them for a colossal gathering to announce our return," I suggested.

Word was already out that we were back in Rome, and people were angling for an invitation to dine with us at our earliest convenience.

"It's quite a phenomenon," Lukan reported. "You would think the Caesar had returned unexpectedly. But it is only us and your memorable meals, with an emphasis on the latter."

Lukan was happy about the celebration we were planning. "No doubt we will spend our entertaining budget for the entire year in one evening. After our protracted absence, and their protracted abstinence, everyone will want to indulge in your cooking. I must get to work straightaway to refill the coffers."

"Our party will launch your new business," I countered. "Then we will keep your colleagues and potential partners well satisfied, even if they are unable to negotiate the most favorable deal with you."

"You and Vivendi are the secrets to my success," Lukan remarked playfully. "A repast here will have even the most recalcitrant dealmaker prepared to agree to whatever terms I suggest."

We invited Vespasian and his wife to attend our gathering. Even though we preferred a more intimate setting for our conversation with them, we weren't able to schedule it before the event. The last thing we wanted was for him to hear about our party and wonder why he hadn't been invited.

In typical fashion, Vespasian took matters into his own hands. He was home when the messenger brought the invitation and decided to respond in person. The messenger returned looking harried, Vespasian at his heels.

"What's this about a big party?" Vespasian bellowed. "I heard just yesterday that you were back in Rome, and I was planning to see you right away. Then this invitation arrived. It will never do. We can't engage in uncivilized banter with a roomful of politicians and praetors milling about."

"You have a point," I conceded.

"So I came here in person to commandeer your evening," he noted happily. "I want to hear all about your Papa and Mama."

I gave him a wicked smile. "And what if we have plans?"

"You'll cancel them," he announced with exaggerated authority.

"Do I detect a certain anxiousness to welcome us back to Rome?" Lukan asked sardonically.

"Not in the least," replied Vespasian. "I simply wanted to give you two a chance to keep from offending me by updating me on your travels over dinner. Here. This evening."

"In that event, we will make sure we are serving something besides stew!" crowed Lukan.

The three of us enjoyed our time together, filling each other in on what had been occurring in Britannia and Rome. Vespasian was pleased to hear Papa was doing well and the peace they negotiated was being maintained. He then updated us on the latest political maneuverings in Rome, none of which were surprising.

"You are a major reason we returned to Rome," I commented. "We appreciate seeing it through your eyes as well as our own."

"My eyes have grown less idealistic and more cynical lately," Vespasian noted.

"I disagree," I countered. "Since you never were much of an idealist, you're not likely to become a disillusioned cynic. You're more of a realist."

"I suppose so, but I can't help being disappointed in our leaders," he replied. "I keep wishing they were like your father – firm, fair and focused more on the welfare of others than on their own gain.

"I did a great deal of thinking in your absence. I knew your return to Britannia would reveal to the two of you where you prefer to reside. I can name many compelling reasons for you to remain in your homeland. If, however, it is to be here, I want to introduce you to those who share our values. You bring something priceless to Rome, and that is your integrity.

"Your Papa and I accomplished much by building a relationship based on trust. I have the same connection with the two of you. It is rare and even more precious when treachery threatens to overcome truth. We can build anything if we trust each other."

"That trust will never change, unless it is to grow stronger," Lukan affirmed. "I welcome your ideas about possible shared endeavors. There is no one I would rather have as a partner than you."

"My involvement can't be obvious," Vespasian explained. "Think of me as the one you can turn to for honest information about the people with whom you might be doing business. I want you to be successful not so you can grow rich, though you inevitably will, but so you might influence how people deal with each other. I want them to understand that honesty and fairness can be as effective as the opposite. Perhaps the Roman propensity for power abuse can be transformed into reciprocity, if not also generosity."

"It would be gratifying to contribute to that change," replied Lukan sincerely, "especially since Gracila and I have decided to make Rome our permanent home."

Vespasian glanced at me, observed a smile I couldn't hide, and let out a boisterous cheer.

"You can do so much here, and I am committed to assisting you," he declared effusively. "But I had to wait until you decided your future, which is why I said nothing before you left for Britannia. I didn't want to influence your choice by arguing why you should live here."

"Your conscience can be clear," Lukan assured him. "We realized when we returned to our too quiet house in the country, that our lives away from Rome are uninteresting and irrelevant."

"Well, there is nothing uninteresting about Rome," chortled Vespasian, "unless you consider the tedium of the gossip mongers. And I intend to make certain your lives are anything but irrelevant!"

Thus it was established. Lukan would have the direct counsel of Vespasian, the most upright man in our circle of acquaintances.

"Now you know why I barged in on you today," Vespasian revealed. "There is no way we could have had this conversation with other ears in the room. And besides, I was anxious to see you both. I missed you."

"And we you," I replied, squeezing his hand affectionately.

Vespasian didn't attend our gathering later that week. Vivendi and I spent days beforehand preparing the food, which far exceeded any of our previous efforts. In one memorable evening Lukan and I reestablished ourselves as the preferred host and hostess, even though we served our guests food and conversation instead of wine and concubines. Thus our entertaining continued, three or four evenings a week.

True to his word, Vespasian helped Lukan make shrewd judgments about potential business dealings. Vespasian's ethics remained unimpeachable, even when he assumed the coveted post of consul and gained greater authority and influence. He never took advantage of his position, which endeared him to us all the more.

Lukan was as successful in his ventures as Vespasian predicted he would be. The combination of credibility, trustworthiness and acumen made Lukan one of the most sought after business partners in Rome.

We had the means to purchase a home of our own. Unassuming by patrician standards, it was a veritable palace to us. Its gracious rooms and elegant, understated interiors featured intricate mosaics and sublime frescoes. A sunny courtyard abundant with blossoms, naturalistic sculptures and peaceful seating areas became my favorite spot except for the kitchen, which included everything I could possibly want.

Vivendi and I continued to explore the city, locating even more exotic foods and spices and inventing incessantly with them. We created unique spice and herb combinations unavailable anywhere: mustard, ginger and rosemary; anise, laurel and basil; cinnamon, caraway and cumin; saffron, sweet pepper and mint. Each one had a hint of other spices – white pepper, allspice, cassia, nutmeg, silphion – making them impossible to replicate anywhere else.

That led to a business of my own. Spices were a status symbol in Rome, since only the wealthiest families could afford them. They could be acquired individually in market stalls, but no one had thought to package mixed spices. My idea was to do just that, and not incidentally, to infuse every container of spices I sold with the blessings of the Divine Mother. People in households throughout Rome would be imbibing love with every morsel of food they enjoyed, even if they didn't realize it.

Lukan began importing large quantities of the spices we used in our kitchen. Vivendi and I mixed them in bulk to create our distinctive varieties, praying and chanting all the while. We packaged various combinations in small terra-cotta pots and sold them to apothecaries and exclusive shops serving patrician households. Tied with silk ribbons and decorated with tiny tin ornaments to differentiate each variety, the spice pots became so popular we couldn't keep up with the demand.

Ironically our business was successful even though wealthy women set foot in the kitchen only to announce the menu others would prepare. Such was the compelling influence of Rome's gossip-hungry, shopping-addicted, status-conscious matriarchs.

"You are the natural business person in the family," Lukan remarked one day after I gave him another large order for spices from India, China and lands throughout the Empire. "You take easily accessible ingredients, combine them in unusual ways and package them to perfection. Then you sell your products for ten times what they cost to produce, and we can't keep them in stock. I should retire and leave the business dealings to you."

"I might declare I am simply selling the latest status symbol," I noted sardonically. "But you know that is not the case. It's true only the upper classes can afford to buy my spice pots. But they are acquiring more than another way to flaunt their wealth. They are eating food enhanced by spices blessed by Matres."

"I love how you counteract the vicissitudes of Roman society," Lukan said wryly, kissing the tip of my nose.

"Of course, our creations aren't half as delectable as the rumor mill has made them out to be," I added. "One would think our dinners come directly from the gods. Eating a relatively ordinary dish during dinner at our house is recounted in ecstatic wonderment because people want to have a superior experience here. The dishes others create with our spice combinations may not live up to the exaggerated descriptions offered by our guests, but they are food for the spirit nonetheless."

"I am not so sure our guests exaggerate," Lukan countered. "I believe they really do experience what they describe to others. It is as much about your magic as it is the spices. You infuse everything with generous portions of peace and goodwill. People feel it somehow, and then they report it was the best meal they ever had."

"As you know, we instill that same vibration in every pot of spices," I affirmed. "It's the secret ingredient. We are managing to spread love all over Rome, and people think they are merely buying a rare blend of spices for their cooks."

"Remarkable! Love as an enlightened business strategy," Lukan mused. "You have transitioned from your mother's stew pot to the dining halls of Rome. Many will benefit from it, not the least of whom are the spice importers, who by the way are charging me exorbitant prices these days. They too have heard of our dinner parties."

My business expanded to include herbs for healing, incense for religious ceremonies and extravagant aromatic oils. Frankincense and myrrh were packaged in delicate marble containers, fragranced oils were sold in blown glass flasks, and medicinal herbs were packed in silk pouches.

This expanded assortment was well received. When it became impossible to run my business out of our house, Lukan and I purchased a small facility where we could inventory, blend and package our products. We began to receive orders from individuals and shopkeepers living outside of Rome, then beyond the borders of Italy. We were spreading Mama's love far and wide, and she hadn't taken a single step away from her village.

Thus we spent the better part of a decade, contented and complete, Lukan with the expanding reach of his trading business and I with my pots and petals, spices and spirit.

∞ ∞ ∞

As my business grew and I could rely on others besides Vivendi to keep it going, I took time off to explore Rome's cultural and architectural wonders. I had seen many of them before, but I wanted to discover the rituals and celebrations they commemorated.

One day I was ascending the steps of the Temple of Minerva on the Aventine hill, intent upon experiencing her wisdom and magic. It was particularly hot and steamy, and I looked forward to the expanses of cool marble and gentle shade awaiting me inside. Near the entrance by one of the columns I overheard someone talking in a low voice to a small group.

"I traveled with him and his followers for over two years," the person was saying. "I have many stories to tell, but each one communicates his message of love, forgiveness and compassion. When we meet, I'll tell you everything."

Love, forgiveness and compassion – those were the lessons Mama shared with me on my first visit after we returned from Rome. I stopped in the shade and appeared to be studying a marble carving, the better to hear what the man had to say.

"He exhorted us to love all," he explained. "But that would mean nothing had he not lived by that standard. I never once saw him judge another harshly, even if that person disrespected him or worse, was cruel to him. He had the capacity to forgive everything, without condition. The light in his eyes was so clear and his intentions so pure, we were in a constant state of wonderment. Yet he wanted none of that. He was the most humble man I've ever met."

I speculated he was referring to Yeshua. He had lived in Judea and was crucified by the Romans. Some said he was a prophet. Others called him a charlatan.

"We are meeting this evening," the man stated. "Please feel free to bring a friend. All are welcome."

I walked to the periphery of the group. When the conversation paused, I inquired, "I couldn't help overhearing your description of this remarkable man. If in fact all are welcome at your gathering, I would like to attend."

My boldness surprised me. I knew nothing about these people. Lukan already had plans for the evening, so I would be going alone, not the safest prospect. Nonetheless, I asked for the location and time of the gathering then entered the temple.

I felt lightheaded. Thinking the heat had taken its toll, I found a cushion and sat down against a wall. Soon I fell into in a deep meditation. Mama appeared as if she were standing in front of me.

"My dear Gracila, this evening you will start on a journey all your own, one that will follow you through many lifetimes," she observed. "It is not an accident that Lukan has other plans. You are meant to go alone.

"Although this Yeshua is gone, he lives on. Allow him into your being that you may serve the divine feminine ever more profoundly in the context of his emanation of the divine masculine.

"Lukan will honor your commitment to the tradition of this prophet, although he will have no desire to become a follower himself. Do not fear this difference between you. It will engender no conflict, in this lifetime at least. Now do what you must, and surrender to the unfolding. You are blessed. All is love."

Mama vanished, and I remained in a meditative state for some time afterward. Although my spirit traveled away from my body, I was perfectly safe. That was Mama's doing. Most likely I was invisible to those milling about the temple.

That night at the meeting I discovered a sacred nest into which I could settle. As fulfilling as my life was after I left Mama's village, and as much as I loved Lukan, I lost my mystical center over the years. That evening I found it again.

Lukan was already home when I arrived. He listened intently as I told him about what occurred that day. He recognized how meaningful the experience was for me, and Mama's presence during my meditation caught his attention. Her powers had credibility with him since he experienced them himself.

"I am gratified you came across a group with whom you resonate so completely," Lukan commented. "I was unaware your spirituality wasn't being nurtured. If I stopped long enough to think about it, though, I might have recognized something was lacking."

"I didn't realize it myself until today," I admitted. "Now after just a few hours, I am feeling joyful again."

"Nonetheless, I haven't been with you as I was before," Lukan persisted. "I have too many priorities, knowing full well my only real priority is you."

"It is not as if you have been attending business meetings all over Rome and leaving me here pining for your return," I reminded him. "I have been as busy as you with my own enterprise. Then today I was stopped in my tracks by Mama, no less!"

"She still knows you better than any of us," Lukan acknowledged. "I am gratified you discovered a spiritual community that means so much to you already."

"Would you like to accompany me to the next gathering?" I asked.

"Yes I would," he replied immediately. "Anything you appreciate so much is bound to be beneficial to me as well."

Lukan participated in the meetings occasionally, but he never felt the same sense of family with the followers of Yeshua's teachings that I did. I saw the perfect harmony between Mama's lessons about the divine feminine and Yeshua's messages about the Source of all that is.

Lukan and I loved each other as dearly as always. But the more involved I became in the teachings of a prophet from the Middle East, the less interested I was in our conversations with evening guests. They became increasingly superficial and downright banal.

After one particularly trying evening, we were getting ready for bed when Lukan commented, "We may have outgrown our dinner parties. What I used to experience as scintillating conversation is feeling forced. I can tell the same is true for you. Perhaps we should have fewer gatherings and be more selective about whom we invite."

"I would love that," I replied. "Tonight in particular the relentless arrogance and bombast were almost unendurable. I wanted to escape to the quiet of our room until everyone had gone home."

"These evenings served an important purpose," Lukan noted. "When we first arrived, they provided a means to introduce ourselves to influential people in Rome. Then they helped establish my business. With the unerring guidance of Vespasian, I achieved that aim. If anything I have too many ventures to tend to now."

"For years we enjoyed our dinner parties," I recalled.

"We were fascinated with the intelligence, education and worldliness of our guests," Lukan reminisced. "Now their banter seems mindless, as if its sole purpose is to upstage others rather than contribute to an exchange of ideas."

"What precipitated this shift?" I asked.

"Things changed in the fifteen years we have lived here," Lukan continued. "The emperor has been corrupted, squandering resources and abusing power in the extreme. Others are susceptible to it, even when they believe they are rising above the depravity. Fear and uncertainty are roiling just below the surface. People mask their intentions and create the pretense of a dialogue to obscure their true opinions. The conversation tonight reflected that, and we felt it."

"Does this mean you and I can enjoy more quiet evenings at home, by ourselves, eating leftovers and perhaps a bowl of stew every now and then?" I asked, feeling lighter than I had in a while. "And if we'd rather read than talk, we could do that. Or if we wanted to make love for a very long time, that would be a possibility as well."

"I take it you prefer my company, in bed and otherwise, to that of assorted blowhards with nothing new to say," he whispered playfully.

"You are correct," I chirped. "But to clarify, I always prefer your company in bed than anywhere else. Given, however, that we can't languish here indefinitely, I might deign to share you with the rest of the world every now and again."

"Only every now and again?" Lukan questioned, feigning shock.

"And only if absolutely necessary," I murmured as I kissed his eyelids, his cheeks, his lips.

We discovered each other again that evening. A sweet appreciation blanketed us both as we experienced our love in ways that were so comfortable to us. I slept more soundly afterward than I had in a long time, tucked into Lukan's body, his arm around me through the night.

∞ ∞ ∞

Things changed for the better after that. We entertained less and more selectively. No one seemed to notice we were living quieter lives. I frequently participated in gatherings of my spiritual community, which provided meaningful sustenance for me.

We didn't see much of Vespasian. He served as Proconsul of Africa then traveled throughout Greece with the emperor Nero. From there he and his son were called to put down an uprising of the Jews. We heard news of him from others but had no direct communication from him.

Rome was becoming even more disorderly. The rule of the Caesars devolved from incompetent to corrupt to downright madness. The level of violence and viciousness accompanying this decline was evident throughout the city.

Lucan and I became so alarmed at what we witnessed, we seriously considered leaving Rome permanently and returning to Britannia. Our parents were growing old and would most likely not live much longer. We wanted to be with them again.

Lukan was assessing how he might divest most of his enterprises, and I was preparing to close my business as well. Our energy and attention were turning away from Rome.

We had not yet taken any action. If we learned nothing else in our years together, it was that we should plan appropriately while remaining open to the possibility of following a different course altogether.

We were home one evening despite the excitement that pervaded the city. After a succession of emperors, four in one year, the army declared a successor. Chaos ensued.

"I wonder if we haven't waited too long," Lukan observed. "It is no mean feat to leave town when people are rioting in the streets."

"I was having similar thoughts," I replied. "But for whatever reason neither of us felt it was time to depart. Things change so quickly, we never know what might happen."

"So you prefer to wait a while longer," concluded Lukan.

"We may not be leaving after all," I admitted. "Every time I think of leaving I have a sense it won't occur, even though there is no legitimate reason to feel this way. With that said, I can't see a clear future for us here either. This may be nothing more than wishful thinking on my part, a desire to return to our early days in Rome when Vespasian was our impromptu evening guest and the emperor was rational and relatively fair-minded."

"I have always trusted your instincts, so let's wait and see how things unfold," Lukan suggested. "We can relish the calm of our home while all of Rome enjoys drama in the streets."

It was a lovely interlude. The power struggles continued, sometimes right outside our door, and we enjoyed our privacy.

It was midday. I was in our garden amidst the birds and blossoms and Lukan was inside reading, when an insistent knock at the door pierced the quiet. The housekeeper ran to see who was there.

"An army officer has a message from Vespasian," she announced.

I hastened to tell Lukan, who ushered the officer into the courtyard.

"I have been ordered to inform you that Vespasian was elected emperor by his army and will be returning to Rome," he decreed. "He asks that you help prepare for his arrival. He sends you a list of the people who are to be involved and gives general instructions on what is to be accomplished.

"The exact date of his arrival is unknown. He requests that you, and others whom you trust, do everything possible to calm the citizens and keep the bureaucrats from pillaging the royal coffers. Those are his exact words. Here are his documented instructions."

The officer handed Lukan a large scroll, sealed with Vespasian's familiar signet. I invited the soldier to refresh himself with a meal and a rest in our home, but he insisted he couldn't delay.

"How will your commander know I have received this message?" asked Lukan.

"He instructed me to bring it to you first," he replied, "and if you weren't to be found, I have a short list of others to be located and informed instead. He wants this information to land in capable hands, although his every hope is that they are yours. He told me that himself."

"Very well," agreed Lukan. "I will prepare a brief written message for you to take to our new emperor, committing to honor his wishes and offering to be the first person in Rome, along with my wife, to welcome him upon his return."

Vespasian provided extensive instructions regarding what he wanted done before his arrival. Most of it was a deterrent to keep dishonesty to a minimum. Lukan was to work with a handful of trustworthy senators, a prefect or two and various military officers.

"It appears our days of solitude have come to an end," I commented, with more excitement in my voice than I had heard in a while.

"And once again your intuition was impeccable," Lukan noted. "We were well advised to remain here. I wouldn't miss this for the world."

"Nor would I," I replied. "Can you believe it? Our dear friend is returning as Rome's emperor. For once, we will finally see things put aright."

∞ ∞ ∞

Our home became a meeting place again, only this time the dialogues and exchanges of information and opinion were riveting. A new optimism was emerging after long years of decadence and despair. Incredibly, Lukan and I were participating in its resurrection.

Another change occurred, however, which we didn't welcome. It was well known we were allied with Vespasian through an enduring friendship, priceless in a city where influence is bought and sold to the highest bidder. Attempts to garner our favor and that of the new emperor began in earnest.

It started unobtrusively enough, in the form of invitations to lavish parties where we wouldn't normally be included. Then more obvious inducements began to arrive: the best foods and wines, entertainment, adornments and even slaves.

Lukan declined all invitations and informed those who sent gifts that they were being donated to help the poor. Eventually word reached all corners of the city that neither Lukan nor the emperor, who had yet to arrive, could be bought at any price.

Vespasian's choice of Lukan as his emissary sent a clear message to everyone. The emperor's favor would not be auctioned off to the highest bidder. Ethics and integrity were on the rise.

We didn't see Vespasian immediately after his arrival in Rome. Because Lukan held no office, he couldn't participate in the formalities that accompanied the induction of a new emperor. We knew, however, that as soon as Vespasian had the opportunity he would call for Lukan to give him a comprehensive briefing.

Sooner than we expected a messenger arrived with an invitation written in the emperor's own hand. It read, "Enough of these interminable rituals and endless lines of people who wish me well but would sooner see me corrupted. I long for simpler times in your homeland. Please join me for dinner tonight that we may reminisce about better days. It will be a private affair."

I was both excited and apprehensive about meeting our dear friend who had just become the ruler of the largest empire in the known world. Would he be the same person we had grown to love, or had he been changed by the power conferred upon him? Would Vespasian still see us, as he commented once, as "a perpetual pool of sense in the middle of a roiling river of nonsense?"

I needn't have fretted over this.

"It's about time you two showed up to congratulate me on my new governmental job," Vespasian effused, giving Lukan a slap on the back when we arrived for dinner. "Everyone else in Rome saw fit to do so immediately after my arrival. You would think I was up to something important."

"Impossible!" laughed Lukan. "Why are you not still in the field expanding the Empire? Whatever did your soldiers think you could do from here? They must have wanted you out of their hair."

"Thank the gods you're not afraid to take me down a notch or two," Vespasian roared. "I am already sick to death of the simpering, duplicitous people who wangle their way to have an audience with me. Give me an honest person, at least every now and then. If they only knew I am more easily persuaded by genuineness than by guile."

"Speaking of guile," I heard an unfamiliar female voice come from a doorway into the room. "I recall a most unfortunate evening when you lacked it completely and fell sound asleep in the middle of Nero's performance in Greece. You were subsequently banished. Obviously, the former emperor didn't value guilelessness the way you do."

Vespasian smiled broadly. "Caenis, these are my dear friends from Britannia, Roman residents these past twenty-some years, Lukan and Gracila."

The moment I saw her I knew. She was the one true love Vespasian told us about the first evening he spent with Papa, Lukan and me. His wife had died, and he was free to have her in his life.

"I am pleased to meet you both," she greeted us warmly. "To say I have heard a great deal about you is an understatement. I am grateful for all you accomplished before Vespasian's return to Rome as emperor. Your work was invaluable, as he knew it would be."

"It was an honor to serve in this way," Lukan assured her. Then turning to the emperor, he continued, "Please know we are committed to continuing our assistance indefinitely. You have only to ask, and you can consider it done."

"Since you make it so easy, let's start with something out of the ordinary," Vespasian suggested. "How about spending a relaxing evening with Caenis and me so the four of us can celebrate our togetherness and forget I was ever named ruler of the land?"

By the end of the evening I made a dear friend in Caenis. She was so like me, outspoken and self-confident. I wondered how she came to be that way, but I didn't dare ask.

Not much later I found out, on the street no less, that she had been a slave freed by the emperor Claudius's mother. Nonetheless, she and Vespasian were barred from marrying because of his position in the senate at the time. He married another. What a pity. They were perfect for each other.

∞ ∞ ∞

Under the previous Caesars Rome became inured to irresponsibility and waste, and worse, downright fraud and treachery. That was the way of life, starting at the top. No one expected anything better from the ruler or elected officials. It took a long time for Vespasian to root out power abuse and build a new platform of integrity for serving the people. The tide turned, albeit slowly.

Lukan was instrumental in helping Vespasian reconfigure the complicated machinery that comprised the official work of the state. He was perfectly suited to the task. On the one hand, he never held public office, so he had no vested interest in maintaining the status quo. On the other hand, he learned a great deal about the workings of government, not to mention the arbitrary way decisions were made, during his years as a diplomat and businessman. He was savvy without being compromised by self-interest. He was astute, and he never sold out.

Vespasian commented often that Lukan was the exception in Rome. No one offered more credible advice to the leader of the Empire than he.

Throughout it all, Lukan remained modest and unassuming. If anything, he grew more humble as his implicit and explicit influence expanded. Well aware of the seductions lurking in the halls of power, he remained alert to their siren songs.

One evening we were engaged in a lively conversation with Vespasian and Caenis during a rare visit to our home. We issued a special invitation for them to celebrate the second anniversary of Vespasian's becoming Caesar. Just the four of us were dining together, a luxury we all cherished.

"I would like to offer a toast," Vespasian announced, holding a goblet of wine in the air. "To true love and its enduring capacity to fill our hearts, challenge our minds and lead us to the heights of achievement and integrity."

As he said these words he looked at Caenis with adoration then nodded toward Lukan and me in affirmation.

"What a splendid decree from an equally brilliant emperor," I exclaimed. "We are honoring you on this occasion, and true to form you have taken it in a different direction. It is so like you to go straight, shall I say, to the heart of the matter."

"My reign as emperor isn't about me, and it never will be," Vespasian declared. "The moment I believe that to be true, I lose my ability to rule fairly and engender justice. I wouldn't be half the person I am today were it not for the love of this woman, who is far more remarkable than I. Her strength of character easily surpasses mine. Thus I commemorate her, and the two of you, on this second anniversary of my stepping into the ultimate seat of power. May I always remember my roots, and honor the ones who have loved me faithfully despite the limitations of politics and privilege."

"Caenis, did you ever doubt your love, even when you knew you couldn't marry?" I asked.

"I never doubted it," she replied, "but I did rail against the rigid structures of the elite that prohibited our legally sanctioned union. Even today we cannot marry. That is remarkable considering that Vespasian holds the highest position in the land. Nonetheless, I have accepted this limitation as the absurdity it is. More importantly, we are together now, and our love is all the more sturdy for the years we sacrificed our oneness in the name of senatorial sanctions."

"When Lukan and I united, we had no rules to follow and no restrictions to limit our choice," I recalled. "We simply committed to spending our lives together in the context of our love. Our parents participated in a ceremony of sacred union that bound us to each other. The law was not involved. That is as it should be."

"And you love each other still, which proves love transcends all," continued Caenis. "It may be enhanced by the affirmation of a sacred union, but it is not torn asunder by the impossibility of a legal one. In a way, Vespasian and I enjoyed our own version of a sacred union all along."

"Except when I was married and we didn't lay eyes on each other," Vespasian refuted.

"Even then we loved each other," Caenis affirmed, "and our union remained intact."

"I can vouch for that," asserted Lukan. "The day we met Vespasian, he told us about you indirectly. He was married at the time, but it was clear you occupied his heart."

"Love is more powerful than the Empire," mused Vespasian. "And the union of two in love is stronger than that of legions in battle. Thus we commemorate love rather than my ascension to the role of Caesar."

"As you wish," I replied. "Once again you have proven to be a prescient potentate."

"I would much rather be a humble farmer," Vespasian protested, "but that fate was reserved for others more fortunate than I. At least I have my love at my side. A simple man can't ask for more."

The four of us shared stories and relaxed together over too much wine for too many hours. Morning light was peeking over the horizon when our guests were preparing to depart. They weren't free to find their way home anonymously and unaccompanied. Enough guards to win a small skirmish camped all night in our courtyard and in the street outside, awaiting the emperor's departure with his ladylove.

"Thank you for one of the most joyful evenings of my life," Vespasian effused. "I cherish our friendship all the more because we can share it as two couples who appreciate each other immensely."

"It is an honor to spend such a relaxed interlude with the two of you," replied Lukan. "We must do this again. And if you can't be released from your duties anytime soon, at least we know another anniversary will occur exactly one year from now."

"Go in peace," I said quietly. "And may everlasting love unite you always, that you may never again be apart."

We remained in Rome throughout the decade-long reign of Vespasian. During that time he created order where there once was chaos, accountability where there was unreliability and agreement where there was conflict. Not everything was perfect, but the city itself and the Empire as a whole were more peaceful and prosperous than they had been in quite some time.

Vespasian faced constant conspiracies to unseat him, thwarting each one with ruthless efficiency.

Lukan continued as the emperor's most loyal advisor until the end. Among other things, he helped bring about the construction of the Colosseum, which was intended to give back to the people the land Nero appropriated as his own private lake. Vespasian didn't live to see the first games in the Colosseum, but his son Titus, who succeeded him as emperor, honored him in an appropriately spirited fashion.

Caenis departed from Earth a few years before her love, leaving him lonelier than we had ever seen him. Ever the taskmaster, he stayed busy to compensate for his grieving and became an even more effective, albeit bereft, emperor.

Vespasian never lost his commanding presence or self-deprecating sense of humor. One of Lukan's colleagues reported that Vespasian faced his own death with typical irreverence, commenting, "Oh, dear! I think I'm becoming a god." How very like our dear friend.

Even now I miss him terribly.

∞ ∞ ∞

I have said little about what Mama and Papa were doing while we were in Rome. Lukan and I never convinced them to visit us, so we returned to Britannia every few years to be with them. On the last visit when I saw Mama alive, we shared a memorable moment of intimacy. Knowing she would be gone soon, she imparted an invaluable message to me.

"Have you ever wondered what will become of you and Lukan when your current lifetimes are over?" she asked.

"We will return to the spirit world for either a brief or an extended respite," I replied without much forethought, "and then be reborn into another lifetime."

"Together?" she queried, delving more deeply.

"Yes, of course," I responded.

"Will you be lovers, always able to create a sacred union?" she pursued. Obviously Mama was getting at something I needed to know.

"Based on your line of questioning, I can only assume the answer is no," I asserted.

"You are correct," Mama affirmed. "You have free will choice regarding whether you return for another lifetime and under what circumstances. You may choose to be born while he remains in the realms of spirit, and vice versa. You may both be born and arrange to know each other but find it inadvisable to be lovers."

"Like you and Papa," I observed. "You gave up so much for us!"

"It felt more that way earlier than it does now," Mama admitted. "One blessing of growing older is the ability to live joyfully without a lover.

"But let me continue. You two might decide to be born of the same gender. Or you might agree to test your love the way Vespasian and Caenis did in order to learn many valuable lessons."

"Lessons that come at a high cost," I inserted.

"Yes and no," Mama countered. "Each lifetime is configured according to the learning opportunities you most want to embrace. They may appear unfortunate. But your purpose is always to grow together more completely and discover the infinite power of your love."

"Will we ever have no need for more lifetimes?" I ventured.

"You will accomplish the ultimate union you both want, after you have loved and been tested, lived together and been challenged many times over," Mama assured me. "Through it all you will discover the one sacred truth of your existence, that all is love and you are love.

"After countless lifetimes you and Lukan will reunite as one spirit. You will remain as one until all are reunited with Source. That is both the end and the beginning."

That was Mama's final gift to me, the affirmation of the power of the love Lukan and I shared and the ultimate eternality of the love residing in all of Creation.

In the end when Mama was ready to leave the Earth plane, she cleaned her hut, put everything in perfect order then vanished into the nether realms.

We received a letter from Papa describing how she had chosen to go and vowing that he would love her eternally. His grieving was so evident I wept for days not for my loss, but for his. Three months later he was gone as well.

Both of our parents having left the Earth plane, Lukan and I had little reason to return to Britannia. His brother replaced his father as king and was dutifully pursuing the traditions of the patriarch. The Roman occupation became a way of life in Britannia, and the negotiations Papa and Vespasian originally established were deeply rooted.

We were growing older as well. As much as we loved Rome, we wanted to spend our last days in our homeland. After Vespasian's death, we began preparations to leave Rome for good. Lukan sold his businesses at a significant profit, and I was busy selecting what we would transport to Britannia. After three decades in Rome, many memories were inherent in each object.

One afternoon as I was going through a chest of serving pieces and having little luck choosing anything to leave behind, a servant came running into the room. "The emperor is here!" she announced.

At first I thought it was Vespasian, so accustomed was I to thinking of him that way. Of course it was his son Titus.

"I hear you are planning to leave permanently," he announced as I entered the courtyard where he awaited. "Can I convince you to stay at least until the opening celebrations of the Colosseum? My father would have insisted you be in attendance. But alas I can only request that you remain longer than you may have planned."

"When will construction be complete?" I asked.

"In three or four months' time," Titus replied. "Not long at all. I would like you and Lukan to be guests in my imperial suite during the opening celebration and as often afterward as you like. It is my gift to you, in memory of my father and how much he treasured your friendship."

"I graciously accept your invitation, especially given that it was delivered in person," I agreed. "It is an honor to have you here. May I offer you some refreshment?"

"Unfortunately I must take my leave," Titus declared. "I will send word regarding the opening celebration as soon as I know for certain when it will occur. In the meantime you can enjoy the pleasures of Rome."

"Thank you for your thoughtfulness," I said in gratitude. "We will celebrate with you and toast your father's generosity toward the people."

Like his father, Titus was true to his word. Our invitation arrived with ample time for us to make plans to attend the celebration. I had an elaborate gown made for the occasion, a rare extravagance I thoroughly enjoyed.

I witnessed the Colosseum during all phases of construction, but being inside the immense amphitheater made me dizzy. It was a monumental achievement, extraordinary in every way.

We enjoyed the spectacle of the opening ceremonies and games, but toward the end of the afternoon I began to feel ill. Something within me was nauseated, not so much by the violence I witnessed that day, which was minimal. Rather, I sensed that centuries of brutality would occur there. Oceans of blood would be spilled in that arena. The carnage and death would rival that of wars, and all for a spectator sport – entertainment. I couldn't wait to leave. Lukan and I politely refused all subsequent invitations.

∞ ∞ ∞

Our final journey home was blessedly uneventful. We arrived in the early spring and headed straight to our farm. To our surprise, we settled easily into the comfortable routine of the simple lives we led there so long ago.

When the carts loaded with our possessions arrived, I was astounded at how much I brought to Britannia. If we used our entire home for storage, we would run out of room. The caretaker hurriedly constructed a shed where we could stash everything, and we stacked the wooden crates there under lock and key. Myriad mementos of our elegantly appointed lives in Rome were in that shed, and yet Lukan and I puttered about in our oldest clothes and ate off rudimentary dinnerware.

Lukan was building a fire in the hearth one evening when he commented, "We have the financial resources to build as large and lavish a home as we want. We could be engaged in construction for the rest of our lives, using the world's finest craftsmen, and not run out of funds. So if you want a different home, just let me know. It will be yours."

"My dearest, you have always been generous with me," I replied. "And equally important, you thoughtfully anticipated anything I might want. The home you built for us when we first met is precisely where I prefer to live now. We left Rome behind. There is no need to create an imitation of that life here."

"I couldn't be happier than I am now, here with you as we warm our feet by the fire," Lukan agreed. "But tell me, aren't there at least a few things you want to retrieve from the shed?"

"Not really," I replied without hesitation.

"Nothing?" Lukan asked, astonished. I half expected him to admonish me for insisting we bring so much with us, but instead he laughed with gusto.

"Actually, there is one thing I want to retrieve from my skirt," I admitted, reaching into a pocket and pulling out an ancient carved sandalwood box.

"Ah, yes, my flea market find! How you do treasure that," Lukan commented.

"The only thing I love more than this box is the ring you had crafted for me in Rome," I replied, holding my hand to the firelight. Two bands, one of gold and one of platinum, were woven together, forming intertwined braids. Each one was carved with sacred letters embedded in engraved strands of equally sacred geometries. In a dream he saw this ring in detail then had it made to his exact specifications.

"The ring, the box and you are all I want," I stated simply. "The ring is the most precious gift anyone could receive from a lover, apart from his love. But to have both is a blessing too profound for words. As for the box, I have no idea why it means so much to me, but it does."

"I remember the day I discovered it, not long after we arrived in Rome," Lukan recalled. "I was on my way to a meeting, in a dreadful hurry, when I saw the box out of the corner of my eye on a rickety table piled high with worthless junk. The box was covered with dust. Who knows how long it had been sitting there unnoticed? I pulled out a coin, tossed it to the vendor, picked up the box and went on my way. It took me a few days to remember I had it. I gave it to you still covered with grime from the street."

"I cried the moment I saw it," I reminisced. Years of rubbing it tenderly created a soft sheen on the wood. The oil from my hands, and my constant fingering of its carvings, brought it back to life.

"It must have some meaning for us," commented Lukan, "but for the life of me I can't discern what it is."

The shed remained locked, and we continued to live simply. I had all I needed.

Our lives unfolded serenely, season upon season, year after year. Our joints grew stiff, and Lukan's battle wounds talked back to him incessantly. But still we kept on gardening, chatting at all hours and making love on occasion. We were happy, even as we were slowing down.

Inevitably our health began to fail. We were weary of the pain that accompanied our every movement, and we could feel our bodies growing weak.

"It might be time for us to make one last visit to the Standing Stones," Lukan whispered one night as we lay close together to keep each other warm. It was summer, but we perpetually felt a chill.

"I believe so," I agreed.

We journeyed to the stones often when we visited Britannia. No one knew for sure how they got there or what otherworldly force planted them upright, in perfect alignment with the equinoxes. But however the magical circle came to be, it created a portal into the nether realms. Every time we sat within it, we were transported in meditation to the highest frequencies of light. The stones were like a temple for us, a sacred place where we could experience our own divinity. The oneness we experienced there was equaled only during our most exquisite lovemaking.

We put our household and inheritance in order, much of which would go to the families who faithfully cared for our home in our absence. We divided the land appropriately and gave it to them, along with their dwellings and an annual stipend. The items in the shed, still unpacked, were to be sold off to help their children establish an independent livelihood when they reached adulthood.

No one knew we were leaving for good. We simply told them we were traveling to see the Standing Stones while the weather was balmy. We packed minimal belongings and food, bade everyone farewell, then set off down the road. I had the sandalwood box in my pocket and the ring on my finger. Lukan, protective to the end, covered me with an extra blanket, then sat down beside me in the cart, grabbed the reins, and we were off.

We arrived at the stone circle after a journey that was longer and more arduous than we anticipated. I was nearly crippled as I tried to climb down from the cart one last time. Lukan took me in his arms and carried me like a child into the center of the circle. Then he returned to the cart, unhitched and freed the horse, and retrieved blankets and a few provisions.

It was midday. The sky was an uncanny blue, alive with the dancing rays of the sun. Birds chirped without a care. Bees buzzed busily, visiting clover blossoms aplenty. A butterfly landed on the handle of the basket Lukan had carried from the cart.

He spread out a thick blanket woven from the wool of the sheep on our farm. We had used it for years, dragging it indoors and out with the temperature changes. It made a fitting bed for us in the grass.

We sat on the blanket, in the sun, and talked of our lives and our love. We toasted Vespasian with goblets of our best wine and commemorated Mama and Papa. I thanked Vivendi and blessed everyone who attended our gatherings in Rome, that they may find a path to peace. I thanked Yeshua and those in my spiritual community for helping me discover my own path to peace.

Then we acknowledged each other. We revisited the many blessings we shared and the love that accompanied them. We recalled the challenges we faced and how our love enabled us to transcend them. We remembered our many nights and days of lovemaking and the transformative experience of oneness.

I cannot recall exactly what we said, for my spirit was already starting to leave my body. I gazed at my eternal love, radiating light and calm certainty about the next step he would take with me. The sun was setting, and it was growing cold.

"It's time," Lukan whispered.

"Yes, my love," I replied. "Hold me as you always have and always will."

"Come here, my darling Gracila," he said tenderly, wrapping me in his arms and covering me with a blanket. "I love you with all that I am, eternally."

"I love you, my dearest Lukan," I replied, "with the infinity of the ages."

I closed my eyes and felt my spirit float above my body. I looked down at us, two old people lying together in love, at peace in the middle of the Standing Stones. Lukan's spirit left his body and joined mine. We bade farewell to our earthly vessels, grateful for having made the transition effortlessly in this blessed portal.

I was just becoming accustomed to my newly unencumbered state when Mama and Papa appeared to welcome us. They encompassed Lukan and me in their love, and together we were drawn into divine light.

ACKNOWLEDGEMENTS

For the past half century I have been blessed to be part of a constantly emerging, joyfully celebratory sisterhood. Each of these dear friends exhibits the divine feminine in all of her unhesitating acceptance, generous support and unconditional love. They are, in alphabetical order:

Susan Blake

Delinda Chapman

Linda Davidson

Choong Gaian

Davida Hartman

Sally Hudson

Trudie London

Sharon Mehdi

Regina Meredith

Pix Morgan

Sandra Tripp

Justine Turner

Wendy Weir

Explore additional books by Gates McKibbin at
www.lovehopegive.com

Epic Steps: *Rekindling Democracy, Unity and Peace*

One, Beyond Time
Love, 24 AD
Hope, 120 AD
Give, 1671 AD

The Light in the Living Room: *Dad's Messages from the Other Side*

Lovelines: *Notes from Spirit on Loving and Being Loved*

A Course in Courage: *Disarming the Darkness with Strength of Heart*

A Handbook on Hope: *Fusing Optimism and Action*

The Life of the Soul: *The Path of Spirit in Your Lifetimes*

Available Wisdom: *Insights from Beyond the Third Dimension*

Forging Faith: *Direct Experience of the Divine*

Printed in Great Britain
by Amazon